MW01050060

Ethan & Juliet

Try Again Series, Volume 1

Marla Holt

Published by Marla Holt, 2018.

eBook ISBN: 978-1-7322754-4-7

Paperback ISBN: 978-1-7322754-5-4

Cover Photo by: Joanna Nix

Cover by: T-Rex Cover Design

To Find out more and for exclusive sneak peeks at Marla's newest work,

[sign up for her newsletter][1]

---

1. https://dl.bookfunnel.com/kxq14cdo4n

Also by Marla Holt

The Other Lane
When Abe Met Lane

Try Again Series
Ethan & Juliet

Standalone
The Other Lane: A Modern Fairy Tale

Watch for more at tinydinostudios.com.

For Norla, Eileen, Jodi, and midwives everywhere

Ethan & Juliet

By
Marla Holt

Chapter One

Juliet slapped her palm against the steering wheel as traffic closed in around her. She should have known better than to get on the highway at eight o'clock in the morning even if it was the fastest way to get from Overland Park to Midtown. And she needed to be in Midtown ten minutes ago.

Fifteen minutes ago, Juliet had stepped out the front door of the birth center into the brittle warmth of the spring morning with no other plans than to go home and nap. She'd squinted past the newly leafed trees and into the sunlight. Juliet had basked in the afterglow of assisting in the uneventful birth of a healthy baby girl. The high of witnessing new life never got old, but the adrenaline of it had already worn off. Exhaustion had pressed down on her shoulders like she'd been carrying both her physiology book and her pharmaceuticals book in her bag at the same time again. She'd wanted to go home and sleep and sleep and sleep.

Juliet had taken one deep, cleansing breath in through her nose and out through her mouth and had just turned toward her heap of a twenty-year-old Toyota when her phone had buzzed in her pocket.

The screen had flashed Gina's name, and Juliet's heart had ticked up a notch when she'd heard panting over the line instead of words.

"Gina? Gina are you OK?" she'd asked.

A whimper had been her answer.

"Gina are you in labor?"

Juliet had heard her friend draw in a deep breath, then in a shaky voice, she'd said, "Regular contractions, getting strong fast. And they hurt more than last time. A lot more."

Juliet had done a mental sun salutation since she hadn't had time for a real one, then she'd pivoted on her heel and walked right back into the birthing center. On her way, she'd asked if Gina was experiencing pain between contractions and if she'd noticed any spotting. A yes to both.

"And Colin is still . . . out of town . . . and it's too early." Gina's voice had been a sharp whine interrupted by hard pants.

Gina wasn't due for three more weeks, but that hadn't been what had Juliet worried. Not by a long shot. "It's not too early. Call Rich to stay with Noah, and I'll be there in a flash."

Gina had groaned as another contraction came on.

"Scratch that, I'll call Rich. You hang tight."

Juliet had snagged Charlie, the midwife she'd worked with the night before and filled her in.

"She needs to get to the hospital," Charlie said.

Juliet nodded in agreement. "She's only a few blocks from KU Med. I can have her there in thirty minutes."

Charlie had offered to take care of the official transfer and meet them there. Then Juliet had been off, only to wind up stuck in traffic ten minutes into a twenty-minute drive. The wait was long enough for every awful thing that could be wrong with Gina to pass through Juliet's mind. When she felt panic crushing her diaphragm, she focused instead on how good it had felt for Gina to adopt her when she'd first moved to Kansas City. How all the nights drinking wine and dancing had forged a sisterly relationship that withstood Juliet's split from Gina's brother.

Juliet's pulse slowed as she remembered and breathed. They were both strong women. Gina would survive this. Juliet would get her to the hospital. The University of Kansas Medical Center was the best hospital in the area, with the best doctors. Gina would be fine, and Juliet could do this. She was a nurse, almost a full-fledged midwife, she was trained to stay calm in these situations, so she would, even when it was one of her best friends in danger.

Juliet practiced breathing in through her nose, out through her mouth, and it did almost as much as a good round of yoga.

Then she remembered she'd offered to call Rich and cursed.

Juliet fumbled her phone out of her satchel, and scrolled through her contacts, keeping one eye on the road in case the car in front of her moved.

"*Durand.*" He answered, with a perfect French accent.

"Are you going by your last name now?" Juliet asked.

A pause, and Juliet imagined a sexy, confident smile sliding onto his face. "Oh, Juliet. It has been too long."

Juliet snorted. "Whatever. Have you talked to your sister lately?"

"I'm on call for the baby."

"Yeah, well, the baby's coming now."

All the flirtation fell from his voice as he said, "Is everything okay?"

"I'm on my way over so I can take her to the Med Center. Colin's still out of town, so I need you to get over there now. Stay with her until I can get there, and I need you to take care of Noah and let Colin know what's going on. If she starts bleeding or can't handle the pain, call an ambulance and don't wait for me, got it?"

From the scraping and scuffling noises in the background, Juliet guessed Rich was gathering papers off his desk. "I'll be there in fifteen minutes." Then he hung up.

It might have been the least amount of flirting Rich had ever pulled off in one conversation. At least he understood the situation. Rich had always respected her professionally, even if he hadn't been good for her in any other way.

When Juliet arrived, Rich was making Noah eggs, but paused to help Juliet get Gina into the car. Juliet's hope that Rich had somehow been horribly scarred in the last two years were dashed the second she laid eyes on him. His thick, wavy dark hair fell in his earnest brown eyes. His olive skin glowed in the morning sun as he gripped Juliet's hand and thanked her for being there for his sister. Looking up at him, Juliet was reminded of the first time they'd met. He was just as gorgeous at thirty as he'd been at eighteen. Possibly more so.

Juliet snatched her hand back and only just resisted wiping it clean on her scrubs. "I'll call with news as soon as I can." Then she joined a groaning Gina in the car.

The drive to KU Med took less than ten minutes, and Charlie met them at the emergency room doors along with a nurse who got them checked in and into an ultrasound. Then they were admitted to the high-risk wing of the Labor and Delivery ward. Juliet helped Gina through contractions while Charlie coordinated with the hospital staff.

After what Juliet considered far too long, the door opened and a man in a white coat entered the room.

Juliet's heart might have stopped beating when he snapped the file he'd been reading shut, revealing his rugged face and bright blue eyes.

It was him.

Juliet knew she would run into him eventually. To have made it four years without meeting him when they worked in the same field was almost a miracle.

What wasn't surprising was the near scowl he wore as he took them all in one at a time. He'd always hated mid-wives, and here were two, along with a patient in distress. That would make him cranky. And if his greasy hair and thick stubble were any indication, it was well past the end of his shift. Oh yeah, he would be in a great mood.

Gina squeezed Juliet's hand, and Juliet tried to give her friend a reassuring smile, but that was when the doctor spoke.

"I'm Dr. Harvey," he said, pulling the last empty chair in front of Gina's bed. "I'll be performing your cesarean today."

"Cesarean?" Gina blinked.

Juliet and Charlie had explained to Gina that they thought she had a partial placental abruption, but the hospital staff hadn't said a word. When asked, the nurse had said they were waiting for the doctor to get out of surgery to confirm the results. The doctor they had been waiting on was now exchanging glares with Juliet's boss.

"She doesn't know?" he asked

"Your staff hasn't exactly been forthcoming," Charlie said. "We warned her it was a possibility."

"It's the only way to deliver safely at this point," he said, angling his head back toward Gina.

"Is the baby okay?" Gina asked, her voice quavering in panic.

"The baby is fine," Juliet said, nodding toward the fetal monitor. "Dr. Harvey means that a vaginal delivery is too risky for you right now."

"And for the baby," Dr. Harvey said. "Stillbirth would be the most likely outcome."

Gina let out a little sob of shock and her heart rate monitor beeped a little faster.

"Ethan!" Juliet sent him a silencing glare as she felt Gina go rigid beneath her palm, then said to Gina in a soothing voice, "C-section is the best way to make sure you don't bleed too much if the placenta detaches, but the baby is okay."

Gina looked to Dr. Harvey who said, "The risk of hemorrhage is high."

After grimacing through another contraction, dulled by the pain medication they'd given her, Gina asked Juliet, "You'd do it?"

She was pretty sure she heard Dr. Harvey's teeth grind.

Juliet made sure she smiled as she said, "In a heartbeat."

Gina nodded, looking determined. "Alright then. Let's do it."

Dr. Harvey explained the surgery and recovery as if his life depended on him doing so in fifty words or less. Then he swept himself from the room with a dark look in Juliet's direction. She didn't flinch. It wasn't her fault his bedside manner was so atrocious that she'd had to translate for him.

"That's it?" Gina panted through a contraction.

Charlie said, "He's abrupt, but if you have to have a c-section, he's who you want."

Juliet nodded and squeezed Gina's hand back, and said, "He's the best," trying not to let anything else show on her face. In her mind, Juliet was poking Gina in the shoulder, saying "Oh my God, oh my God," over and over, and maybe throwing a "He's the one!" in there.

Juliet hadn't seen him since she'd finished nursing school. Her life was completely different now, but Ethan hadn't changed at all.

He was still broad and sturdy like a rugby player, only three or four inches taller than she was. His shaggy, dark hair still escaped from beneath the surgical cap that matched his blue eyes. He still couldn't take the time to talk to his patients and was apparently working so much he couldn't even be bothered to shave. The Dr. Harvey she remembered had always been miraculously clean shaven, even at the end of a twenty-four-hour shift. He looked more ruffled this morning than he used to get, but Juliet had to admit she liked the beard. It matched him somehow.

Gina huffed, her face still contorted in pain. "I hope he's better at surgery than he is at conversation."

A nurse with a consent form arrived then, and Juliet focused again on Gina, and not on the way Dr. Harvey's eyes had looked at her in annoyance. Not that she wanted him to look at her at all, she wanted him to focus on Gina. Juliet did not want to talk to him, or about him. She'd avoided all reference to him for four years. All she had to do was to make it through this surgery, and she could go back to forgetting he existed.

Only once the surgery started, Juliet had trouble not watching him. She was positioned by Gina's head, so she couldn't see his hands, but the poise of his shoulders, the stillness of his body as he worked, the soft whisper of his voice, efficient with his words as he directed the staff. Juliet noticed every breath he took. He was impressive, and despite herself, Juliet felt a pull in her belly to be near him as he worked.

She wasn't the only one. When she'd been in nursing school, Dr. Harvey had been the young, handsome doctor who notoriously never dated nurses. Which meant each of Juliet's classmates had wanted to be the exception to the rule and flirted shamelessly whenever he was near.

Despite her attraction, Juliet hadn't bothered. She'd had Rich back then, and they'd been talking about getting married. While she'd noticed Dr. Harvey's sparkling blue eyes and unshakable confidence, she'd also noticed they came with an air of entitlement and a healthy dose of arrogance. He didn't just not date the nurses, he spoke to them over breakfast with half-teasing condescension, and sometimes even a hint of derision. Even among his fellow obstetricians Ethan incited controversy and lead discussions with a tone that implied anyone who disagreed with him was an idiot.

Rich's soft charm and poise had been magnetic by comparison. Rich's passion had been so intoxicating that even when Juliet had met him at fourteen, she hadn't been able to imagine loving another man. Most days she still couldn't, but she was no longer as naive as she had been four years ago when she thought she and Rich would get married, have babies, and live happily ever after.

In that moment of regret, Dr. Harvey raised his eyes to hers and held. It lasted only a moment before his eyes were back on his work. She wondered how he remembered that night, and if he despised her for being there with a birthing center patient.

"Birth," she remembered him saying about at a group breakfast one morning, "could go from normal to dangerous in a split second. Why would anyone endanger themselves and their child by choosing not to have every modern option available?" It had maybe been those words, more than anything else that had kept Juliet from seeking him out again, not when she'd been angling for the job at the birthing center near the end of her nursing degree, and not after she'd started her midwifery program two years ago.

A cry broke through the quiet stillness of the operating room, and Juliet left her memories to share a tearful smile with Gina as Dr. Harvey said, "It's a boy." He handed the baby off to a nurse and returned his attention to Gina.

Juliet stayed with Gina until the surgery was over since Gina's husband had arrived just in time to accompany his new son to the nursery.

When they wheeled Gina to recovery, Juliet escaped back to the room and collapsed into the nearest plastic chair.

She let relief wash over her. Abruption could be so, so bad, but they'd gotten here in time.

Every muscle protested in exhaustion as she checked her watch. It was after eleven. She'd only slept four hours in the last two days. Juliet couldn't remember the last time she'd eaten, and she'd have to be here another couple of hours at least.

The door opened, and Juliet sat up, expecting to see a nurse wheeling Gina in. Instead, Dr. Harvey leaned against the door frame.

"She's doing great," he said. "She lost a lot of blood, and she'll be here a few days, but she will be alright."

"Thanks," Juliet said. It wasn't information a doctor confided in a colleague, but family. She sat up straighter. "Your bedside manner is still abominable."

"A compliment so soon?" he chuckled, then sobered, his eyes narrowing in on her. "You were smart to bring her straight here."

Juliet sat up straighter and squared her shoulders, looking down her narrow nose at him. "I'm not exactly new to all this."

The corners of his mouth twitched, as if he were trying to smile at her, but couldn't bring himself to follow through. "You're wasted at that freestanding place."

Juliet thought, that considering the circumstances, she was just what they needed, but said, "Are you offering me a job?"

"How about breakfast? Dino's?" It was the diner across the street, the usual gathering place.

The allure of eggs and hot coffee was too good to pass up. "I sometimes dream about Dino's breakfast."

A real smile lit up his face this time. "Great. I've got paperwork to finish up, then I'm done. Meet you downstairs in an hour?"

Juliet nodded, knowing her confusion showed on her face, but he smiled like maybe he didn't despise her after all.

Chapter Two

Of all the times to grow a beard, Ethan had to choose the week Juliet Hawthorne walked back into his life. If he'd known she would be in his hospital, Ethan would have shaved.

Not that she'd looked at him with anything but reproach in her eyes. But good Lord she had gorgeous eyes. They were a pale green that was so sharp he suspected her stare could slice him open. There might be something wrong with him, because Ethan didn't think he would mind if she did.

The only way he'd made it through surgery was to remind himself that nurses were off limits. Ethan had never dated a nurse, or anyone else who worked at the hospital. It created too many conflicts when people's lives depended on there being no kinks in the system. Keeping his interactions light with everyone but family was how he'd kept his life running without a hitch over the last ten years. At work he was professional. Everywhere else he was sincere but casual. There were fewer distractions all around that way.

He had been ready to make an exception for Juliet once upon a time, on both the casual and professional fronts. Seeing her again, Ethan had slipped right back into his crush. Dating Juliet Hawthorne wouldn't be a distraction on the ward, but a boon. Her instincts were as sharp as her eyes and her reaction time even better. She could make patients smile and could to set them at ease with only a word. He wanted her skill on his team.

He'd wanted her to take the open L&D position when she'd graduated nursing school. Ethan had recommended her application personally. If she'd stayed, he could have made her his nurse just like his dad had done with his mom.

That partnership had lasted a lifetime, and Ethan could picture Juliet slipping into his life just as seamlessly now as she'd done then. She'd work with him during the day, and then they'd go home together at night. Cook dinner together. Shower together. Sleep together. Make a family together.

That dream had been so tangible then, and while he'd left it dormant for years—along with the rest of his social life if he was honest—all it took was seeing her again for the longing to reawaken. He was certain he could convince her to give him a chance now that she'd agreed to breakfast. He would tempt her away from the birthing center. The pay couldn't be that good. Ethan knew he could offer her more. And maybe over breakfast he'd find out if there was any truth to that ridiculous rumor that she was training to be a midwife.

Why anyone would want to become a midwife was beyond him, but that was peripheral. What mattered was that she was here, chatting with an intake nurse by the front doors. One of his favorite things about Juliet was her ability to hold a conversation with anyone. He'd requested she work with him often during her practicum for that reason. He didn't have time for niceties, but she knew enough about her field and how he worked that she anticipated his diagnosis, his plan of action, and sometimes, even the insensitive words that came out of his mouth.

Juliet Hawthorne was Ethan's perfect complement.

She'd even snapped at him, right in front of a patient today. She'd been right. He would have reprimanded anyone else for calling him out like that, but he would not complain about Juliet saying his name. Though he had a few more pleasant scenarios in mind.

As he approached, he noticed the jumble of woven bracelets that still crowded her watch face. He even liked that she was a hippie. When her long red hair wasn't braided, it fell in gentle waves to her waist. He remembered with great clarity the black and gray sun and moon tattoo on her hip. Ethan had studied it and let himself believe, for a few short hours, that she could be his.

The smile that curled Juliet's lips as she left the other nurse faded as her eyes landed on Ethan. The good mood that'd had him whistling through the last hour of paperwork plummeted.

"Is everyone else already there?" she asked, her eyes darting.

Never one to show his disappointment, Ethan leaned against the wall next to the door, crossing his arms, as he looked down at her. He was not a tall man, only five-ten. Juliet almost met his eye level. "Everyone else left hours ago."

"And you stayed?"

"You don't see abruption every day I wasn't going to miss out on that."

Juliet bristled and stepped up to him, "Do not dehumanize Gina like that. She's practically my sister."

She was close enough to kiss, but Ethan ran the tip of his nose across the bridge of hers instead. "And your gratitude for saving her life is appreciated."

Juliet hissed like a cat and pushed him into the wall with a strength that surprised him. "Glad to know you're still an arrogant ass," she said, and was out the door before he could retaliate. He didn't know whether to be aroused or insulted.

Ethan caught up in a few steps. "I didn't mean to offend you," he said.

"Yes, you did." She didn't look at him.

He might have been testing his boundaries with her, but he hadn't wanted to make her mad at him. "Well, you are gorgeous when you're angry."

Juliet snorted and adjusted the strap of her bag over her chest, a small hiking pack, he realized. Not a purse. "I'm too tired for this shit," she said.

"How long has it been since you slept?"

Her shoulder rose in a shrug, and Ethan watched her exhaustion overtake her annoyance, like a cloud moving in front of a full moon. "Cat naps for two days."

"When's your next shift?"

"Not until Monday. Clinic hours. You?"

"Been on since six last night. I'm on call tonight, then the next two days off." He was just glad she'd have time to rest and recover.

"Sounds like you haven't had any more sleep than I have."

"I got a full eight before I came in yesterday."

Ethan held the diner door open for her, and he smiled when she looked up at him as she passed. He couldn't stop smiling at her, even though Juliet hadn't crossed his mind in months.

Ethan had dated plenty in the last four years. He had only ended his latest off-and-on-again thing with Cynthia, a cute blonde science teacher who worked with his sister-in-law, two months ago. Things with Cynthia had been nothing more than convenience. Juliet was different. She was the spark of something real he'd been missing in his life. The energy from her presence was already invigorating him, even though by all rights he should be exhausted.

"If you got here last night, then what's with the three-day stubble?" she asked. A small smile curved her lips.

She was teasing him. He'd take that.

A hand skimmed his chin. He usually went to pains to remain clean shaven, even shaving partway through a shift if he had a chance. Ethan prided himself on always appearing alert and professional. It was something he'd learned from him parents. His father, who never let his patients see him ruffled, had been everything Ethan had ever wanted to be.

A pang of grief pinged through his chest. Even five years later, he didn't think he'd ever be able to think about his father without missing him. His mother, who was still alive and well, thank God, had no qualms about telling her son when he looked like a slob.

"I thought I'd give the whole beard thing a try."

Juliet led the way through the pastel pink and blue diner to a two-top table by the far window and turned her coffee mug over before she sat down. She looked eager for coffee, but did she realize she'd led him to the same table?

"Getting in on that trend a little bit late, aren't you?" she asked.

"I'm not as interested in fashion as I am in not being mistaken for a first-year resident."

Her eyes evaluated his face, and she didn't look impressed by what she saw. "You're trying to look older?"

"Last week a patient thought I was twenty-six."

"So?"

"I'm thirty-six."

"Most people would take that as a compliment."

"Twenty-six-year-olds in this field don't know what they're doing,"

"I'm twenty-six," Juliet said, and smiled up at the waitress who delivered menus and filled their coffee mugs. Juliet asked for a glass of orange juice like he wasn't even there.

Ethan wanted to apologize. He wanted to explain that, at twenty-six, doctors would still be in medical school, but he had a feeling that would only make things worse, so he sipped his coffee as she perused her menu.

She folded it into her lap a minute later and said, "Did you consider that it might be more a reflection of your behavior rather than your appearance?"

Ethan snorted into his coffee. "I keep forgetting we don't get along."

"Are there any women you do get along with?"

"A few. Would you like references?" His sisters-in-law came to mind. Any other woman was either his mother, or a woman that had told him in one way or another that he was emotionally unavailable, but Juliet didn't need to know that.

Juliet pretended not to hear him as the server returned with her orange juice and took their orders.

Ethan asked, "How long do you have left on your CNM?"

"Only my final practicum."

That answered that question. He had no clue what to do with a midwife. "Are you doing that at your birthing center?" he asked.

Juliet shook her head. "I can't and keep my job. I'm doing it here. Well, in the hospital birth center."

They called it a birth center, but it was a wing of the L&D designed for low-risk cases. They had birth tubs and queen-sized beds, but all the regular hospital equipment was still there, just less obvious. They had a small team of midwives that oversaw the care, but they were still bound by hospital procedure—unlike at the freestanding place she worked at, where, as far as he could tell, they did whatever they wanted, danger to mother and child or no.

"So, you'll be around more soon?"

He was officially pathetic, only she'd missed it somehow, because she said, "Don't worry, Dr. Harvey, I'm sure you'll barely see me."

"Juliet," he said, and she raised her eyes to his. Her direct gaze was so intense he almost had to look away. "Call me Ethan."

ETHAN WAS ANTAGONIZING her on purpose. Juliet wasn't sure why she was surprised, he'd always been that way. At least now he had a reason, even if it was bullshit. Juliet had seen herself angry. Her face and neck turned red, and blotchy and made her hair look even more orange. Sometimes she bit the inside of her lip until it was raw and bleeding When she was really, properly furious, Juliet cried. But Ethan had seen none of that. At most, he'd seen her annoyed. From the way he kept staring at her and grinning his alluring half-smile, he found her annoyance gratifying.

Juliet didn't want to feed his ego by being impetuous. She wanted to be cold and sullen, to make him see the vast gulf of distance between them. Except, Juliet liked that little half-smile, and for four years she'd remembered him scowling and accusatory. She had convinced herself that even if she ever saw him again, he would be the one who was cold and distant with her. That he was smiling was a relief.

And Juliet almost didn't want to admit to herself that she liked teasing him.

It was refreshing to flirt, because that's what they were doing, no matter her reluctance. She'd shut down that part of herself for so long, not trusting men, and not trusting herself with men, that her participation surprised her. The unexpectedness of Ethan's good mood on top of her exhaustion had her guard down.

The waitress came by and filled both their coffees. Juliet enjoyed the comfortable silence as she watched the rest of the diners enjoy cheeseburgers and ham sandwiches with fries while she waited on a vegetable omelet.

When Ethan cleared his throat and asked, "How are things?" Juliet knew what he meant, but she chose the shallow answer instead of the one he wanted.

"Good. School keeps me busy. Work too. Not much time for anything else."

"But you're doing okay?" he asked. "Things are...calmer?"

Juliet preferred the flirting to the appraising, cautious concern. "I'm not a living soap opera if that's what you're asking."

"I shouldn't have left you alone that day."

Juliet rolled her eyes. "If you really thought that, you would have contacted me a lot sooner."

Ethan dropped her gaze, and stared into his coffee until their food arrived, then attacked his pancakes, covering both his sausage and bacon in syrup as he went. Juliet tried not to watch him eat the meat as she cut into her omelet. She was halfway through when Ethan asked, "Are eggs vegetarian? I've never been clear on that."

"Some people don't eat them, but some vegetarians also eat fish. *I* can't eat anything with a face, and I wasn't getting enough protein, so I eat eggs."

"Fish are delicious," Ethan lisped around a mouthful of food. He swallowed. "Freshly caught, breaded and fried with hushpuppies. Or grilled with zucchini and peppers."

Juliet sat back from the table, covering her mouth with her fingertips. "I think I'm going to be sick."

The farce earned her a chuckle, and she picked at a piece of tomato that had fallen out of her omelet. The hushpuppies and zucchini sounded tasty, maybe she could convince him to make them for her sometime and forget the fish.

Juliet's fork halted halfway to her mouth when she realized what her errant thought implied, and she put her fork down and made a show out of checking her phone. She'd said goodbye to Gina and Colin before she'd left, and she couldn't think of a reason for anyone else to text her, but she planned to feign a text from Gina. Instead, she found a text from her sister. Her actual sister, Colleen, whom Juliet almost never talked to.

COLLEEN: *Help! I have an interview at a hospital next week. You work with these douchebags all day, right? How do I make them look good?*

Colleen was three years younger than Juliet and had a degree in marketing. She'd been working at a little coffee shop in Denver since she'd graduated the year before, applying for job after job after job with no luck. Juliet supposed this was another one of those, and as much distance as there was between the two, Juliet felt for her sister. Juliet's scholarship had paid for school and Rich had paid for everything else. When she'd graduated, she'd only applied for two jobs and been offered both. Colleen had worked all the way through school and was still struggling to find her footing.

Juliet must have stared at her phone too long, because Ethan asked, "Is everything okay?"

"It's my sister," she said, slinging her bag over her shoulder. "I have to go."

"Your actual sister or is there a problem with Gina?"

"My actual sister." Juliet stood and rifled through the zippered pocket where she kept her emergency cash. This breakfast had not been in her budget.

"I didn't know you had a sister." Ethan stood with her. His voice was soft, a mix of awe and concern.

"There's a lot about me you don't know, Dr. Harvey."

His hand covered hers as she tried to place ten dollars on the table. He crumpled the bills back into her fist. "Ethan," he said.

Juliet tried to ignore the thrill of pleasure that pulsed up her arm. It was less intense than the one that had hurtled through her core when he'd brushed his nose over hers. The presumed familiarity had almost been too much for her as, even if for just a second, she'd remembered the feel of him in the dark.

"Fine, *Ethan*. I have to go." Juliet tried to free her hand, but his grip held firm.

"It's on me," he said.

"I—" Juliet met his eyes and had to stop herself from smoothing the unwashed, overlong locks out of his lashes.

"Have dinner with me," he said with a hint of desperation in his voice.

"Will you let me pay for breakfast if I say yes?"

"No."

"Then no"

He let go of her hand then, but Juliet folded the money back into her pocket, as he said, "Please have dinner with me?"

"We just had breakfast."

"That was work related."

That was the flimsiest excuse Juliet had ever heard. Never in her life had dating Ethan Harvey sounded like a worse idea, and that was saying something.

Juliet shook her head, and said, "You have got to be kidding me," and backed a few steps away.

Ethan chuckled as she all but fled from the diner.

At home, the apartment was quiet, but Alex's beads were spread over the coffee table and piled on the breakfast bar. There was even a bowl in the fridge with Alex's spare pair of glasses folded inside. Juliet shook her head and let them be. Her roommate had done stranger things with her art supplies. Alex, however, was nowhere to be found, for which Juliet was grateful. Somehow her roommate would know what had happened and demand an explanation. Instead, Juliet turned her phone to silent and collapsed into bed.

When she awoke a few hours later, the sun was low in the sky and the stereo played Alex's strange '80s music in the living room. Juliet showered then seated herself at the breakfast bar in front of where Alex cooked pasta in their kitchen.

"You have been out forever," Alex said. When Juliet only nodded, she asked, "You want wine or coffee?"

"Coffee first."

Alex set a mug of fresh coffee down in front of Juliet a minute later.

"You are a saint." Juliet inhaled the steam before taking her first sip. Alex's coffee was always hot and strong. She'd been a barista for a while and had taught Juliet how to make good coffee at home.

"You remember you said that the next time you step on a sharp bead."

"Speaking of, why are there beads in the fridge?"

Alex shrugged, her curly blonde hair bouncing on her shoulders. "I had berries for breakfast." She stirred her pasta sauce like she wasn't concerned. At least she hadn't eaten one of her beads by mistake. "How many babies have you helped into this world today?"

"Two," Juliet said. "We had a little girl at the birthing center last night, and the second I finished there, I got the call from Gina."

Alex froze mid-stir. "Gina? How'd that go?"

Juliet explained her morning at the hospital, leaving out any details about Dr. Harvey.

"Jesus that's scary," Alex shuddered as she put a pot of water on to boil. "I don't know if I'd be able to tell the difference between that kind of pain and regular labor."

"How often have you had to handle a laboring patient on your own?"

"Never," Alex raised the box of noodles like it was a glass of champagne, "And here's hoping I never have to."

"Amen." Juliet raised her coffee mug to the toast.

A few moments passed in silence as Juliet watched Alex slice a baguette from the farmer's market. "So, you spent the whole morning with Gina?"

"Yup."

"Any sign of . . ."

"I had to call him to watch Noah."

"And?"

"And, he was there to help his sister. He'd be an asshole not to have been."

Alex narrowed her eyes. "Rich is an asshole. Hot, but an asshole."

"He's good to his sister."

Alex sat a basket of bread and a saucer of garlic olive oil on the counter. "Doesn't make up for how he's treated you."

"I know," Juliet said, accepting the glass of wine her friend offered next. "I'm hoping I can manage to avoid him."

"Good," Alex said, "because if you sleep with him again, I will have to kick your ass and his."

"Please do." Juliet picked at a slice of the bread, her hunger warring with the desire to share with her roommate. "I should call and check in on Gina though. I've been gone too long."

"She has a full staff of nurses looking after her and you haven't slept for two days. She can wait another thirty minutes while you eat dinner."

Juliet shrugged and dipped another bite of bread in the olive oil. She knew what Alex said was true, but Juliet felt guilty leaving Gina alone at the hospital even so.

Chapter Three

Ethan woke to the sound of someone calling his name. He checked the time on his phone. It was after ten. He hadn't meant to sleep the whole day away, but at least he hadn't missed a call from the hospital. Sitting up and rubbing his eyes, he heard his name again from outside his bedroom door.

"Ethan are you in there?"

"Yeah, Mom. Hang on."

His bedroom was on the bottom floor of his condo, dark, cold, and almost entirely underground. Not only was it handy when tornado season came around, it was easy to keep dark even at noon. The only problem was that he had to fumble for the light, for his clothes, for what time it was and where he should be upon waking every damn day.

"Well, hurry up. Your dog hasn't seen you in days."

His dog. It was his mother's dog. The miniature poodle had been her birthday present to herself five years ago, not long after she'd moved in after Ethan's father died. Helen hadn't wanted to live alone, and he was at the hospital so often, she'd decided she needed a dog. A year ago, when she'd moved in with Henry instead, the dog hadn't moved with her. She still came by to visit and let the dog out when he was gone overnight, which he appreciated, but knew it was all a ruse for her to check in on him.

Still, Camille wasn't Ethan's dog. His mother had purchased her. His mother was still her primary caregiver. To Ethan, the dog was a constant reminder of what his mother didn't have any longer—a husband. A partner. And then Ethan would miss his father more.

Ethan's father, William Harvey, had died of prostate cancer six weeks after his diagnosis. His dad had been a stubborn ass who had been a doctor his whole life and hadn't thought he needed to see anyone about anything. Ever. Anger still licked at Ethan's insides like tongues of burning flame when he thought about how treatable prostate cancer was when doctors caught it early. Even the aggressive types, which his father admittedly had, had decent treatment rates. But the Harvey's hadn't even had a chance to try.

His father had collapsed in his office one day, been diagnosed the next, and never gotten back up out of his hospital bed. Though it had been five years, Ethan still felt the hole in his gut where his father's encouragement and approval had been. Placing his dad's ancient, cracked leather office chair behind his own desk, storing his dad's collection of medical texts, old and new, in his living room, being the best damn obstetrician he could be still didn't make up for the fact that his dad had died before Ethan had been able to make good on the promise he'd made to him when he started medical school.

It had been a promise his older brothers had made too. Their parents would help pay for medical school so long as the soon-to-be young Doctors Harvey promised to be dedicated to their studies, their practice, and when the time came, their families.

Ethan had done the first two and attempted to do the third. Finding a partner had proved trickier than he'd expected, and he'd sealed his fate by working in hospitals when he'd accepted a fellowship at University of Colorado Medical Center. His emphasis in school had been maternal/fetal medicine, and the fellowship allowed him to concentrate on the tricky, high risk patients that had always been his favorite. He loved his job and took pride in what he did. In the ten years since he'd graduated medical school, he'd never once lost a mother. He never would if he had anything to say about it.

Still, hospital schedules did not lend themselves well to dating, and Ethan hadn't had a relationship that had lasted more than a few weeks since med school. Even with Cynthia, they'd been on for two months, off three, then back on for a month before they were off again. They were over for good this time though, and the only person he'd been serious about since his med school girlfriend had been Juliet, and they hadn't even had a chance to start.

It wasn't like he hadn't tried to find someone to start a family with. But the connection he'd been looking for hadn't happened, so Ethan tried to find contentment with taking care of the family he did have. It had been a stroke of luck that a similar full-time position had opened up in Kansas City at the same time his fellowship had ended, and Ethan had moved home to be nearer to his brothers and their families. Being around to keep his mom company, even if she drove him nuts, was something he took just as much pride in as not losing patients.

In the spirit of family loyalty, Ethan pulled on a pair of running shorts and a t-shirt and followed his mother's footsteps up the stairs into the kitchen, knowing the earful he was going to get when he arrived. Camille wiggled around his feet as he emerged from the basement, and he bent to pet her as his mother started up the coffee pot.

"You're still insisting on sporting that ridiculous beard, I see," she said.

Right in one.

"I want to see what it looks like all grown in." He opened the refrigerator door and stared into the light, finding the shelves mostly bare.

"You look like you're homeless," his mother said.

"Give it a few more days."

"In a few more days, you'll look like a homeless man who stole a white coat and a stethoscope."

"Mom, please," he said, "you know I rarely wear the coat." She sniffed, but he knew better than to take her comments personally. Helen liked everything a certain way, and while she would be vocal about not liking his beard, or his car, or how he slept in the basement, she'd never do more than complain.

"Don't they have a dress code at that hospital?" she asked as he pulled an expired carton of eggs from the fridge.

"Yes, and I am not violating it." Ethan cracked a couple eggs into a bowl, sniffed them, then cracked a couple more. "You hungry?"

"No," she said. "I ate dinner like any reasonable person would have by now."

"It's breakfast for me." He reached for the salt and pepper.

"You know if you opened your own practice, you could keep more regular hours."

And there it was. Ethan was glad his back was to his mother, so she couldn't see him grimace. This was a conversation they'd been having more and more often ever since Ethan had turned thirty-five. She "wanted him to have more meaning to his life." Meaning she wanted him to get married a settle down like his brothers had done.

"I like working at the hospital."

"I was talking to Logan this morning and he mentioned that he could use a full-time obstetrician on his staff."

Logan was Ethan's oldest brother. He ran a family practice clinic in the next suburb over and, as his mother reminded him often, rarely worked outside regular office hours. But working for Logan would mean pap smears and birth control consults and wasting his expertise on a handful of high-risk cases a year.

He gave her the argument she'd expect a surgeon to make. "I'd get no time in the OR if I worked with Logan."

"Maybe not every day, but you'd be able to schedule more of them on your own time instead of going into the hospital at all hours."

Ethan dumped his eggs into a pan and pulled two coffee mugs from the cupboard. It might be almost midnight, but his mother, even in her seventies, never turned down a fresh cup of coffee. "I'm happy where I am," he said as he slid a mug to her over the counter.

She reached for the sugar bowl next to the toaster. "You will never meet a woman looking like a homeless man."

Ethan smiled into his coffee and thought of Juliet.

JULIET TIMED HER RETURN to the hospital so it coincided with when Gina's husband went home for the night. She stayed through three feedings to help Gina work out nursing issues. Then, Juliet rocked the baby, cuddling him so his mother could sleep. She lost track of time as she sat rocking him in the dark room until long after he was asleep. She never got the chance to hold newborns. As both a nurse and a midwifery student, her job was to tend the mother, but Juliet still loved holding babies whenever she had the chance. It didn't make any sense but holding a newborn every now and then helped with the pain of never getting to hold her own baby.

So much turmoil had led her to midwifery, and she could date every single heart-wrenching incident to the moment she ran smack dab into Rich's chest during a school dance her freshman year of high school.

Every year, the state foreign exchange student program hosted a weekend meet up of all the exchange students in the state. For whatever reason, that year it had been in Goodland, Juliet's tiny hometown in northwestern Kansas. They'd kicked off a weekend with a dance that Juliet had helped organize, and in her haste to relay a message from one senior to another, Juliet had almost bowled Rich over.

He'd thrown his arms around her, as much to steady himself as to keep her from falling, but after he'd looked down at her, Rich hadn't let go.

Juliet still sometimes wondered why. At fourteen, she'd been lanky. Her hair had been bright orange and frizzed into uncontrollable curls. Her freckles had stood out stark against her pale skin, and she hadn't yet mastered makeup or figured out how her clothes should fit. But Rich's eyes had changed as he held her in the middle of the bustling dancefloor, focusing into awe out of wide surprise.

He'd introduced himself as Riccardo, but told her to call him Rich, everyone did. For the first hour, Juliet had thought he was an exchange student since he'd spoken as often in French or Italian as he spoke in English. It had only been after he'd explained he was from Kansas City, and that his mother was Italian, and his father was French did Juliet realize he'd been there as part interpreter, part goodwill ambassador.

After they'd danced the rest of the night, Rich had kept Juliet by his side the entire weekend, even though he'd been the coolest senior there and Juliet had only been a freshman grunt. Not only had Juliet's esteem risen several degrees in the local population, but before the weekend was out, Rich had given Juliet her first kiss. He had pulled her behind one of the historic buildings they were touring and asked if it was all right if he kissed her just before he'd laid his lips to hers. His kisses had been soft but insistent, and they'd only sneaked out of the little alley when a chaperone caught them.

They'd exchanged email addresses and phone numbers before he'd left for home. They'd stayed in touch throughout

Juliet's high school career, mostly via text. Juliet had learned the hard way about email. In her sophomore year, she'd forgotten to log out of her account on the family computer, and Colleen, the snoop, had read an exchange that had led to a sit-down discussion with her parents about how she was too young to be having sex, even though she hadn't had sex. And how, whether he lived seven hours away or not, a nineteen-year-old was too old for her.

Juliet had dated boys from her high school to mollify her parents after that. Dating had not stop her from talking to Rich, who had never kept secret that he saw other women, and that he planned to until he and Juliet could be together.

Juliet thought of dating Daniel Holtzman and Colton Wright and their ilk as gaining experience to be ready for Rich. When she'd gone for an overnight visit to the private university he'd attended in Missouri during her senior year, Juliet had played along when he'd whisked her away from her host under the pretense of taking an old friend out for ice cream.

There had been no comparison between Daniel Holtzman and Rich Durand. Daniel had been a linebacker and approached sex like he was going in for a tackle. Rich had worshipped every inch of Juliet he could in the two hours they'd had. When Juliet had gone back home and then to prom with Colton Wright, the student body president, the blanket he'd laid out in the pasture with the candles and pilfered wine had been sweet, but even pretending he was Rich hadn't helped her enjoy herself.

That summer, Juliet had been feigning indecision about where to go to school, still weighing her parent's expectations against what her heart wanted. But after her visit to Rich's school, after fending off Colton Wright's fumbling advances for weeks, she'd accepted the scholarship offer from the University of Kansas nursing program so she could be closer to Rich.

Her friends had told her Rich would have grown bored by the time she moved. Her parents had wanted her to go to the University of Colorado in Denver instead. It was a more prestigious school they'd said, and closer to home, they'd make up the cost difference of going out of state. What they hadn't said was that they hadn't wanted her to move for a boy.

Even Colleen, who'd been a confidant before the email incident, had told Juliet that the chances of Rich being sincere were slim, and that Juliet had gotten the reputation as a slut for making out with a bunch of dudes—and that Colton had only taken her to prom so he could lose his virginity.

Juliet hadn't spoken to her sister for the rest of the summer, and she'd ignored her parents. Instead she'd corresponded with her new roommate, who had turned out to be Alex, and called Rich every day.

What no one had understood, was that Rich and Juliet were soulmates. What they'd had was powerful and real. He'd read her Italian poetry over the phone. She'd texted him her gripes. He'd helped her find her way to nursing during her junior year when she'd been disconsolate after volunteering at the hospital for a few weeks and hadn't understood why. Juliet had known from the beginning Rich would be a part of her world, and she'd been confident enough in him to cut the naysayers out of her life.

When Rich had showed up to help her move into her dorm room, Juliet had introduced him to her parents with a smug smile. Her parents had been polite, but worn tight, disapproving frowns. It hadn't stopped Juliet and Rich from being inseparable for the next four years. Until they suddenly hadn't been.

Juliet had already been leaning toward labor and delivery work when her application for the obstetrics practicum had been accepted, and after spending time with the midwives in the hospital birth center versus the endless c-sections in the regular labor and delivery ward, she'd grown enamored with the style of care.

When a woman was vulnerable, she needed the support of other women who knew what she was going through. When Alex, who had dropped out of nursing school to pursue her jewelry making business, had landed a job as the receptionist at the birthing center, Juliet had been one of the first people to know they were hiring.

Even though she'd made friends with a few of the nurses at KU Med, and had a recommendation from her mentor, Juliet had been undecided. After Ethan had dropped into a breakfast conversation, surrounded by ten other people, that he would put in a good word for her if she applied, Juliet had chosen the birthing center.

After she and Rich had fallen apart—after the abrupt conclusion to her night with Ethan, Juliet had run. She'd chosen the option that had taken her away from all of it. Not to hide, but to heal. The birthing center had been soothing and invigorating and bursting at the seams with love. She hadn't worked there more than two months before toying with the idea of getting her CNM. At the time, she'd been finishing up her yoga teacher training, and had thrown herself into that instead.

Teaching yoga had been fun. She still taught one flow class and one prenatal class each week, but it hadn't given her the same satisfaction as being in the birthing room had.

It had taken Juliet two years to gather the courage to apply to the program. Even then, it had taken getting burned by Rich a second time. He'd convinced her to give him another chance. When he still couldn't remain faithful to her, Juliet knew if she didn't go after what she wanted, she'd be doomed to repeat her mistakes forever. Juliet had cut Rich out and enrolled. For the last two years, her life had been nothing but work and school. Everything else had been a distraction.

Now her certification was so close she could taste it. With it, Juliet would have the means to be independent. She would never have to depend on someone else for a place to live or help to pay the bills. She would stand on her own two feet and be free to become her own woman. She had once thought that might never happen.

A knock on the door frame woke her from her musings, and she startled, losing the baby's grip on her finger.

Ethan stood in the doorway, blocking the meager light from the hall. "Visiting hours were over ages ago."

Juliet shushed him, returned the sleeping baby to his bassinet and shooed Ethan into the dark, quiet hallway. "What are you doing here?"

"Got called in for an emergency C-section, then I thought I'd check on the one from yesterday. How's she doing?" He leaned against the wall with his arms crossed, and Juliet wondered if he had the ability to stand on his own.

"She's recovering well."

"You staying all night?"

Juliet checked her watch. It was nearly three in the morning. "Wasn't planning on it." She'd meant to go home and try to nap and get back to a normal sleep schedule.

"Is it too soon to do breakfast again? The cafeteria breaks out the cinnamon rolls about now."

He stood too close to her. Much too close. Awareness prickled as the nurse coordinator at the desk spied on them, but Juliet couldn't bring herself to step away from the smiling man with bright blue eyes.

"Are you going to ask me out every time you see me now?"

Ethan stood straight and reached his right hand to touch her. His eyes were tender, and she knew he was remembering too much about her past. He knew so much without actually knowing her.

"We could be friends, at least." He let the tips of his fingers graze her cheek as his hand fell away.

Juliet wasn't surprised by the spark she felt when he touched her. It had been there the day before when he'd run his nose over hers. This touch was more intimate than that one. The whisper of his fingers down her cheek made the nose thing seem vulgar by comparison. To remind him he didn't have permission to touch her, Juliet took one measured step back.

"I'm going home," she said, then turned on her heel and walked away. Juliet didn't need whatever he was offering.

"Sleep well, my fair Juliet," he called after her.

She flipped him off as she retreated. Like she'd never heard the Shakespeare jokes before.

ETHAN CHUCKLED TO HIMSELF as Juliet sauntered off his ward. It had been too long since he'd played this game. If he could get her riled up, she'd still be thinking about him when she got home. Then she'd think of him when she woke up the next morning, and later.

"What else do we have going on, Elsie?" he asked the nurse behind the desk.

Elsie was a no-nonsense nurse in her sixties who ran nights in L&D. The lights might be dimmed, but nights were usually the busy shift. The night was almost too quiet.

"Two labors in progress, one induction, and a nursery full of two-day old babies." That meant that the mothers on the ward would leave soon, and all the new laboring women would arrive at once tomorrow.

"You call me if you need me tomorrow."

"Dr. Taylor is on call tomorrow."

"If you need an extra set of hands, I'm here."

"I'll mark it on the calendar, Dr. Harvey." She was already scribbling something on the desk calendar.

"You're a doll, Elsie."

She glared. "Go chase after that pretty midwife if you want to flirt, Doctor." Then she flipped open a file and blocked him from view.

Chapter Four

Juliet and her sister had communicated more in the last twenty-four hours than they had in the last twenty-four months. Juliet answered Colleen's original question by telling her to avoid comparing the way a hospital did business to how cattle are herded through runs, it might imply that they were lining patients up for slaughter.

COLLEEN: *Right, so instead of saying that my sister is a midwife who hates hospitals, I should say she's a nurse who's inspired a great respect for the health care industry in me.*

JULIET: *I don't hate hospitals.*

COLLEEN: *I can't lead with them being a necessary evil either.*

Juliet had to think about her response for a long time. She'd considered leaving the conversation at that but didn't think it would be fair when her little sister had asked for her help for the first time since high school.

After she'd flipped Ethan off and left the hospital, Juliet had sat in her car in the dark parking garage and typed to her sister that the best way for the hospital to sell itself was to put the patient first always, not doctors, not insurance companies. Patients first, always.

Two messages interrupted the playlist Juliet was streaming on her phone while she did yoga the next morning.

COLLEEN: *I can work with that. Thanks.*

COLLEEN: *3am, huh? Were you just getting off work?*

JULIET: *Sort of. Gina had another baby. I was hanging out with her at the hospital.*

Colleen's reply was swift, and Juliet cringed when she read it.

COLLEEN: *Rich's sister? You aren't fucking him again are you?*

"She's so much more than Rich's sister," Juliet muttered out loud, but didn't think it would help her already rocky relationship with Colleen if she admitted to preferring her ex's sister's company.

JULIET: *He's not the only man in my world.*

Why everyone thought her legs spread the second Rich arrived was beyond her. Juliet hadn't slept with Rich in two years, and she hadn't wanted to.

COLLEEN: *Yeah, but sometimes I'm not sure you know that.*

Juliet had texted back that she wasn't seeing Rich and had left her phone to recharge in her bedroom while she showered and ate breakfast, but when she came back another text was waiting for her.

COLLEEN: *That means there's someone else, right?*

Juliet didn't know what had gotten into her sister. They barely talked, and when they did it was about school or work or their parents, it was never ever about boys—well, unless Colleen was taking a jab at Rich.

JULIET: *Not for a while, unless you count the doctor that asks me out every time I see him.*

Juliet dropped her shoulder bag onto the passenger seat of her car as Colleen responded.

COLLEEN: *And is this doctor old? Ugly? Creepy?*

JULIET: *He's an arrogant ass.*

Juliet pocketed her phone so she could start her car.

She was opening the door to Gina's room when her phone pinged again.

COLLEEN: *Better an ass than an asshole.*

Juliet snorted, knowing Colleen meant Rich, only to look up from her phone and realize that the man in question was smiling at her over the head of a wiggling toddler. Something beneath her ribs twisted. It was like a long-abandoned dream come to life, Noah, with his dark hair and olive skin bore enough of a resemblance to his mother to be able to pass for Rich's son.

Before Juliet caught her breath, Gina said, "Hey! We finally have a name!"

The baby was asleep in his mother's arms, and Juliet breathed in once through her nose and out through her mouth as she approached the bed, ignoring the man who was sitting on the other side.

"Well don't leave me hanging," Juliet said. "What is it?"

"Isaac." Gina grinned.

Juliet felt her lips curl to mirror her friend's smile as she stroked the baby's cheek, his dark hair already hanging over his forehead.

"Perfect."

"And very Old Testament," Rich said, letting Noah slide down his legs onto the floor to play.

"Not intentionally." Gina stroked a fingertip over her baby's fat cheek.

Rich's teasing grin was infectious, or maybe Juliet was as susceptible to him as everyone thought, because she found herself smiling along with him as he said, "All you need now is an Abraham and a Jacob and you'll have a complete set of patriarchs."

Gina spluttered. "Oh no. No way. After that disaster," she gestured with her hand toward her door, "there will be no more little patriarchs."

Juliet took the opportunity to evaluate her friend from a nurse's point of view. Gina's lips, usually a bright pink, blended in with the too pale skin on her face. She leaned heavily against the pillows on the bed, when Gina never slouched. She still wore an IV portal, which meant they were still giving her pain meds, and fluids to help her recover from the blood loss. While Ethan had been quick and precise with the surgery, Gina had still been through an ordeal.

"I don't blame you one bit," she said. "But it's okay if you change your mind."

Gina gave her a dubious look that had Juliet changing the subject while Rich chuckled in the background, his eyes on the toddler at his feet.

"I stopped by to see if you were tired of hospital food yet."

Gina's tired eyes lit up. "Yes, yes, yes! What can you bring me?"

"What do you want?" Juliet asked.

"I have been dreaming about lamb all day. Do you hate me?"

"Not at all," Juliet said. "You could probably use the iron."

"The braised lamb at that Mediterranean place Juliet and I used to go to was amazing," Rich said, then asked Juliet, "They still a couple blocks over?"

Had he not been back since they'd broken up? If not, perhaps they had even less in common than she'd thought, because "that Mediterranean place" had been one of their favorite restaurants.

"Sure are." Juliet met Rich's eyes for the first time since her arrival. The open expression of equal parts regret and longing he bared to her was too much, and she looked away.

"Why don't Noah and I grab us all lunch?" he said to Gina. "Braised lamb for us." His eyes shifted to Juliet. "And the veggie and hummus platter for you?"

She nodded, "with—"

But he cut her off, "Baba Ganouj and extra pita. I remember."

Gina rescued Juliet from Rich's too tender smile with a barked, "Extra pita for me too!"

After Rich and Noah had gone, Gina dropped her head back onto her pillow. "How am I going to take care of Noah when I go home? I can't even move." For emphasis, she tried to raise baby Isaac in her arms and winced.

Juliet moved the infant to the bassinet and said, "That will improve. And where is Colin? Isn't he on paternity leave yet?"

Gina rolled her eyes. "He's finishing up some contracts or something and officially starting tomorrow."

"Do bar managers work on Sundays?"

Colin worked as a sales rep for a local brewery.

"I think he's setting stuff up for other reps. Which he should have had done already, but whatever. If he's home for the next four weeks, I don't care."

"I can help out more now that's school's out."

Gina stretched her arms up over her head. "You're sweet, but don't waste your summer on me."

"It's not a waste," Juliet said. "I'm here for whatever you need."

The expression on Gina's face turned tight, even as her voice softened. "You should do something for yourself this summer. Take a vacation. Have a fling, or hell, just go on a date."

Juliet tried to look relaxed as she stretched her yoga-sore legs out in front of her. "Vacations are expensive. I don't have the energy for a fling, and there isn't anyone I want to date."

Gina raised her eyebrows. "No one?"

"Your brother and I are through. Forever."

A sad grin pressed at Gina's pale lips. "I know. He misses you, but believe me, I understand why."

Juliet did not allow herself to absorb the fact that Rich missed her, and Gina didn't give her much time as she said, "I didn't mean Rich. I was asking about the doctor with the muscly arms who was asking about you this morning."

"Dr. Harvey was asking about me?" Juliet's words left her mouth in an embarrassingly breathy rush.

Gina's grin turned sly. "So, you two do know each other."

"We worked together a lot when I was finishing up nursing school."

"He said the same thing. Sounds rehearsed."

"What?"

"The whole, 'we worked together' thing sounds like a line you two came up with to hide how well you know one another." Gina gazed down at her newborn, her expression turning mushy as she asked, "Why is that?"

"It's not a line. It's the truth."

"Then why are you blushing?"

Juliet buried her face in her hands, then peeked at Gina through her fingers, trying, and failing, not to look guilty.

"He's the one, isn't he? The doctor with the crush you took advantage of to hurt Rich."

That was, word for word, how Juliet had once explained what happened with Ethan. Only, Juliet didn't feel that way anymore. "That may not be exactly what happened."

The knowing gleam in Gina's eyes said enough, but the other woman only said, "He wanted to know how we knew each other," as if Juliet had asked what they'd talked about.

Juliet waited for Gina to get to the point.

"He looked jealous as hell when I told him you used to be engaged to my brother. Rich and Noah weren't here yet, of course."

"Rich and I were never engaged," Juliet said.

"My brother may have never got up the guts to pop the question, but you two were done for from the start. Even I could tell he was a goner when he first came back from Goodland." Which was saying something, since Gina had been finishing up her journalism degree at the University of Missouri three hours away.

Juliet nodded, her eyes on the floor. "We talked about getting married after . . ."

Gina sat forward and covered Juliet's hand with her own, the one with the IV port in it, letting Juliet know she didn't have to finish that sentence. Annoyance warred with gratitude. On the one hand, Juliet didn't want to talk about the twenty-four hours that had led to her and Rich's initial breakup. On the other hand, it could be that she hadn't moved past it yet *because* she refused to talk about it.

Juliet and Rich had broken up four years ago. Outside her one night with Ethan and a handful of dates courtesy of Alex, Juliet's only serious lover since then had been Rich. They'd reconnected when Noah had been born, and Rich had wooed her back into bed within days of the event. They'd spent one month in a cocoon of lust-induced stupor, meeting for a tryst whenever the other could spare a moment, having coffee or lunch. It had only been when Juliet asked how come they never went to his place that it came out that Rich had been living with another woman—in the same apartment he and Juliet had lived in before.

It had taken all of Juliet's willpower to not kick him in the balls. No matter how he begged her to give him a chance or how many times he promised to break up with Rachel, Juliet had told him that they were through, that she wouldn't be made a fool of again.

Juliet had stayed firm in her resolve for the past two years.

Instead of talking about Rich, Juliet told Gina about Ethan treating her for breakfast and about their other short encounter.

Gina said, "You should go for it."

"I can't," Juliet said. "If the school found out I was dating a doctor from my program, I'd get kicked out before I could even come up an excuse."

Gina shrugged, "So? Who says you'd be together that long? Doesn't mean you can't enjoy your summer with him."

Juliet shook her head, but part of her wanted to know who Ethan was outside of work. Would he taunt her at every turn? Would they argue about the differences about the need for epidurals and episiotomies? Would he make her laugh? Would every time be as electric as that one stolen night?

Juliet wasn't sure she was ready to find out. "Next semester's only eight weeks away. That's not even worth it."

"I don't know," Gina said. "I could have a lot of great sex if I had eight weeks and no kids."

Juliet couldn't help her laugh. "You are an awful influence."

Gina winked and laid her head back against her pillows as a knowing smile played at her lips.

Rich returned with the food a few minutes later, and they passed a pleasant lunch, eating while their attention was on Noah and Isaac. They talked about their work, Rich, a university Italian professor, Gina, a freelance writer, and Juliet's yoga classes. Rich didn't flirt in front of his sister. Though he did drop that he was currently single into the conversation.

Juliet excused herself to go when Gina's nurse arrived. Rich left with her, claiming he was taking Noah home for a nap.

"Join me for coffee sometime soon?" he asked as they stepped into the elevator, a sleepy toddler's head lolling against his shoulder.

"I don't think that's a good idea," Juliet said.

"It's just coffee, Jules."

Rich was the only one to ever call her Jules. It simultaneously annoyed her and made her yearn for the time when the endearment had made her feel special.

"It wouldn't be just coffee for long," she said.

"Only when you're ready for it to be more."

Juliet looked him up and down. He was still so gorgeous. His espresso colored brown eyes had always been expressive, and his thick dark hair hung over his brow in a way that invited her to brush it back along his scalp. His height made Juliet feel small, even though she was not short. She could almost feel the way his long arms wrapped around her waist when he held her.

"It can't be more, Rich. Not after everything."

"You'll forgive me if I try to change your mind?" He offered her a crooked grin, and despite her resolve, Juliet felt a twinge of longing.

"Why?" she asked, her heart racing to hear the answer.

"I miss you," he said. "Every day. It's not the same without you."

The elevator opened to Juliet's level in the parking garage. "I can't," was all she said, and left him standing there.

When she checked her phone before starting her car, she had another text.

COLLEEN: *Is the persistent doctor cute, at least?*

Chapter Five

S undays were for baseball.

It had been that way as far back as Ethan could remember. If their dad hadn't treated them all to a Royals game
on Sundays, they had been camped around the TV at home.
All the Harvey brothers had been enrolled in little league.
Little league had turned into high school ball. For Henry,
who'd won a scholarship, there'd been college games too.

The Harvey brothers were all doctors, yes, but they all
agreed baseball was what they really had in common. From
time to time, they still went to games together, but like their
father before them, Logan and Henry liked to make games a
family affair, taking their wives and kids. Sunday afternoons
though, were just for the brothers. It was Ethan's favorite
part of the week.

They gathered at Logan's place in the country, where
Logan had built a theater room in a failed bid to impress
his teenage daughters. Paige and Vanessa, Henry's and Logan's wives, took up residence in the kitchen, giving the men
their space, even though Paige was probably the biggest baseball fan of them all. Helen, Ethan's mom rounded up all
the grandchildren for their weekly Sunday cooking lesson at
Henry's place. Each child made a dish from scratch and at

the end of the afternoon, they sat down for a big Sunday feast.

That afternoon had started early, the Royals game was supposed to start at quarter after one, but the game before it ran long, so the network didn't air the Royals until after half past one. They were playing Cincinnati, and an hour and a half in, this game was looking to be a long one.

The Royals were down.

Which, while annoying, was not spurring Ethan's usual desperate optimism that the team could pull off a win if only he hoped hard enough. Instead, Ethan found himself reclined in his usual leather chair, working on his third Coors Lite of the day, doing what he'd done for the last three days: allowing memories of Juliet to resurface.

There had been the expected ones, the image of kissing her in the rain, the way she'd looked with the morning light shining through the ferns in the bedroom windows as she slept. He recalled her complete concentration by his side in the operating room, or the way she coaxed a laboring woman to breathe. But then there were others that had surprised him, like her rolling her eyes at him at Dino's and choosing the chair farthest away from him. The way she'd attempted to socialize, but also not offered any personal details.

Then, out of nowhere, her age would strike him like a blow to his stomach. He hadn't realized Juliet was that young. If he had taken a second to think about it, to do the math, he might have guessed, but he never had. Somehow, he'd assumed she'd been an older student, that she was perhaps closer to thirty. That Ethan was ten years older made him squirm with discomfort, but not enough to regret his desire to woo her properly this time.

Loud cheering from both his brothers pulled Ethan from his thoughts and he focused on the projection screen just in time to see the replay of a Cincinnati runner getting tagged out over home plate. Ethan joined in the cheering, but his tardiness didn't go unnoticed.

"Where is your head today?" Henry asked when the game had gone to commercial. "You completely missed that play."

Henry was the tallest of the three brothers, and still had most of the muscle he'd built as a hitter in college. With his sandy brown hair and tan skin, he looked like he worked out-doors, but it was really because he and Paige spent most of their time off hiking outside the city or working in their garden. Henry didn't immediately strike one as a pediatrician, but he had a soft voice and a playful manner that leant itself well to working with children.

"It was a busy week," Ethan said, draining his beer and reaching for another.

His brothers exchanged a look. Logan, the oldest, looked most like their father—the way Ethan though a doctor should look. He was taller than Ethan, with long, lean physique of a runner. His hair, the same chestnut shade as Ethan's, was graying at the temples and he wore studious round glasses on his intelligent square face.

While his brothers took after their dad, Ethan looked more like their mother's father. He had a shorter, broader build. The kind that could devolve from broad to stout with very little effort, so it was a good thing he preferred to be active. Growing up, he had always resented being the youngest and the smallest. In situations like these, it didn't take much for his brothers to make him feel like he was twelve again. The look they shared said doctor or no, unmarried, childless Ethan didn't know what a busy week was. Ethan had to tamp down the similarly pre-pubescent surge of defensiveness.

He wanted to ask them how often they worked outside their regular office hours, but perhaps they were right. If he hadn't felt like he'd lived three weeks over the past three days with the way his mind wouldn't shut off, he would have agreed with them.

While Henry had complained about a long lingering strain of the flu, Ethan had stared unseeing at his beer bottle. While Logan had ranted about the new boy his youngest daughter wanted to invite to the Fourth of July party, Ethan had been figuring out how to ask Juliet out again.

She'd been all he'd thought about all weekend.

He'd even googled her after work yesterday when he couldn't fall asleep. On top of her job and going to school, it turned out that Juliet also taught yoga classes. The website he found said she specialized in prenatal classes and showed photos of her leading class in a form fitting gray outfit on top of a pink mat. He could see the muscle definition in her arms as she balanced on one leg, the other leg contorted up and out behind her, held in place with a hand around her ankle. She looked like a dancer, graceful and strong. He no longer wondered at the unexpected strength she'd exhibited when she'd pushed him against the wall the other day.

"You lose somebody?" Logan asked, and from the concern now on his brothers' faces, Ethan could tell he'd missed more of their conversation.

Ethan shook his head but told them about Juliet's friend anyway. His brothers listened to him explain how Juliet's quick thinking had saved her friend's uterus, possibly her life. He didn't name her, just in case his brothers remembered. Instead, Ethan allowed them to remind him that he couldn't think about how things could have gone wrong. It was a pep talk they gave each other from time to time, but Ethan specialized in high risk cases *because* he could keep his head and his hands steady under pressure. It didn't change how failing a growing family in their time of need was his number one fear. He never wanted to know what it felt like to lose a mother.

The sympathy his brothers offered between plays eased the stress that had been building in his shoulders and creeping up his neck into his jaw. He wanted to tell his brothers about Juliet, but he didn't know how to explain her. She was the only woman he'd been enamored with since Amanda, and his brothers knew that. Ethan couldn't confide his feelings toward her to them when he didn't even know how to get ahold of her—short of showing up at one of her yoga classes. That was a level of pathetic he wasn't ready to stoop to yet. But he had to tell her she was the missing puzzle piece. The part of him he hadn't known was missing until he'd found her.

At the top of the seventh inning, Logan tapped the empty twelve pack with his toe. They never finished the whole thing, but today, he said to Ethan, "There's another one in the fridge. Why don't you go get it?"

On his way to the garage he had to pass through the kitchen where Vanessa and Paige sat sipping wine at the breakfast bar, a half-finished antipasti platter between them. Their conversation cut off when he appeared.

"Holy hell, you have a beard," Paige, Henry's wife, said. She slurred enough to imply that the women had been drinking just as much as the men.

"I'm trying it," he said. After a week, the dark hair looked like he meant it to be there instead of looking like he'd forgotten to shave for a few days.

"In twenty-five years, I have never seen you with a beard," Vanessa said.

"Have you and Logan been married that long?" Ethan asked.

"Don't change the subject," Paige said.

"I'm getting another case of beer."

"But we want to talk about your beard." Vanessa giggled. It had been a long time since he'd heard his sister-in-law giggle.

"It's just facial hair," Ethan said, then descended into the garage and pulled a new twelve pack out of the refrigerator.

"I've begged and begged your brother to give a beard a try," Paige said, "and he won't."

Vanessa grabbed his arm as he passed, "Is it for a woman?"

"No."

"That was a mighty quick answer."

"And an accurate one."

"It's not Cynthia again is it?" Paige asked, her lips forming into a pout. "I like her, but she isn't right for you, and we need a third girl up here." It was a common refrain from his sisters-in-law.

Ethan shook his head, knowing anything he said would only be fodder for their gossip. He was glad they couldn't see inside his mind to the endless replays of what it had felt like to be on top of Juliet. Inside her.

"Tell us if there is a woman, though," Vanessa called after him as he retreated down the stairs. Just over the sound of his brothers yelling at the umpire, he heard her say, "Oh, there's totally a woman."

Chapter Six

O ver her lunch break, Juliet deleted three texts from Rich without reading them. He'd texted her all weekend, suggesting they meet at coffee shops they'd never been to or a new jazz bar. Juliet had been dying to go to that Jazz club—just not with him. She stopped reading the texts after the fifth then deleted them outright when they kept coming.

Each time Rich's name popped up on her phone, Juliet's heart raced. Part of it was habit, the old excitement of waiting to hear from him, but dread thudded in her chest more often than not. Juliet had known this was coming. Until one of them moved away or got married, Rich and Juliet would never be completely over. There was too much history.

It wasn't like Juliet didn't feel the tug. She did. She missed their connection. The constant ache had been her fast friend for the last four years. But there was more to it than that. Juliet had messed up big time. Sure, Rich had betrayed her first, but Juliet had been the one to land the final blow in her relationship with Rich. It had taken her two years to forgive herself. And after her second failed attempt at a relationship with Rich, Juliet had been in man exile. It was just better for everyone if Juliet kept her brokenness to herself.

Even if Ethan still tempted her.

Juliet stopped by the reception desk to check in with Alex before heading back to the office. Instead of giving Juliet the rundown on the afternoon appointments, Alex said, "Did you see the cookies?"

"There's cookies? Was Celia here?" Celia was the pharmaceutical rep who hawked them birth control and plied them with goodies.

Alex shook her head. "She's not due in until Wednesday. These are from Dr. Harvey."

Juliet's mouth went dry. "Dr. Harvey?"

Swiveling in her chair, Alex pinned Juliet with a hard look. "Seems you left a little bit out of your story when you told me what went down with Gina."

"That he was the surgeon was neither here nor there."

Alex snorted. "Right. And have you slept with any other OB-GYNs?"

Juliet rounded the desk, flapping a hand at her friend while fighting a blush. "Will you keep your voice down?"

"You're not changing your story now, are you?" Alex asked in a stage whisper.

"No." Juliet leaned against the desk and crossed her arms. "But that's ancient history. I don't even know him that well."

Alex nodded. "Sure you don't. I mean, how many guys remember the favorite cookie of a woman they spent one night with four years ago?"

Standing straighter, Juliet frowned. "What?"

Alex grinned. "He sent snickerdoodles."

"So?"

"From the vegan bakery."

All Juliet's blood drained from her head. "Shit. Really?"

"Oddly specific, right?" Alex's grin was reaching Cheshire cat proportions.

"How does he even know that?"

And just like that, the teasing grin on Alex's face fell, perhaps remembering, like Juliet was, all the times they'd talked over what had happened.

"I'll tell you the same thing I told you back then, I think he was paying a lot more attention to you than he let on."

For the last four years, guilt had been Juliet's dominant emotion when it came to Ethan. Alex had convinced Juliet that Ethan had been aware of what he'd done that night, but he'd still fallen into bed with Juliet without all the facts—or any of them, and she was ashamed she'd put him in that position.

"So, what do you think this means?" Juliet asked, not trusting her own conclusions.

Her roommate rolled her eyes. "If you need me to say he still has the hots for you, I will, but you know it already. What I want to know is what you'll do about it."

"I can't do anything about it," Juliet said. "I've worked too hard to get kicked out of the program over some guy."

"You know you sound crazy right? Nobody is gonna care."

"It's the first rule in the practicum book."

"I remember," Alex rested the end of her pen on her lip. "Do you think that's part of the doctor handbook? I always wondered if they put that rule in the nursing handbook because most nursing students are women. Do the majority dudes get the same treatment?"

Juliet shrugged. "Probably not."

Alex scowled. "Man fuck the patriarchy."

"You have to do more than parrot the catchphrase if you want to change anything, you know."

"Honey, I challenge the patriarchy through my very existence. Now, leave me alone," Alex shooed her away. "I have prenatal appointments to schedule and arbitrary social boundaries to topple."

Juliet waved and made her way to the break room where she indeed found a half-empty box of snickerdoodles. She grabbed three, munching on them as she collected the paperwork she needed to finish and submit to Kelly for billing. Try as she might, Juliet couldn't keep the memory of her night with Ethan from creeping into her present.

It had been her last shift for her senior practicum. She almost hadn't made it in after her doctor's appointment that morning. She'd been so late she'd had to provide her supervisor with a signed doctor's note so she could graduate. The night had been a blur until they'd taken one patient in for an emergency c-section due to fetal distress. The baby had low oxygen levels at birth, and despite everything, had passed away by the end of Juliet's shift.

Somehow, Juliet had held it together. She had cancelled her plans with Alex and told herself she could go home and curl up beside Rich when it was all over. She would tell him about her awful day, about her doctor's appointment. He would stroke her back and tell her that losing the baby was just one of those things, that it couldn't be her fault, that she'd done everything she could. Then he would kiss her, make love to her, and even if she didn't feel better, she would at least feel less alone.

When she got home that night, Rich wasn't there, and he still wasn't answering his phone. He hadn't left a note. The only sign he'd been there after work was his favorite coffee mug, half-empty, sitting by the sink. He always drank a mug after work, so Juliet wouldn't have thought twice about the discarded mug if there hadn't been a second coffee cup. Juliet had washed all the dishes that morning after Rich had gone to work.

She had stared at the wall over the kitchen sink and allowed all the small suspicions she'd brushed off over the last couple months accumulate in her mind. The missed phone calls, the late nights, the vague answers about where he'd been had sounded less and less like a busy semester and increasingly like something else. Countless times she'd told herself Rich wouldn't have cheated. They'd been soulmates. They'd known it since high school. He'd waited for her. She'd moved across the state to be with him. They'd been living together, they'd been planning to get married, they'd been—

There'd been a crash as Juliet had hurled his coffee mug against the far wall, the lipstick stained mug had shattered next to it moments later. She had dialed Rich's phone number again, and had left him another message, this time allowing the blinding pain in her belly force all her words out in a rush.

"This is the third time I've called you today, and it's the last time. Remember how I was supposed to call and let you know how the doctor's appointment went? Well, you should have fucking answered your phone, Rich. Because it was bad. Really fucking bad. I lost the baby, and we lost a baby at work tonight, and you're off screwing some random chick instead of home where I need you. And I'm so pissed and so sad and so broken, and you were supposed to be here, and you're not, and I don't think I can forgive you." She paused to choke on a sob. Juliet had refused to let him hear her break down. "I'm not stupid, you know. I know you've not always been faithful, but I have been. And I was so excited to have your baby. And now I'm not, and we're over. I'm done. You and your fuck buddy can go to hell."

Then Juliet had grabbed her keys and left. She was exhausted, but she hadn't been able to stay in that apartment alone. Juliet had walked, circling her neighborhood until she was back at the hospital, wiping the silent tears that flowed down her cheeks. Her limbs were shaking, and she realized she hadn't eaten all day.

A group of people in scrubs had left the ER doors and had walked up the hill toward Dino's, and Juliet had followed them in. She'd seated herself at the little table in the corner where the group from the hospital couldn't see her from their booth and had stared at her coffee and pie, willing her tears to stop.

Juliet didn't know how long she'd sat there, and she hadn't noticed anyone approach until he'd plopped down in a chair next to her. Maybe if she kept staring at the table, he would go away.

"You gonna eat any of that pie?" Dr. Harvey asked.

Juliet pushed the pie towards him without looking.

"Thanks. Peach is my favorite." The clatter of metal against porcelain told her he'd dug in. "You should have joined us," he'd said between bites.

Juliet had raised her head to him. She had meant to tell him to go away, but when he'd seen the tear tracks marring her cheeks, he'd dropped his fork.

"Ah, hell, Hawthorne." He'd yanked a few napkins out of the dispenser and held them out to her in a wad. "You had the early neonatal death tonight, didn't you?"

She'd nodded, taking the napkins, but held them in her fist instead of wiping her eyes.

"Your first?"

Juliet had nodded again and before she could stop him, Dr. Harvey had pulled her into his arms, murmuring the exact words she'd wanted to hear from Rich. His warm, steady hand had rubbed small circles over her back, and for the first time all day, Juliet felt safe.

Shock and anger had given way to despair. Juliet had buried her face in his scrubs and sobbed. She'd forgotten where she was and who she was with. All she'd felt had been pain for herself and pain for that poor woman back at the hospital. At least that woman had her husband.

The smell of the hospital soap had reined her back in as she had remembered she had been crying all over Dr. Harvey. Juliet had pulled back, trying to catch her breath. "I'm sorry," she'd said. "You don't even know me and—"

He'd clasped one of her hands. "Shhh. Don't apologize." He'd wiped her tears away with the strong, steadfast fingers. "We all have these days." His voice had been sturdy and calm, and she'd thought someone should tell him to use that voice with patients instead of his usual brusque aloofness.

"It's been an awful day." She hadn't been able to tear her eyes away from his. His expression had been so clear and earnest and so patient, like there had been nothing more important in the world than comforting an acquaintance.

When he'd squeezed her hand in comfort, Juliet had shied away. "Dr. Harvey—"

"Please, it's Ethan."

"Thank you, but I should get home."

Ethan had sat up a little straighter, but he'd kept his grip on her hand. "Are you on your bike? Is there someone I can call for you? A sister, your mom? A boyfriend?"

Juliet had shaken her head no. "I walked."

Ethan had checked his watch and cursed. Juliet had checked hers, 2:15 A. M. "I can't let you walk home on your own."

"It's fine."

"Come on. I'll go with you."

Juliet hadn't had the energy to decline his offer but had dried her face and blown her nose as Ethan had paid for her pie. When he'd grasped her hand again and led her out the door, she hadn't protested. A light rain had dotted their shoulders with cool water, but Ethan hadn't hurried her through it. He'd allowed her to set their pace as they had walked the few blocks to her apartment.

"No wonder you always ride your bike to work," he'd said when they turned the corner onto her street. "It's so close."

Juliet had shrugged and realized she still had hold of his hand. She'd squeezed to make sure she hadn't been imagining it. The world had blurred around the edges and numbness had set in, but when Ethan had squeezed back, she realized he hadn't stopped talking.

"If you get the job, it'd be an easy commute."

Juliet had heard the smile in his voice and recognized his attempt to cheer her up. It had been Rich's apartment, so she said, "I have to move." She hadn't blamed him for faltering for a second. He hadn't known she'd been going through more than just a tragedy at work.

"That's too bad," he'd said. "Do you know where you're going?"

"I'm trying not to worry about it until I find a job." It had been an outright lie. If she'd had anywhere else to go, she wouldn't have come back here. She'd already known she'd end up on the futon in Alex's studio apartment the next day.

"Smart."

He'd remained at her side as they'd approached her building. She'd lived in the apartment above the Italian restaurant. Juliet had stopped and looked up to where, in the daylight, you could have seen her rubber tree plant through the living room window.

"I'd eat nothing but pasta if I lived here," he'd said, and the smile on his face hadn't erased the concern from his eyes. When Juliet hadn't answered, he'd stepped closer and cupped her cheek with his palm. "Is everything okay, Juliet?"

"Have you ever felt like your whole life is falling apart?" Juliet's voice had cracked, and new tears had mingled with the rain on her face.

Ethan had stroked her cheek with his thumb. "Once. About a year ago."

"That's me, tonight."

"Juliet . . ." He'd trailed off. He'd searched her eyes with his own, as if he'd been begging for a way to fix everything for her—and his gentleness, his earnestness, had made her think that maybe he could have. "Juliet," he'd said again, this time with anguish in his voice.

He'd never said her name before tonight. He'd always called her by her last name. Until he'd said it, she hadn't been sure he'd known it.

And then he'd kissed her, his lips damp from the rain, but firm. The arm around her waist had been sturdy, and Juliet had sunk into him even as he'd ended the kiss and angled his head to judge her reaction. Juliet hadn't shied away from his gaze but hadn't hidden her pain and confusion either.

When Ethan had looked back with sad determination in his eyes, Juliet had said, "Come upstairs with me."

"Are you sure?"

"I don't want to be alone."

Ethan had nodded, and Juliet dropped his hand to unlock the door. Inviting him up had been a horrible decision, but Juliet hadn't been able to face going upstairs by herself. The choice had been eighty-five percent self-indulgence, ten percent attraction, and five percent revenge. The small part of her that had wanted to hurt Rich hoped he'd arrived home and would be there to see her come home with another lover.

The apartment had been dark and silent.

Juliet had flipped on the lamp by the door and had balanced on one foot as Ethan took in the shabby apartment. She'd hoped that tree pose might balance the world that had been coming apart around her. "Can I get you something to drink?"

Ethan had shaken his head no. He'd stepped in close, had raised his arm, but had been hesitant to embrace her. "What's wrong, Juliet?"

She'd stepped into him and wrapped her arms around his waist and rested her head on his chest. She'd felt the warmth of his skin through the rain-soaked fabric. His arms had closed around her, and she'd felt sheltered, like his touch had the power to remove her from her new reality. "Everything's changing, and it hurts."

He'd circled his arms around her back and had swayed side to side. "This is about more than graduating?"

"Yes."

"You want to talk about it?"

"Maybe later."

They'd swayed together in silence for a while before Ethan said, "I think it's only fair you know I've had a crush on you all semester."

Juliet had laughed a reluctant, sad laugh. "I think you're a pompous ass most of the time."

He'd stood back enough to look at her and tilted her chin up to meet his eyes. "No, you don't," he'd said.

Juliet had gulped, because he'd been right. Part of her had liked that he'd paid special attention to her. Part of her had craved his praise. And it would have been a lie if she said she hadn't fantasized about him.

He'd grazed her lips twice before he'd pressed of his mouth against hers. His tongue had darted out to taste her bottom lip before he'd pulled away. "This feels selfish when you're upset."

Juliet had arched her back so her breasts had pressed into his chest. "Please, Ethan. This is what I need."

Whether it had been because of her verbal confirmation or because she'd called him by his first name, Juliet hadn't known, but he'd told her to lead the way to the bedroom.

They'd been on the bed, stripped of their clothing in a matter of minutes. Ethan's hands had been everywhere. Juliet had hardly been able to breathe for the intensity of his touch. She'd been numb for so long, since even before she'd lost the baby. Ethan's hands on her body had felt like waking up.

Then his fingers had been between her legs, and she'd been gasping for air.

He'd cursed when he'd slipped a finger inside her. Juliet had bucked into his palm and had ignored her guilt and anger and despair in favor of the luxury of Ethan's attention. All she'd felt had been the pleasure building as Ethan increased his pace and had sought a breast with his free hand.

Juliet had hissed as he'd rolled her nipple between his fingers, then she'd said, "Please, Ethan. I need you."

"I don't have a condom." His voice had been a rasp, like he hadn't been able to breathe either.

"Top drawer on your left."

He'd left and come back in a second, then he'd positioned himself above her. Then he'd cursed as she'd raised her hips and pushed herself onto him.

With a kiss, they'd fallen into a rhythm. Juliet had arched to meet his thrusts and had rotated her hips and ground against him until she'd been the one cursing. When Ethan had joined her moments later, he'd let out a string of foul words then collapsed on top of her. Juliet had closed her legs around his hips and laughed—actually laughed.

"What's so funny?"

"I don't normally curse like a sailor," she'd said, and Ethan chuckled against her neck, and for just those few moments, Juliet had felt alive. Nothing else had mattered by this moment and this feeling and this man.

Then Ethan had asked where the bathroom was.

She'd told him, then she'd burrowed into the covers and reality settled back in that quickly. Juliet hoped he wouldn't notice Rich's toothbrush or shaving kit. But when he'd come back, Ethan joined Juliet in the bed. He'd spooned her and nuzzled her ear and run a hand in lazy circles over her slightly rounded belly.

"Do you feel better?" he'd asked.

After a deep breath, Juliet had said, "I do. Nothing's fixed but thank you." Her body, at least, had felt alive.

He'd kissed her neck, just below her ear. "Anytime, love." He'd kissed his way down her neck and over her shoulder. "You can talk to me, you know."

Juliet had only nodded. She hadn't known how to tell him about everything he'd walked into, not when he'd thought this was the beginning of something. She hadn't known how to tell him it couldn't be.

Ethan had been quiet for so long, she'd thought he'd fallen asleep.

Then he'd traced a hand from her ribs to her hip, over stomach and back a few times, the feel of his fingers had turned more purposeful with each pass. "Are you-" he'd paused, and she'd heard him swallow. "Juliet are you pregnant?"

The afterglow of what they'd done had disappeared just like that. Despair had settled back around her like a shroud. Of course he'd noticed. How could he not have?

When she hadn't answer he'd said, "I'm guessing you're not quite twenty weeks?" His hand had settled over the skin under her belly button, just where she'd started to show.

"I'm eighteen weeks," she'd said, "but they told me today that the baby stopped growing two weeks ago."

Juliet had heard the grief in his exhale before he'd said, "I'm sorry." She hadn't needed to see his face to know he'd worn a frown. "You've had an awful day, haven't you?"

"The worst day ever."

He'd stroked her belly, then he'd kissed her shoulder. The tenderness of it had brought tears to her eyes. He should have been angry, but instead he'd comforted her. "Do you know what you will do yet?"

She'd known what he meant. "I haven't decided, but probably the D&E."

"Good," was all he'd said, and this time, they had fallen asleep, his hand still over her womb.

When Juliet remembered Ethan from that one night, she wanted to have a thousand more nights in his arms, but the comfort she'd felt hadn't been real. She'd been angry and devastated, and he'd been looking for an excuse to get her alone.

That he had any interest in her at all considering the fall-out from their night together, was something Juliet couldn't wrap her mind around. She never would have guessed he'd had a crush on her. He'd always been annoyingly present that semester, but he'd hardly spoken to her unless she was assigned his patients and even then, he used his usual brusque, efficient way of speaking.

Somehow, Ethan had always been a part of their group when they went to Dino's. His manner had been different at those breakfasts. He'd joked and laughed, but almost always with the men—and they'd spoken about sports, about medicine, about movies and TV. He might have flirted with their server, but if he'd been trying to impress Juliet, all he'd done was annoy her.

And yet, there had been that tension between the two of them, her never allowing herself to get too close, even though he'd been impossible to avoid.

How had he learned her favorite cookie back then without ever knowing about Rich?

Juliet scrubbed at her eyes. She didn't want to think about him anymore. But her mind wandered in and out of her memories of him for the rest of the day, finding the hints of his crush through their early interactions. She was just leading her students out of *savasana* after a demanding vinyasa class when it occurred to her that instead of flipping Ethan off the other night, she wished she'd let him buy her a cinnamon roll.

Shaken, Juliet ended her class. She'd found she was most honest with herself in those moments of rest or meditation after a physically demanding yoga sequence. That she might want to date anyone, especially Ethan, surprised her. She hadn't allowed herself to think along those lines since she'd gone back to school. She hadn't deserved to.

When she thought about her last semester of school, Juliet knew she should stay far, far away from Ethan Harvey.

But when she thought about how much she'd wanted to kiss him when they'd been standing nose to nose the other day, or how he'd let her sob on his shoulder, she knew there was enough there to become something. And she knew she wanted more than she had now. Maybe she'd even earned the indulgence of kissing Ethan after all her hard work.

When Juliet checked her phone after her yoga class, hoping for another text from Colleen, all she found was another one from Rich saying he hoped they could meet and talk to clear the air. He said he wanted to make things like visiting Gina and the boys easier.

He had her there. She'd spent the last four years avoiding Gina and Colin's if she knew Rich would be around, and they'd all been great friends once. They'd gone dancing on Saturday nights and stayed in playing cards on Wednesdays. Juliet wanted seeing Rich to be no big deal, so she invited him to join her and Alex when they went out on Friday night. She'd listen to what he had to say and then maybe she'd finally feel free of him.

Chapter Seven

On Monday, Ethan sent Juliet the cookies he'd over-heard her mention once at Dino's, a move he'd held onto for four years. The next day he sent lilies. The day after that, he sent a peach pie from Dino's. On Thursday, just after he'd received confirmation his chocolates had been deliv-ered, his phone rang. When the ID showed the Birthing Center was calling, his heart hammered. He hadn't heard a word from Juliet, though his phone number had been en-closed in every gift.

"Juliet?"

"Nope, sorry. This is Alex Stafford, I'm the receptionist."

"Hello, Alex." He switched to his doctor's voice, deeper, more authoritative. "What can I do for you?"

There was a pause. Then she sighed. "I'm also Juliet's roommate."

The leather on Ethan's ancient office chair, the chair that had been his father's, creaked as he sat up straighter. "I'm lis-tening."

"I get that you're trying to do the wooing thing, but if you don't stop sending things to Juliet at work, she's going to die of embarrassment, and then you'll never get to sleep with her."

Ethan felt a blush creep up the back of his neck. "I—"

But Alex cut him off. "Sorry, that should be 'sleep with her again,' shouldn't it?"

Ethan's jaw worked for a moment before he choked out, "You know about that?"

Alex's dry laugh chafed his ear drum. "Do I know how my best friend lost her whole life in one night and dealt with it by hooking up with the hot doctor? Yeah, I know about that."

His mind whirred as he processed what the woman on the phone was saying. She knew everything about Juliet, and he clearly needed help.

"Okay." he grabbed his pen. "So, no more gifts at work?"

"Weeeell, I'd probably lay off the gifts altogether if I were you. I mean, besides the fact that Juliet doesn't work today, which is why I'm calling. Juliet's pretty skeptical of materialistic bull shit."

"Do you have any suggestions? Or are you telling me to get lost?"

There was a squeak, like a spinning office chair that needed oiled. "Oh no, I am team Hot Doctor all the way. And while the cookies got her attention, you're currently striking out."

"How do I fix that?"

"Did you know we live above a bar?"

A strange turn in the conversation. "No."

"Well we do, and I'm taking Juliet out tomorrow night to celebrate the end of the semester. If you happened to show up around oh say, half past nine, you might find her more receptive to being wooed."

It had been years since Ethan had hung out in a bar for a woman. Sometime in his early thirties, he'd found himself preferring to hang out with his brothers and colleagues rather than trying to find a single woman. But this time, the woman would already be there, and the Royals might still be playing, and he could try out some new beers and eat some peanuts and not be Dr. Harvey, but Ethan. He wanted Juliet to see him as Ethan.

"What bar?" he asked.

"Tokyo Nights."

"Tokyo Nights?" It didn't sound like the kind of place that would have the Royals game on.

"It's very popular," Alex said, hearing his skepticism. Then she gave him the address. "Don't be late."

RICH WAS ALREADY AT the bar when Alex and Juliet made it downstairs. They were running late because Alex had talked Juliet into letting Alex do her makeup. Alex had offered suggestions about how to make Rich go away for good the entire time, including a joke about Alex using herself as a decoy that Juliet did not find amusing.

Juliet told Alex she had nothing to worry about, but when they spotted Rich at the bar, a gimlet in his hand and a disarming smile on his face, Juliet felt her stomach drop. Alex scowled at him and said to Juliet, "I'm not sticking around to watch this." Then she disappeared into the crowd on the dance floor.

"You are gorgeous," Rich said when she stopped in front of him

Juliet looked down. She had dressed to tease him. She didn't have much in the way of curves, but the white sundress was cut low enough to show some skin. The flirty skirt hit a few inches above her knees, and the halter top showed off the lean muscles in her back and arms. She hoped she looked lithe and strong, but soft.

Instead of answering, Juliet shrugged, took the gimlet he'd ordered for her, and asked, "So, what happened to Rachel?"

Rich's smile fell. He frowned into his drink. He'd always been a Manhattan drinker—no cherry. That didn't look to have changed. When he met her eyes again, he seemed to have resigned himself to having this conversation, because he wore an expression of calm sincerity.

"I broke it off with her two years ago," he said. "After you stopped returning my phone calls, I admitted to myself what I'd always known: that I was only with Rachel because I couldn't have you, and that wasn't fair to her."

Juliet swirled her straw through the ice in her glass. Attempting not to let the old anger simmer over she said, "Seems to me that if it wasn't for Rachel, I would have stayed with you," she paused for effect, then said, "Probably forever."

He didn't respond outside of a slow nod. At least he wasn't making excuses.

"You've been single for the past two years?" she asked.

He shrugged, the hint of a grin tugging at the corners of his mouth. "More or less."

Juliet had a feeling it was less single rather than more.

"What about you?" he asked.

"I've been too busy to date," she said, which was basically true. Between school and work and her yoga classes, Juliet had made sure she had little energy to spare on men. Alex, on the other hand, had taken it upon herself to try to set Juliet up with some guy she'd met whenever she could. It had never led to anything. She wasn't looking for a relationship. Might never again.

Rich slid closer to her on his stool, his thigh grazing hers. "You're lonely, Jules. I can tell."

She was, but she wasn't going to tell him that. "I'd rather be working toward my dream alone than wondering if my boyfriend is screwing someone else while I'm at work."

He winced.

"Can you ever forgive me?"

"My life crumbled like a cardboard façade in the rain because you weren't there when I needed you most—"

He cupped her cheek, and she let him because she had never seen him look so sad, so remorseful, not even two years ago when he'd tried to convince her it had all been a mistake. "I'm sorry," he said. "I was so scared, Jules, so scared."

Rich had said that before, and Juliet wondered what he was afraid of. Her? Their baby? Getting married and raising a family? Hadn't that been the plan all along? They hadn't talked about getting married in high school, but there had been a lot of *forevers* thrown around.

Juliet wasn't sure she wanted to know the answer.

"I can't," she said, and brushed off his hand, then downed the rest of her drink, trying to calm her hammering heart. Rich ordered her another, and something tempted Juliet to throw that one back as well, but she sipped as Rich stared into the dregs of his Manhattan. He sighed and gave her a sad smile.

"When Gina told me you'd gone back to school to become a midwife, I was so relieved."

Juliet blinked. "Why?"

She'd been talking about going back to school during their brief reconciliation, and he'd told her that if being a midwife was what she wanted, she should make it happen.

"Because I knew it would make you happy," he said. "It does make you happy, doesn't it?"

Juliet gave him a real, broad smile. They spent the next thirty minutes discussing her classes and her clinic hours. Last semester, she'd been able to help with some pap-smears and birth control consultations. In the fall, she would work with pregnant women and attend and manage births.

"That's not a far cry from what you're doing now, is it?" he asked.

Juliet shook her head and told him how a nurse could check heart rates and assist, but it was the midwife who made the important decisions, even if that was the decision to just sit back and let the mother do her thing.

"So, you're power hungry is what you're saying," Rich said. "You always did have to be in charge."

Juliet laughed, and rested her head on his shoulder. The gin had relaxed her, and despite everything, Juliet couldn't deny she enjoyed his company.

Rich brought his arm up around Juliet's shoulders and squeezed. "Thanks for being there for Gina." His breath feathered over her ear. "I'm glad she has you."

"I'm glad I was there too."

Soft lips landed on her cheek, the scrape of day-old whiskers brushed her jaw, and Juliet willed herself not to melt into him even further.

"Dance with me?" he asked.

"All right," Juliet said, and let Rich lead her into the gathering crowd on the dance floor.

ETHAN WASN'T LATE, but he was nervous as hell. This place did not have the Royals game on. Tokyo Nights, more a nightclub than a bar, was in an old building in a rundown part of town near the West Bottoms right next to the river. The neighborhood was in the early stages of gentrification, if the presence of the nightclub was any indication. The decoration inside was trendy and modern, lots of white with dark wood in long sleek lines. The sharp, white bar ran the length of the club on the far wall. One end served liquor, the other end played host to a row of busy sushi chefs. They'd lined the other three walls with booths, and in the middle was a full dance floor.

It wasn't hard to spot Juliet's red hair in the mass of people. He shouldn't have been surprised to see that she was dancing with someone. Ethan didn't like how jealous he was of the tall, dark-haired man's hands on her hips. He held her too close as they moved to the heavy beat. Alex had said Juliet would be more receptive to being wooed tonight, but Ethan hadn't anticipated competition.

Ethan retreated to the bar, where the menu boasted over forty different kinds of sake. He played it safe and ordered a bottle of a local microbrew instead. He claimed the last empty stool, and never lost sight of Juliet's white dress in the crowd. Juliet danced with the same guy as the song changed, smiling and laughing as they somehow talked to one another over the music. The way this guy touched her was propri- etary, as if he knew Juliet's body well. The reason Juliet hadn't responded to his gifts crystalized in his mind. Alex had said she was Team Hot Doctor, which meant Team Tall, Dark, and Handsome likely already had Juliet's vote.

Ethan decided to leave when he finished his beer. This was not his scene. He was uncomfortable, the music was weird, and Juliet didn't want him here.

He had just tipped the bottle up to drain it when a pretty blonde at least ten years his junior approached him with a bright smile. She wore chunky black glasses and a short black dress.

"Waiting for someone?" She squeezed her way in beside him and flagged the bartender.

"Just getting ready to head out, I think," he said with a polite smile. She was cute, but he wasn't interested in anyone but Juliet.

The blonde placed her order then faced him, "You can't go yet, I need you to rescue Juliet from Rich."

For a second, the woman's words didn't make sense, but then everything clicked. "You're Alex?"

"Ding. Ding. Ding." She ran her finger over the line of his jaw in a move that had him wondering how many drinks she'd had already. "The picture on the hospital web- site doesn't do you justice. You're way hotter in person." She cocked her head. "Or maybe it's the beard."

Ethan decided it was best to ignore her. "Why does Juliet need saving? She looks like she's having a good time." He failed to keep the hard edge out of his voice.

"You don't recognize him?" Alex looked confused for a second, then shrugged. "You probably didn't get a good look at him that morning." Alex turned toward the dance floor and nodded in Juliet's direction. "That's the baby daddy."

Ethan followed Alex's gaze to where Juliet and Rich still danced, and Ethan tried to recognize him. He remembered that morning with cold clarity, but he'd never taken a good look at the other man on purpose.

Humiliation still bubbled up inside Ethan like boiling water when he remembered the morning after he'd slept with Juliet. They'd been in bed; his hand had been splayed over the curve in her stomach where her baby had stopped growing in her womb. It hadn't mattered to him that the baby had been someone else's, because it had been just as obvious to him that whoever he'd been, he'd abandoned her. Ethan had decided he'd be there for Juliet, if she'd let him.

He remembered holding her closer as the sun broke over the horizon, feeling as though he'd finally found what had been missing all this time. He must have dozed again, because the next thing he'd known, there'd been a bang, and then the thunder of feet on the wooden stairs to the loft bedroom. After a pause, a man's harsh voice had said, "What the fuck, Juliet?"

They had both jumped and tensed at the slamming door, Juliet hadn't flinched at the voice, as if she had been expecting it. She'd pulled herself out of Ethan's arms and had sat up, covering herself with the sheet. Ethan hadn't dared move.

"Maybe I want to ask you the same thing," she'd said.

In the quiet that had ensued, Ethan had understood. The father had very much still been in the picture, and Juliet's situation had been more complicated than she'd first let on.

"Where were you last night?" Juliet had asked.

There had been more silence while Juliet and her boyfriend had stared at each other and Ethan had grown so uncomfortable he'd almost said something just to break the tension.

"Get dressed," the man had said. "And get him out of here." Then he'd stomped back down the stairs.

Juliet had been up and throwing his scrubs at him before Ethan had been able to even move.

"I'm sorry," she'd said, pulling on a shamrock green robe. Even after all these years, the color of that robe stuck with Ethan, the way it had made her messy hair stand out like flame over a spring meadow. "I should have made sure you were gone before he got back."

At those words, Ethan's shock had worn off, and anger had taken over. He'd held his temper in. He'd been in another man's bed, and if someone turned the tables, Ethan would have been roaring his discontent and throwing the other guy out on his ass, clothes or no. All Ethan had said as he pulled on scrubs still damp from walking in the rain had been, "That would be the father then."

Juliet had only said, "That's him."

She'd crossed her arms and clenched her jaw. Rage had flared across her red cheeks, but Ethan hadn't known if the emotion had been at getting caught, or anger at the man who'd been pacing in the living room below.

"Are you alright?" he'd asked.

A dry laugh had escaped her lips. "No, but you should go."

"I can stay if—"

But she'd cut him off. "I can take care of myself," she'd said. "He might cheat and lie, but he isn't violent, so there's nothing you need to worry about."

Ethan had wanted to argue, but she hadn't even been able look at him. In the end he'd said, "I should go then," and he hadn't been able to keep the bitterness out of his voice.

Juliet had preceded him down the stairs, then had marched across the apartment and opened the front door. Ethan had followed and had left without looking at either one of them.

When the door had closed behind him, Ethan had waited for the explosion. He'd heard the man say in a sneering voice, "Did you have fun?"

Then it had come, Juliet had screamed at the other man that he'd left her alone when she'd needed him. That she hadn't known what she'd been doing. She'd been so heartbroken that she'd fucked a doctor she hadn't even liked because otherwise—Ethan hadn't stayed to hear the otherwise.

The anger he'd felt at being used had waned throughout the years. More often these days, he felt like he had been the one to take advantage of her. He'd seen her devastation. He should have made her a cup of tea and tucked her in bed and called someone to come take care of her. Instead he'd kissed her, not to make her feel better, but because he had wanted to for months.

That Juliet would still be with her absent and unfaithful boyfriend four years later was not something he'd expected.

The bartender plunked Alex's drink on the bar, something that smelled like lime. The thud brought him back to the present. "They're still together?" he asked.

"God no. They broke up that day, but he comes sniffing around when he's bored with whatever girl he's seeing. He claims he's changed, and Juliet almost always falls for it."

Indignation and jealousy reared, mixing with the beer in his gut like a large stone hurled into a placid pond. That anyone would treat someone as beautiful and kind as Juliet like a toy made him want to march across the club and invite the other man for a word outside. Instead he laced his words with sarcasm, "Sounds like a nice guy."

Alex shrugged. "He would be if he could keep it in his pants. Anyway, I'm gonna send her over." She dropped the drink she hadn't touched in Ethan's hand. "You give her this and just be your sweet self." Alex pinched his cheeks then runway walked toward the dance floor. Was he the only one not enjoying himself?

Chapter Eight

Alex broke in on Juliet and Rich. She shoved herself between them and claimed she needed a girlfriend dance. Rich bowed out with an offer to buy them dinner. Alex listed off three different sushi rolls, all with fish, and shooed him away before Juliet could say a word.

"What are you up to?" Juliet asked over the music.

Alex bobbed to the K-Pop and said, "Who me?"

"Don't play innocent with me."

"I thought you weren't gonna sleep with Rich."

Juliet scrunched her nose. "I'm not."

"Coulda fooled me with all your hair flipping and giggling."

Juliet hadn't realized she'd been flipping her hair. She couldn't deny the flirting. When she was around Rich it just sort of happened.

"He's fun to flirt with."

Alex herded Juliet to the edge of the dance floor. "I've got someone better for you to bat your eyelashes at."

Juliet didn't like the grin on her friend's face. Whenever Alex had set Juliet up in the past, it had happened just like this.

"Nuh-uh. Not another one."

"Ah. Give him a chance. You might like him." Alex positioned Juliet so she was facing the bar. "Dead ahead. The guy in the blue shirt with the beard."

Juliet didn't have to scan the crowd at the bar to find him. He was looking right at her, and the intensity in his frown stopped her heart. Juliet couldn't tell if Ethan wanted to scold her or have her for dessert.

"Oh my God. What did you do?"

Alex gave Juliet a little push. "Go talk to him. He's waiting for you."

Then her friend disappeared back into the crowd, and Juliet was on her own.

In the past, Juliet would have one drink with Alex's setups before letting them down easy. It wasn't the poor guy's fault Alex had given them false hope, but with Ethan, Juliet didn't think it would be that easy.

The quality of Ethan's clothes grew more obvious as she approached him. Though they looked casual, a pair of brown boat shoes, jeans, and a sapphire blue shirt with sleeves rolled to the elbows, the fabric almost shone in the dim lights above the bar. He looked ill at ease, and Juliet knew she never would have invited him to meet her here. As she evaluated him, Ethan leaned over and said something to the guy on his left, who looked over his shoulder at Juliet, then gave up his stool, sliding closer to the girl on his other side.

"Smooth," Juliet said as she sat down beside Ethan, accepting the drink she knew Alex had ordered for her. "So, what brings you here?"

His half grin sent a tingle down Juliet's spine, but then he spoke, and Juliet remembered why she'd been ignoring his gifts. "Why the hell do you still give that asshole the time of day?"

"You don't know anything about it."

Juliet looked over her shoulder to find Alex and Rich claiming a booth nearby. Though Rich sat across from Alex, his eyes flicked between Juliet and Ethan. Ethan had followed her gaze, nodded once at Rich, then turned his attention back to Juliet.

"I know that he's done nothing but hurt you for four years—probably longer."

"I will kill Alex for this," Juliet said through clenched teeth, as she watched Alex flip a blonde curl over her shoulder. Rich's eyes followed the flirty gesture.

"Seems like she's a good friend," Ethan said.

Juliet turned her back on Rich and took a long, slow sip of her gin. "And what did my friend promise you about tonight?"

"Only that you'd be here. She did not warn me you were already on a date, or that she'd have to bribe you to talk to me with alcohol." Ethan touched the rim of her glass, then brushed his fingertip over her knuckles.

Juliet shivered, but to cover it up, rolled her eyes at him. If he wanted to think she was on a date with Rich, that was fine. She wouldn't correct him.

"Alex does this all the time, you know. She tries to set me up with guys she thinks I'll like. She thinks it will make me feel better to meet someone."

Ethan grunted, spinning his empty beer bottle between his palms. "Does it work?"

"I don't need to feel better," Juliet said. "And I don't need strange men trying to make me feel better."

Ethan chuckled this time, and Juliet shot him a look that told him to tread carefully. He tapped a finger on her nose and said, "At least this time it's a man you know you like, love."

Juliet batted his hand away. "Stop that," but she wasn't sure if she meant the little touches, the term of endearment, or his trying to force her out of her mood. All of them worked in his favor even though she didn't want them to.

When he only stared back at her, Juliet asked, "Why are you here?"

"I don't suppose you'd buy I was in the mood for raw fish and expensive beer?"

It was Juliet's turn to let out a snort of a laugh. "I took you as more of a steak and apple pie kind of guy."

"Most of the time, but I'm not afraid of sushi. You want some?"

"I don't eat fish."

"Right, no faces."

His knowing grin was as maddening as it was endearing. Even worse, it looked good on him. Feeling warm, she held her loose hair away from her neck as she admired his freshly washed hair. She'd never seen it when it hadn't been flattened by his surgical cap. He had enough natural wave that Juliet suspected if he cut it any shorter than falling in his eyes, it might be just plain curly. She kept her fingers on her glass so she wouldn't reach up to test the texture of those curls.

"I didn't think you owned anything but scrubs," she said.

He raised both his eyebrows. "Would the scrubs have worked for you?"

"They did before." The words slipped out before Juliet realized she'd thought them, and flame licked at her cheeks.

Ethan smiled then inclined his head toward the dance floor. "Would you like to dance?" But he already had her hand in his, pulling her that way.

"What if I'd rather not?" she asked, staying rooted to her stool.

"I'm happy to skip ahead to the kissing and undressing portion of the evening," he said.

Juliet gave into the slight pressure on her arm and stood, pressing against his chest. With her heels, they were the same height. "So *that's* what you're doing here," she said, grazing her nose against his in the same way he'd done to her the week before. The teasing action sent a thrill of power through her. "What makes you think you're that lucky?"

Ethan's hands had landed on the dip of her waist the moment she'd leaned into him. He pushed her back just far enough for his eyes to focus in on her. One hand climbed her arm to cup her cheek. "I'm here because I want to be with you, whatever way you'll have me."

All the control she'd triumphed in the moment before fled in the bare honesty in those words, and because of them, Juliet wanted to know what he had to offer.

"Do you even dance?" she asked.

"Only one way to find out," he said, and she let him pull her onto the dance floor.

It turned out that Ethan did not dance. He was a good sport and gave it a shot, even when Juliet teased him as he flailed next to her. Three songs in, Juliet couldn't handle his lack of rhythm anymore. She took hold of his wrists and placed his hands on her hips, holding them there as she stepped into him so they connected from shoulder to thigh. "Like this," she said and swayed her hips to the beat.

For a second Ethan stiffened, surprise rising from his jaw to his eyebrows at the intimate touch. Then his fingers dug into the flesh on her hips. He followed her lead, and though his movements lacked grace, he kept time to the music.

"Now this, I understand," he said into her ear, then nuzzled his nose into her neck. It tickled, and Juliet laughed as she slung her arms around his shoulders to put a little distance between them, and to get his upper body into the action.

Though he was still stiff through his back and shoulders, when the next song started, Ethan adjusted to Juliet's new tempo. It was a slow song but sounded more like the DJ was just slowing down a faster track. His hands met in the small of her back. They swayed together, and Juliet wondered if he was also remembering how they'd done the same pseudo dance just before they'd slept together. She was about to ask when Alex appeared at her shoulder, and Juliet leaned back to hear what her friend had to say.

"Food's ready. Rich ordered you a vegetarian roll, but he's super pissy about your dance partner, so I'd advise you to stay away."

Juliet wasn't sure when it had started, but she found she enjoyed dancing with Ethan. When Juliet looked over her shoulder to see Rich's scowl, Ethan's hands tightened on her back.

"I'm happy here," she said.

"You're welcome. Repay me by getting lucky tonight. One of us should, anyway." Alex winked at Ethan. Juliet frowned at her friend, who blew them a kiss as she joined Rich at their booth.

"Sorry about that," Juliet said.

"Why is he here?" Ethan asked as his eyes followed Alex. His teeth clamped together so hard, Juliet heard them clack. Rich stared at Ethan too. He looked livid enough to breath fire.

Juliet shrugged. "He wouldn't leave me alone, so I told him I'd hear him out."

Ethan scoffed. "Is that all it takes then? Wearing you down?"

"I told him no," Juliet said, not sure why she was defending herself. She should tell him to shut the hell up and leave her alone, only, she had been thinking about him all week. And now that Ethan was here, with his arms around her, he was a lot harder to brush off.

"What I'm not clear about is why you gave him an opportunity to ask in the first place."

The fatigue of the week and the soreness from the extra yoga she'd been doing to take her mind off things overcame her then, Juliet rested her chin on Ethan's shoulder. He smelled fresh and clean, like a stream running through the woods. And Juliet didn't want to talk about Rich anymore. "Rich and I have a long history."

"So do we," he said, his words a seductive caress she'd never heard from him before.

"I'd say it's pretty short."

Ethan chuckled as the song changed. Instead of adjusting to the tempo, he stopped. Juliet hadn't realized she'd let him take the lead. "Do you want to get out of here?"

With a deep sigh, Juliet dropped her forehead to Ethan's shoulder. She had experienced zero male attention for months, and now she'd been propositioned twice in one night, because yes, Rich had suggested they spend the night together while they'd been dancing. "I think I need to go to bed alone tonight."

"I only want to get coffee, talk."

"It's almost midnight."

Ethan chuckled. "And I could kill for a cup of coffee."

Juliet considered her options for a minute, the divey diner a few blocks away, the even scarier twenty-four-hour coffee shop a few blocks beyond that. Or she could invite Ethan upstairs and make sure she kept her hands to herself. She trusted herself.

"Come on. I have coffee upstairs."

ETHAN ALLOWED JULIET to lead him out the back door to the smoking patio. The paved square was crowded with twenty-somethings, the smoke hung heavy like fog in the muggy late spring air. Beyond a gate was a metal door with a keypad. She typed in the code and led him up two flights of sweltering stairs and down a stuffy hallway, before pulling him inside her mercifully air-conditioned apartment.

The apartment was shabby, with the exposed brick and open duct work he'd expect to find in a loft like her last apartment, but this place was all one level. The large living area was separated from a galley kitchen by a breakfast bar. Large windows lined with ferns and small tropical trees adorned the front wall. The furnishings appeared thrifted, but they all went together as if cultivated with intention. The effect was cozy, and Ethan regretted not spending more time making his drab condo into a home.

Ethan's gaze drifted off to the hallway and he wondered if her new bedroom resembled her old one with big windows and a menagerie of plants.

Juliet kicked off her shoes and went straight for the coffee maker. Ethan followed, seating himself at the breakfast bar to watch her skirt swell and twirl around the thighs.

He had been honest when he told Juliet he only wanted to talk, but dancing with her downstairs, having her hips connected to his, made him aware of where her body was in relation to his in the small apartment.

Ethan's body still hummed with the sparks he'd felt where they had connected on the dancefloor. When she'd laughed at his lack of rhythm, Ethan couldn't help but remember her, laughing and cursing underneath him. He wanted to know the difference, between a happy laugh and a teasing laugh and a sated laugh. He wanted to know why she'd taken the job at the birthing center when she was shoo-in for the position at the hospital. Why was she was going into midwifery? And what did she plan to do when she graduated?

Ethan wasn't proud that the midwives he worked with made him uncomfortable. They were all capable nurses, but they were still just nurses. As much as he reminded himself they were OB trained nurse practitioners, he couldn't get past that they weren't doctors.

Juliet switched the coffee pot on and faced him. Her green eyes blinked up at him, and he almost believed she liked him.

"What did you want to talk about?" she asked.

Despite all that was on his mind, Ethan smiled and said. "I don't know. What'll make you smile at me more?"

Juliet rolled her eyes Ethan's grin fell. "You're trying way too hard for a guy who's already in my apartment."

"Sorry," Ethan said, and used his best grave doctor face. "I never know where we stand."

She shrugged as if to say she didn't either. "You want pie? We still have some of what you sent."

"I never say no to Dino's peach pie."

Juliet must have gathered dishes and utensils from memory, because her assessing gaze never left his face. "Interesting that you sent me *your* favorite."

She dished out two pieces of pie then came around to join him.

"I sent the peach because it's what you ordered that night. I figured that meant it was your favorite too."

Ethan cut into his pie while Juliet chased a piece of crust around the edge of her plate with her fork. He was halfway through his slice when he noticed she wasn't eating.

"Wait, you don't like peach pie?"

The coffee pot gurgled, and Juliet jumped up to retrieve mugs.

"That night," she said as she handed him a mug of black coffee, "I asked for a slice of whatever pie it was they needed to get rid of."

Ethan gaped at her, more embarrassed now about the gifting spree than he had been on the phone with Alex. He'd meant to show her that he knew her better than she thought he did, but it had only proved the opposite.

Her eyes looked so sad as she remembered that night that Ethan said, "The other reason I came tonight was to apologize for embarrassing you at work. That wasn't my intention."

Juliet blew on her coffee, also black. "I prefer to keep my social life separate from my work."

"I'm the same. No more I promise." Ethan took a sip of the coffee, it was strong and rich, and she hadn't even asked him if he wanted cream or sugar. He smiled into the mug.

"What?" she asked.

"You know how I like my coffee."

"Lucky guess," Juliet said, but her mischievous smile reached her all the way to her eyes.

JULIET DIDN'T KNOW what to do with Ethan. When she'd known him before, he had only shown his cocky arrogant side. But tonight, his inexperience on the dancefloor was nothing short of adorable. Juliet liked watching him fumble. It made him less of the god the others had made him out to be in nursing school. Juliet liked him a little vulnerable. The humility he'd shown in allowing her to lead him on the dance floor made him more accessible. That receptiveness made her want to touch him, tease him, taunt him to find out which side would come out next. Juliet knew better than to trust that desire in herself, or to trust herself around men period.

"When did you meet Alex?" Juliet asked.

After explaining their phone call, Ethan asked, "Do you go to that bar often?"

He picked at the crumbs on his plate, so Juliet shoved hers over, and he dug in. "I used to, before they remodeled it last year. It used to be this seedy dive bar, and I could afford the drinks then. But I like to be dance, so I let Alex drag me down about once a month."

"You're a good dancer," Ethan said.

Juliet raised one shoulder and let it drop. "I'm passable."

He studied her as he washed down his pie with gulp of coffee. He never took his eyes off her, and by the hard set of his jaw, Juliet knew what he would say.

"What happened that night?"

The emotions from that night were not ones Juliet liked to revisit often. "You were there," she said.

"I was, but I want to know why. How did I fit into your plan?"

Anger rose along with her blood pressure and Juliet wanted to throw the rest of her coffee in his face. "You know, every time I think it wouldn't be a bad idea to let myself kiss you, you open your mouth and something vile comes out."

A brief grin flickered over his lips, and Juliet could tell he was trying not to gloat, as if he hadn't heard the second half of the sentence. Instead he said, "It's an honest question," as if he was owed more of an explanation.

"Jesus, Ethan, I didn't have a plan. I had just lost my baby, and when I got home, my boyfriend wasn't there again. I needed someone, and you were there."

"You weren't using me as an excuse to leave him?"

"Is that what you've thought all this time? That I conned you into sleeping with me that night?"

Ethan shrugged as if to say yes, but he wasn't going to admit to it.

"I barely had the brain power to notice you were there, let alone plan a diabolical scheme."

"But you were planning to break up with him."

Juliet nodded and took a deep breath. "Of course, I was."

"What happened after I left."

"We yelled for a while. Then we cried. Then I moved in with Alex."

Ethan's gaze remained on her face, but he tapped his fork against his plate. "What kind of man cheats when his girl is pregnant? He should have been worshiping you, waiting on you."

Juliet couldn't help her snort. "His girl?"

"Weren't you living together?"

Ethan didn't even seem conscious of the sexism.

"We were basically engaged, but that didn't make me his property."

The way he narrowed his eyes and pursed his lips said he didn't appreciate her interpretation. "He should have behaved better."

Funny, Juliet thought the same thing about herself. She'd failed herself that night by not being strong enough to face her troubles alone. And even though Rich had apologized later, some of the things he'd said to her in the heat of the moment still stung when she remembered them. The self-recrimination must have shown on her face, because Ethan stood and wrapped and arm around her shoulders. His skin was hot against hers.

"Hey," he gave her a reassuring squeeze. "Don't do that. You were going through so much alone."

When Juliet didn't respond Ethan stepped closer to cradle her from behind, even as she still sat on the stool. He tipped her chin up and back with soft fingers on her jaw and their eyes met. A thrill ran down her spine, and she tried not to shiver.

"I was going to be there for you. I was going to help you find a job, find a place to live. I was going to take you for your D&E. Hell, I would have done it myself if that's what you wanted. And I sure as fuck wouldn't have been out screwing another chick when I could have been home with you."

Ethan didn't move, didn't blink, waiting for her response. And Juliet wondered if he'd meant to tip his hand like that or if he'd gotten carried away, because if he was serious, that was one hell of a hand. Perhaps it was even too much to acknowledge yet.

"In all fairness," she said, "I wasn't meant to be home that night. I was supposed to be the DD for a girl's night and crash at Alex's."

"And I would have been drinking beer with my brothers instead of cheating on you."

Juliet closed her eyes and Ethan's hand fell away from her chin as her head dropped back onto his shoulder. That was the best thing he could have said. "I'm trying really hard not to like you."

"Why is that?"

His voice rumbled through his chest and against her back, and Juliet leaned further into him. Ethan wrapped his other arm around her waist and placed a single kiss just below her left ear, and Juliet started to forget about school, about her practicum, about how she couldn't date a doctor she worked with.

"Because I shouldn't."

Another feather-light kiss. "It's alright. I give you permission."

"God, you're so arrogant."

"And you're stubborn." He took her unpierced ear lobe between his teeth for short nibble. "But you're also brilliant. I could watch you work all day."

Ethan kissed a line down her neck, leaving a trail of fire on her skin where his lips had been. Juliet's exhale came out as a breathy sigh.

She arched back, wrapping her arm so she could grip the hair at the base of his neck and guided his lips onto hers.

Heat zipped through her, pooling in her core. Why had she waited so long to kiss him?

Ethan's lips were soft and hot, almost searing hers as he covered her mouth, then he ran his tongue over her bottom lip. Juliet nipped at his in response, and he paused long enough to smile against her lips, then pulled her off the stool so she stood facing him.

Like magnets, their lips slammed back together, and their tongues danced. Ethan had no trouble finding the rhythm this time around. When his hands skimmed down her sides, his fingers dug into her hips as he pressed against her. Juliet moaned. He backed her into the counter, massaging his thumbs downward until she was rocking against him in time to the circular motion.

Juliet rocked into the hard ridge in his jeans once, twice. She whimpered, and he groaned when she did it a third time, then they both stilled, because she'd already said no.

Juliet pressed her palms into his chest trying to catch her breath. "I meant what I said earlier." She needed time to figure out what was happening and how she felt about it.

Ethan sighed, released her hips and took a step back. "I know. I'm sorry."

She grabbed his hands and entwined her fingers with his to soften the blow. "Don't apologize. It was fun."

Pulling on their joined hands, Ethan rested his forehead against hers and said, "Why don't we do this the right way?"

"Which is?"

"Go to dinner, talk, find out what we have in common."

"And you want to try that over dinner?"

"Why not?"

"I'm never going to become a meat eater," she said, angling her lips to meet his against her better judgement, but only for a second.

A grin spread over his mouth and he touched his nose to hers. "I like being an omnivore." Then he kissed her forehead. "We're doing this though, you and me?"

Juliet nodded, uncertain she was saying yes for any reason other than how good it felt to be touched by someone who hadn't hurt her.

Ethan kissed her again, then said, "I'll call you," before he left Juliet alone and aroused and hoping she wasn't setting herself up to hurt even more.

Chapter Nine

E than leaned against the metal door watching a group of twenty-somethings vape behind the club while he wrestled his pulse back into submission.

What he really wanted to do was have Juliet buzz him back up, because he wouldn't be able to think about anything else until they finished what they'd started. Ethan reminded himself he had to work in the morning, and he didn't want to press Juliet any more than he already had.

Ethan hated that she was afraid to like him. He was certain it had something to do with the man who still played with her like a cat with a mouse. Juliet had said that Rich didn't own her, but the way Rich had been watching her said he still thought of Juliet as his.

He pushed himself off the wall and headed toward his Land Cruiser parked in the lot across the street, scolding himself for never seeking her out again. Perhaps things would be different if he'd been there for Juliet in all the aftermath. Perhaps she'd have suffered less with one more friend to lean on.

It wasn't the first time Ethan thought he should have rustled up her phone number at some point over the last four years. His gut had told him to find out what happened to her, to see how she was coping, but that one stupid comment he overheard. . .

"I fucked a doctor I don't even like!"

When she'd asked him to stay with her, he'd had no trouble believing that she was, at the very least, attracted to him. Maybe she even liked him enough to confide in him. But the words she'd said in the morning, combined with the way she wouldn't look at him after Rich had shown up—it was so much easier to believe she didn't want him when he was angry with her for not telling him the truth.

Ethan never had shaken his guilt at sleeping with her instead tucking her into bed. He still wouldn't have left her alone but crashing on the couch until someone else could stay with her would have been more appropriate. He'd been nursing that damn crush for months, since the first time she'd been in the OR with him, calm and confident when all the other nursing students shook with nerves. She hadn't taken her eyes off him that day, and he'd worked better because she was watching.

Then the students had all gone with them to Dino's, and though she'd been at the far end of the table, he'd heard every word she'd said. All Ethan had been able to think about after that was unraveling her hair from her braid and entwining his fingers in the strands while he kissed her breathless.

Ethan spent the next four months avoiding getting too close to Juliet so he didn't do just that. When she was finally in his arms, he lost all control.

Arriving at his condo, Ethan let Camille out and refreshed her food and water. Then he paced the house, tidying in a restless way as he prowled from room to room. He cleaned with no efficiency, tripping over the dog who followed him everywhere. After he'd washed the coffee mugs he'd left scattered around, he was still too wound up to sleep.

In the second basement bedroom, he kept his exercise equipment: hand weights, a treadmill, a weight machine, and his favorite, a rowing machine. He'd rowed in college, and while he didn't have time to get out on the river anymore, he could mimic the action in his basement, rowing until he was too tired to think.

Ethan changed into a t-shirt and athletic shorts, opened the '90s playlist on his phone, and rowed to a rotating soundtrack of grunge, hip hop and R&B until he could barely keep his eyes open anymore.

ETHAN SAT IN HIS BROTHER'S dark theatre room, Logan to his left, Henry to his right. A baseball game he wasn't all that interested in was on tonight—an east coast team playing a west coast team—and he was having trouble paying attention. His mind kept straying to Friday night and his hands on Juliet's swaying hips, her breath on his lips, the feel of her body pressed against his.

At commercial, Logan muted the sound and the three of them sat there in silence, each waiting for the other to start conversation again. Ethan took a swig of his beer, then cleared his throat. He felt both his brothers' eyes land on him, but he kept his eyes trained on the way the blue glow from the screen reflected off the knees of his jeans.

"So, how do you guys feel about midwives?"

Henry snorted derisively and said, "What?"

Logan asked, "You're not thinking of hiring one, are you?" barely concealing his horror at the idea.

"Yeah, that's what I thought." Ethan drained the last gulp of his beer.

"Why do you want to know?" Logan asked.

Ethan shrugged and went for the cooler. "Just wondering. They're getting more popular again." He was desperately trying to sound unaffected, but both Henry and Logan were watching him warily.

"They are," Logan said.

Then Henry finished, "But they're not doctors."

Ethan flipped the bottle top between his fingers. "You don't think that they fulfill a different function—that maybe they couldn't be a complement to what we do? What I do specifically?"

Logan and Henry shared a look over his head.

"Maybe," Logan said at the same time Henry said, "What are you really asking?"

Ethan could feel the skepticism and wariness pouring off his brothers. Some private practices were hiring midwives to work alongside OB-GYNs, but the Harvey brothers were not part of that group. Sure, Ethan worked with midwives at the hospital, but that was basically a separate ward. They didn't cross paths often, and their father, while a brilliant doctor, had always been prejudiced against nurse practitioners taking away good patients. Some of that had stuck with each of them. While Ethan wasn't ashamed of Juliet, he knew he'd be a little embarrassed to introduce her to his father because of what she did.

His father had been a good man. Stern and strict, but kind and understanding. He would have seen who Juliet was, nurturing and strong and confident and how she complemented Ethan before he worried about her career. His father would not have been pleased with her career choice though.

Ethan could see his dad calling him into the office at his parent's old house, telling him to take a seat on the other side of the desk like he had when Ethan was seventeen and been caught shirtless in Marigold Porter's bedroom, his hand on the clasp of her bra. Instead of a lecture on self-control and ruining his career as a doctor before it even started, it would be about how a woman with such a career could possibly fit into the life he envisioned for himself?

Ethan wasn't sure he had an answer to that question yet. He didn't know how a midwife would fit into his life. But Juliet was so much more than just a midwife. He wanted her in his life every way he could fit her in, and his brothers were the best test group he could think of for trying out the idea.

"I, um, I'm dating one."

For a beat there was only silence, then Logan laughed, "Holy shit."

Henry said, "You finally find a girl, and she's a fucking midwife."

"Almost. She's got a semester left before she's certified."

This time Henry whistled and said something lewd. Logan shook his head. "Never took you for a cradle robber."

That was exactly what Ethan had been afraid of. He knew his brothers were mostly teasing, but these were the exact criticisms other people would pick up on. The reasons why Juliet herself might object to a lasting relationship.

"She's twenty-six."

He could see his brother's doing the math in their heads and hoped Logan wouldn't point out that Juliet was closer in age to his oldest daughter, who was twenty-one, than she was to Ethan. Ten years wasn't all that much. It didn't feel like anything when they were together.

"Does Mom know?" Henry asked.

Ethan shook his head. He wasn't ready to confront what would likely be the biggest hurdle in settling into a relationship with Juliet. He could handle his mother's light disdain for the way he lived, but he knew she would hate the idea of Juliet on principle, and by extension, the woman herself.

"She is going to rip you a new one," Logan said.

"And tear your girl apart."

Ethan blew out a breath. "Thanks for your encouragement, guys. It really means a lot."

Henry shrugged, "Shoulda chosen a conventional nurse then."

And there it was. The exact thing he could hear his dad saying in that metaphorical office. Choose a nurse. One that didn't aspire higher than her training. One who didn't want to compete for your patients but assist you with them. That's the woman who would make a good partner both at work and at home. But Ethan didn't want any of the nurses he knew. Sure, he had the rule about not dating people he worked with for professional reasons, but it wasn't that difficult to enforce when he wasn't attracted to any of them like he was to Juliet. He had to think that her profession complemented his well enough that they could make a partnership work.

Their mother had been a nurse before she married their father. She had worked for the original Dr. Harvey from nursing school all the way up until Logan was born. She had been vocal enough for both herself and their father that they wanted the same arrangement for their boys. Doctoring was hard work, and they each needed a partner that understood the demands of that sort of life. So far, none of the three sons had complied. Vanessa was a winc rep, who got them cheap trips to Italy or France, and always had a new label to share with the family. Paige taught high school English, and spent too much time reading, according Helen anyway. Ethan, who had been unapologetically single since medical school was her last hope.

"It's not like we're getting married, we just started dating."

"Then why are you asking?" Logan asked.

Ethan glared at him, then turned to his right and found Henry looking at him with raised eyebrows, so Ethan glared at him too.

"I can't want to tell you about the woman I'm dating?"

Henry laughed, and Logan said, "You haven't dated a woman in ten years."

"Eleven. Paige was pregnant with Jason when he and Amanda broke up."

"Right, so in eleven years, you've only told us about one other woman. You'll forgive us if we're hearing wedding bells."

Ethan set his eyes on the ceiling and gritted his teeth. "She's the same one," he said, "The woman from a few years ago. The only nurse. . ."

Silence reigned as he trailed off. The light on the projection screen changed signaling the game was back on.

"The same one?" Logan asked at the same time Henry said, "Wait, you mean the redhead, from way back when?"

When Ethan blew out a breath and nodded at Henry, his middle brother cursed.

"The pregnant one that had you messed up for months?" Logan asked.

At the same time, Henry clapped him on the back and said, "Congrats, man. You bagged the unicorn."

Ethan imagined how little Juliet would appreciate being compared to a unicorn and told his brothers about how they'd reconnected. He finished with, "If I bring her to Fourth of July, you'll only give me a hard time, though, right? Not her?"

Logan hosted a big Fourth of July party every year. The entire family came to town for the food and the frisbee and the fireworks. It was practically more important than Christmas.

Logan punched him playfully on the shoulder, and Henry laughed. "You better have a date set by then, because all the cousins will be wanting to put your wedding in their calendars."

IT WAS MONDAY BEFORE Juliet heard from Ethan again. It had been a long day, but a good day. She'd done her usual clinic hours at the birthing center and was headed out the door to yoga when the mother who had been due the day before called. They were having contractions regularly, but it was early still. Charlie told them to have dinner, go for a walk, then call back, then Charlie headed out to grab dinner for herself. Alex was already gone for the day, so Juliet paged the on-call nurse and double checked that the birth room was ready.

There were still two hours until her yoga class was supposed to start, but Juliet was antsy. She liked to get there early. Their room at the community center was empty the hour before class started, and Juliet would usually run through her own practice, maybe meditate for a few minutes before she led others. She had a more peaceful, meditative practice planned this week after the rigor she'd put her students through the week before. She wanted to be in the right frame of mind to lead it.

A car door slammed, and Juliet hopped up, thinking Eleanor had arrived early, but when she got the door, she found John helping a panting, cringing Maureen up the porch steps.

"We were going to wait, but the contractions just kept coming," he said.

Juliet assured them that was the right thing to do and got them into the birthing room. She checked Maureen's heart rate and did a quick blood pressure check since she'd been on the high end of normal. Then she listened to the baby's heart with the doppler and got the tub started, explaining in between that Charlie would be right back.

The frequency and intensity of Maureen's contractions continued to pick up over the next twenty minutes, and Juliet, who had paged Charlie and called and texted that she needed to hurry. Finally, a text that Charlie was stuck behind a wreck on the highway and looking for a way out made Juliet's heart rate tick up a beat. When, a minute later, Juliet heard Maureen grunt at the end of her contraction, she took four long breaths in and out through her nose before heading back into the birthing room. She might have to do this alone.

It was as thrilling as it was terrifying.

"Was that a push I just heard?" she said with a smile on her face.

"I couldn't help it," Maureen's voice was almost a moan. She leaned with her forehead on her husband's shoulder as the two of them rocked gently.

"That's a good thing," Juliet said. "It means your baby is coming soon."

Maureen managed a small smile, and Juliet checked mother and baby's heart rates again. Everything was fine, and when another contraction came on, Maureen squared her feet and instead of swaying or rocking, she bore down. She was definitely pushing.

Juliet watched as Maureen braced against her husband for leverage. When the contraction was over, Juliet suggested they help get Maureen out of her dress. Maureen fanned herself once free of the garment. The room was already getting warm after Juliet adjusted the thermostat so the baby wouldn't be cold once on the outside.

Juliet let them know that Charlie was on her way but stuck in traffic. As she was explaining that she was almost a qualified midwife herself, Eleanor arrived.

"I'm totally hiring Juliet when I have my babies," Eleanor said as they helped Maureen, whose legs were tired, onto the birthing stool. "She's the best."

Maureen relaxed after that and lost herself in her contractions. Juliet shot Eleanor a thankful smile, then crouched in front of Maureen and pulled on a fresh pair of gloves. Eleanor retrieved the tools they might need, as well as some blankets for the baby.

It was more difficult for Juliet to see how quickly the baby was coming in the birthing chair, but Juliet remained kneeling on the floor beside Maureen, and in a few minutes the baby was crowning. Juliet encouraged Maureen to reach down and feel her baby's head, and the woman's eyes lit up with surprise and delight. With renewed determination, Maureen pushed her baby out just as Charlie slipped into the room.

Juliet handed the baby up to the mother, a little girl, she saw, but didn't say anything while mother and father took time to meet their new little one. Allowing Charlie and Eleanor to take over, Juliet saw to the paperwork she needed to get done and arrived only fifteen minutes late to yoga class, where she led a peaceful, calming practice with a smile so big her cheeks hurt by the end of it.

Juliet couldn't stop smiling. Alex teased her for it as Juliet settled into her third job for the day. But Juliet couldn't help it, she'd caught her first baby, and it had been magical.

Helping Alex mount her jewelry on earring and necklace cards and organize wholesale orders for local stores was the easiest of Juliet's jobs. It meant that not only did Juliet get to stay up late drinking wine with her friend, but Alex paid a little bit more than her share of the rent as compensation. They had just polished off a bottle when Juliet's phone rang, and her grin widened.

She'd been waiting to hear from Ethan all day. Even if they only had the summer, allowing him to show her a good time beat being angry and defeated like she'd been for months, possibly years. Juliet hadn't even realized she'd wrapped herself so tight until she'd had to slough off some of her protection to kiss Ethan. It was freeing, to let go and give herself permission to feel good for a change.

"I caught my first baby today," she said, without salutation.

Ethan laughed. "Are you telling me specifically, or are you greeting everyone this way today?"

"I'm telling you, you dope. I thought you'd appreciate it."

"It depends what you mean by 'caught,'" he said, a chuckle still in his voice.

So, Juliet explained what had happened, and when Ethan said, "Delivering your first baby is incredible," Juliet reminded him that Maureen did all the work, Juliet was just there for support.

"You're such a hippie," he said.

Juliet blew a raspberry into the phone and took a sip of wine from the new bottle Alex had just opened. "How'd you get Alex to relent and give you my phone number?" she asked. He hadn't ever asked her for it, and up until Friday, Alex had refused him the information.

"Actually, I found it on the Facebook page for your yoga classes. Nice pictures."

"You googled me?"

"I googled you."

"Find anything else good?"

"Your personal profile."

Juliet blushed. She rarely used Facebook for anything but yoga, but Alex tagged her in photos when they were hanging out together outside the apartment. Most of them were over lattes, or dancing at Tokyo Nights.

"I have an Instagram account too," she said.

Alex giggled. Juliet tossed an earring card at her head.

"What do you Instagram?" he asked.

Juliet felt her face flush bright red and Alex yelled out her screen name. "My plants, yoga selfies, or you know, what I'm knitting that day. Stuff like that."

"You knit?"

"Alex already makes fun of me enough for that—but it relaxes me. I took it up after—" Juliet cut herself off. She'd seen a therapist for a while after she'd lost the baby, and it had been she who suggested Juliet take a knitting class. While Juliet had fallen in love with knitting, she really didn't want to talk about that with Ethan.

Ethan didn't need her to finish the sentence and changed the subject for her. "Are you free next weekend?"

"I work Friday 'til late, but I should be free by mid-afternoon on Saturday. You?"

"Can I pick you up at eight Saturday night?"

"For what?"

"Dinner and drinks?"

"We're not going to a sports bar, are we?"

Ethan chuckled again. "No. I'm taking you someplace nice. I owe you that much."

Juliet's voice was nearly a whisper when she said, "Ethan, you don't owe me anything."

But he only said, "I'll see you Saturday."

When Juliet hung up, Alex tossed the earring card back at Juliet. "I take all the credit."

TUESDAY NIGHT JULIET volunteered to make dinner for Gina's family, but instead Gina arranged for Rich to take Noah for the evening and Gina's husband kicked Juliet out of the kitchen. He told her to go gossip with Gina while he caught up on the dishes and ordered a pizza.

Juliet sat next to Gina on the sofa. Instead of wine, they sipped sparkling water, and Juliet cuddled Isaac when he wasn't nursing. They talked about the baby, and Juliet told her about the news that her sister finally got her first real job at History Colorado, Colorado's historical society. This, of course, gave Gina the perfect lead-in to bringing up her only sibling.

"What's going on with you and Rich?"

Juliet snuggled Isaac closer, and said. "Nothing. We hung out at the bar a bit the other night. He wanted to take me out for real—to start over he said. But I told him I couldn't be anything more than his friend."

"And does this have anything to do with the guy you blew him off for?"

"He told you I blew him off?"

Gina nodded, a sly grin stealing over her lips. "He was ranting about how you left with some older guy and saddled him with Alex for the night—and he was speaking French."

Gina and Rich grew up speaking three languages at home. Their mother had taught them Italian and English. Their father had only spoken to them in French. When he'd hightailed it back to Europe just as they were both hitting puberty, French had become the language associated with the negative and the secretive. Rich speaking French was a big deal.

"Damn," was all Juliet said.

Gina stuck out a foot and poked Juliet on the knee with her toe. "Soooo. Who was the guy?"

Juliet felt herself go red. "You've met him."

"The doctor?" Gina nudges grew more emphatic. "No way! You slept with him again?"

"We didn't sleep together," Juliet said, not making eye contact. "But we talked, and there was some kissing."

Gina giggled into her glass. "Finally. Have you even been with anyone since Noah was born?"

There had been a couple of guys she'd slept with over the past two years, mostly a bad mix of Alex's matchmaking games and too much gin, but Juliet shook her head and said, "Nothing serious."

"But you're serious about the doctor?"

Juliet shrugged. "I think he'd like to be, but we'll be working together this fall, and being involved with him could get me kicked out of the program. We haven't talked about that yet, but I keep thinking about that summer fling thing you brought up a couple weeks ago."

Gina's eyebrows rose in surprise. "Do you think that's the right choice for you?"

Juliet's blush deepened. She understood Gina's skepticism. Juliet had always been a relationship sort of girl. Thinking of the guys she dated in high school, Juliet said, "I think I can pull it off."

Gina nodded, but her expression remained unconvinced. "Just, be careful. Okay?"

"Always," Juliet said, but her plans regarding Ethan were anything but.

Chapter Ten

When Juliet heard the door buzzer from her room while she was still getting dressed Saturday night, she cursed pulled her dress over her head while still searching for her cell phone with one eye.

Juliet heard Alex giggle and rolled her eyes. Alex had been dressed and ready to go for thirty minutes. She'd been waiting to descend upon Tokyo Nights until she had seen Juliet safely out the door. As much as Juliet had been looking forward to tonight, Alex had been gushing about Juliet's date all week as if she were the one going.

For the evening, Juliet had switched out her usual rope bag for the matching clutch. It wasn't exactly formal, still being made of rope, but it was all she had.

The smoldering look Ethan gave her stopped her dead on the hall threshold. Worry about her lack of non-athletic accessories, or how the dress she wore tonight was only a yellow version of the one she'd wore the week before evaporated in the heat radiating off him. The equal parts desire, admiration, and tenderness in his eyes had sparks igniting in her stomach.

A shy smile spread over her lips as she took in his patterned button up paired with a navy pair of chinos. The blue in the plaid brought out the color in his eyes. Ethan's gaze stripped past her skin as it lingered over her exposed shoulders and partially bared back. Heaven help her, but she wanted more of that heat.

"Shall we?" He asked, holding out his hand.

It was then that Juliet realized she'd been staring. She shook off her daze and crossed the living room to take his hand.

Alex winked and shouted, "Be safe now, kids!" as Ethan led Juliet into the hall.

Ethan chuckled, and Juliet tried not to blush. Sex was exactly what she wanted out of the evening, but she wasn't worried. She'd been on birth control since she'd lost her baby. And Ethan, for all his other faults, had always lectured the younger guys at the hospital, the ones who did date the nurses, about using condoms. She'd always kind of liked him for that.

"How's your week been?" he asked after he'd helped her into the car.

"Good. Quiet. You?"

"The opposite. You know babies. They all want to be born at the same time."

"That's not a good week?"

"It was a great week, just not a quiet one."

"No, it wouldn't be." She paused then glanced around the inside of his car. The upholstery was sparse and dated, the seats sturdy. There was a fishing pole and tackle box behind their seats and a pair of old muddy boots tumbling around the cargo area. "This is one giant vehicle."

He laughed. "This is the Cruiser. She's the only car I've ever owned."

She snorted. It looked like it had been twenty years old when he'd bought it, and that was probably close to twenty years ago. "I'm surprised it still runs."

Ethan patted the dashboard. "Old Betsy gets me around just fine, on or off road."

Juliet held in her cringe. "There are roads where we're going, yes?"

"Tonight, yes. Next time, maybe not." He flashed her a teasing grin, and she schooled her face into a cool, bring it on, sort of expression until Ethan put his eyes back on the road.

After driving a few blocks in silence, she said, "So you're outdoorsy?"

"I like to hike, camp, fish occasionally."

"Hunt?"

"Not my thing."

"Good, that might have been a deal breaker."

Ethan chanced a quick grin in her direction as he pulled through a stoplight. "I went to medical school in Denver, my residency just outside, and I spent about as much time in the mountains as I did in the hospital. I usually head out that way for my vacations. What about you?"

Juliet was surprised that he'd gone so far away from his family for so many years, but said, "I can't remember the last time I took a proper vacation."

"But what would you do?"

She let out a sigh and relaxed back into her seat. "No cell phone, empty to-do list, and a trashy novel or two at some faraway place, preferably equipped with a hot tub and a mini bar."

"Not much for sight-seeing, I take it?"

"The longer I live in the city, the more I find myself wanting more quiet and less schedule."

"There's plenty of time before school starts. Maybe we could get away for a few days," he said.

"Let's not get ahead of ourselves," she said, and he nodded, but she could already see him plotting their trip in his head. She imagined he saw them at a little cabin by a mountain lake. She'd read on the rustic rocking chair on the porch while he set off toward the lake with a fishing pole over his shoulder. They'd fry the fish he'd caught for dinner, him of course forgetting that she didn't eat fish, until she only ate the biscuits and salad she'd put together. Later, he would lay her down on a blanket in front of the fire and cover her body with his own. It was a nice fantasy, one Juliet found herself wanting even as she knew she could never have it. Juliet hadn't been paying much attention to their destination until Ethan pulled into one of the parking garages along Ward Parkway, "The Plaza? How touristy of you."

"Gotta visit the hometown attractions sometimes."

Juliet grinned, and didn't wait for him to open her car door. When he offered his hand again, she took it, enjoying how good it felt to be allowed to touch someone again as he led her into the fondue restaurant. It was her favorite, and she couldn't keep the grin from turning into a beaming smile.

"You've been conspiring with Alex again, haven't you?" She asked.

"I don't know what you mean," he said as he took her arm, wearing a smug smile of his own.

Ethan ordered them a bottle of wine and made sure Juliet wouldn't be offended if he ordered a steak for himself. They discussed their meal options, and then settled into conversation about their backgrounds and families. When Ethan said that his father had been a doctor and that both his brothers were as well, she heard the genuine love and admiration in his voice as he spoke about his family. She already knew there was more to him than his curt doctor persona. He could be tender and thoughtful and sweet, and she guessed he had his family to thank for that.

"Was it a foregone conclusion that you would all be doctors, then?" she asked when he finished telling her about his brother's practices.

He shook his head. "Our parents expected us to be successful at whatever profession we chose, but they didn't push us toward medicine. We were just talking the other night at dinner about how much we all wanted to be like dad when we were kids. That probably had something to do with it."

"Tell me about him," she said. "What was he like?"

A smile overtook Ethan's whole face. "He was stubborn, you know? Always thought he was right about everything. Granted he usually was, but if he was wrong about something, he'd never outright admit it. He'd make amends, because he was a good man, honest, kind, demanded respect, but he was a stick in the mud. And the best doctor I've ever met."

"Wow, you really loved him," Juliet said. She couldn't give the same glowing praise of her own dad. He was steady, and understanding, but distant. Distracted. And she couldn't remember the last time they'd had a family dinner that didn't center around a holiday. Ethan made it sound like his entire family gathered regularly. She was jealous of that type of closeness—craved to be included in it even.

"When did he pass away?" she asked, noticing the past tense pronouns as well.

Ethan's lips twitched, and Juliet nearly felt as though she were prying, but his voice was steady when he said, "Almost five years ago now."

"And your mom?"

"Officially, she lives with Henry, but she has her excuses to make herself at home with all of us. If I were to move across the country, she'd probably still fly out twice a week to walk the damn dog."

"You have a dog?" she asked.

Ethan told her about his puff ball of a dog and his mother's habit of dropping by unannounced. Juliet couldn't help the jealousy that tugged at her stomach, even as she acknowledged that she was in big trouble if Ethan wanted something serious with her. She had a feeling he didn't do casual either. How could he with such a close family?

Instead of addressing the issue of their future, Juliet told Ethan about her insurance salesman father and her elementary school teacher mother. When he asked, she told him about her little sister who had moved to Denver years ago, and how they had never visited one another in their new homes. To make her life sound less pathetic, Juliet told him about Alex, "who is like a sister to me," she explained. She would have mentioned Gina as well, but that felt too close to Rich for a first date.

The food and the wine were so good, that sometime while they'd been talking, Juliet had cleared her plate and there were only a few crumbs at the bottom of their fondue pot. The bottle of wine sat empty on the table. By the time he was signing for the check, Juliet felt a warm glow radiating off her skin, and decided that this date had been the best idea she'd had in months.

"What now?"

He stood and helped her from her chair, taking her left hand in his right. "I thought we'd take the opportunity to enjoy the evening now that the sun's set. Might actually be cool enough to be outside."

"I'd like that," Juliet said, and walked close to Ethan, so her arm brushed his side with every step.

They strolled in comfortable silence, occasionally commenting on shop windows, but mostly, enjoying the relief from the heat and the buzz from the wine. More than once, she wanted to push him into one of the darkened shop's doorways and run her tongue down the side of his neck, just to see what he would do.

When they'd meandered a few blocks, Juliet nudged him with her elbow. "So, why'd you choose obstetrics?"

He wrapped his fingers through hers and said, "It's beautiful. What's better than helping new life into this world?"

Juliet smiled up at him. She hadn't expected such a romantic answer. "It's not all just delivering babies."

"No," Ethan squeezed her hand and returned her grin. "But the beauty often outweighs the tragedy. What about you?"

"Same," she said.

"I don't understand the midwife thing though. Was it just so you didn't have to go back to school for so long?"

"Not everyone has wanted to be a doctor since birth, Ethan."

His grin turned to a smirk, confirming her suspicion that he liked it when she used his first name. "Even so, I think you'd make a formidable doctor."

"I suppose that's a compliment?" Juliet asked.

"The highest." Ethan's hair fell into his eyes, and Juliet flicked the locks over his brow, and giggled as his eyes brightened. He liked her. Despite the cookies, and the dancing, she hadn't believed until that moment that she was anything other than a curiosity to be explored, or a conquest to be won, but he really wanted to know the answer.

"I believe in the midwifery model of care. I trust a woman's body to know how to labor, and I think gentleness and patience and understanding go a long way."

"But you don't want to be able to do a c-section in an emergency?"

"I can't bring myself to eat a chicken nugget, and you think I can cut into a live person?" She asked. It wasn't entirely true, she knew how to perform episiotomies—not that she had ever done one or planned to—but if the situation called for it, she could do it.

"Not similar in the slightest, I assure you."

Juliet cringed, an episiotomy was still nothing compared to a cesarean. "I'll leave the surgery to hotshots like you, thank you."

Ethan laughed and told her stories of the guys he went to medical school with who drove flashy cars and cut their hair to look like doctors on tv. "So you see," he said, coming to a stop in front of a gelato cart, "I'm down-to-earth by comparison."

"I don't think it counts if you have to claim to be down-to-earth."

Instead of defending himself, Ethan only said, "Gelato?"

More because she wanted to sit next to him on the edge of the fountain than because she wanted dessert, Juliet said yes.

An hour later, Ethan took the last free space in the parking lot behind Juliet's building. He trailed off on the point he was making about not joining his brother's practice as he cut the engine. Juliet waited, knowing he was debating whether walking her to her door looked too desperate.

"You should come in for coffee," she said, before he could stare at the steering wheel too long.

He smiled and followed her up.

Chapter Eleven

The club was busy, the patio filled with smoking kids talking over the music with slurred voices. Juliet didn't spare the crowd a glance and led Ethan past them up the stairs to her apartment. He didn't know how she lived with the noise.

He'd been too distracted to notice the week before, but despite how loud it was outside, the residential part of the building was quiet.

The exposed brick in the hallway gave way to the shabby interior of Juliet's apartment. She dropped his hand and headed straight for the coffee pot, effectively cutting off his plan to back her into the wall. So, Ethan followed her into the narrow galley kitchen, and leaned against the stove while she brushed past him again and again while she brewed coffee. He crossed his arms to keep himself from wrapping them around her waist and pulling her into a kiss.

"What's your schedule like this week?" He asked.

Juliet shrugged, still fussing with the coffee maker. "Not as busy as I would like, but busy enough."

"I barely have time to sleep this week," he said, as she turned to face him at last. "But I'd like to see you."

Juliet stared at him for a long time, her lips slightly parted, her shoulders relaxed, her eyes searching. They stood that way for minutes, and he wondered where her mind had gone. Ethan wanted to know what she was thinking. Her gaze was too heavy for him to interpret. They'd had a nice evening, he thought. An easy sort of connection as they'd gotten to know one another—and yet their kiss from the week before had never been far from his mind. Her skin had been so soft, her body so warm and pliant against his own. He remembered spooning against her, years ago, as he splayed his hand over her belly, planning to be the man that took care of her.

"What?" he asked, just as the coffee pot gurgled and spluttered. She ducked out of his gaze and poured the coffee. She handed him a squat handmade mug glazed in a purple blue green iridescent finish. Juliet sped past him, planting herself on the threadbare gray sofa in the adjoining living room without saying a word.

When Ethan joined her, she said, "I was sort of hoping we could have this conversation over breakfast—if you can stay that long that is."

"I can stay," he said.

Juliet smiled into her mug as she sipped her coffee. He didn't think that was what she'd been worrying over, but he'd let it slide for the moment. Instead, he asked about the bowls of beads left around the apartment, and she told him about Alex's jewelry business, about how she helped when she could. Then he asked about her knitting, and she showed him the baby hats she was working on for her prenatal yoga classes.

"Don't you ever do anything for yourself?"

Juliet raised one eyebrow. The move was adorable. Ethan wished he could mirror it back to her, but he could only move his eyebrows in unison.

She set her half-drunk mug on the coffee table, then pulled Ethan's from his hands. "I thought that's what this was," Juliet said as she pushed him back against the cushions and slid a leg over his lap until she was straddling him.

"Is this enough?" he asked, even as he watched her lips descend until they met his. His hands automatically went to her waist, drawing her body against him.

"Maybe not yet, but it could be," she said between kisses, then pulled back and ran her tongue down his throat. Whatever blood hadn't made its way south surged there.

Any reservations Ethan had after their last encounter dissipated as his hands traveled to her thighs and his tongue met hers in an intense duel for dominance.

A sigh of a moan escaped Juliet's lips as his hands crept higher up her legs, beneath her skirt. Her hands ran over his shoulders, into his hair, down his arms. Her hips pressed down into his lap, and instinctively, he pressed up into her.

"My God," he said against her lips as she found the bulge in his pants and ground against him.

JULIET HADN'T FELT so good in a long time. She was on Ethan's lap. His lips were kissing a line down her neck as his hands rubbed their way up her inner thighs. A fire was building in her blood, her heart thumping. She didn't seem to be able to catch her breath, but it was exactly what she wanted.

Juliet pressed into Ethan as he brought his lips back to hers, and he moaned. One of his fingers brushed the fabric of her panties, and she whimpered just as the door burst open.

One of Alex's drunken giggles broke the passionate silence, followed by a man's voice saying, "Watch it there," as bodies stumbled over the threshold. Juliet flew off Ethan's lap before she recognized the voice. By then, Alex had righted herself and pulled the man into a loud, sloppy kiss that he nevertheless seemed to be enjoying.

Juliet looked down to Ethan, who was staring at her as if he wasn't sure where she'd gone, but Juliet couldn't keep her eyes off the amorous couple who hadn't noticed them yet.

"Rich?" Juliet asked.

Ethan was the first to move, whipping his head around to see the couple at the door behind them. By the time the other two untangled themselves, Ethan was on his feet, with his arm around Juliet's waist in a possessive hold.

"Hey, Juliet," Rich said as he swept his hair out of his eyes. "Fancy meeting you here."

"I live here."

Ethan's grip tightened on Juliet as Rich's eyes flicked between them.

Alex, who didn't even have the grace to look ashamed of herself tugged Rich's hand as she giggled again. "Sorry for intruding. Have fun lovebirds." And then they were gone again.

Juliet's whole body, singing with pleasure and anticipation mere seconds ago now felt numb. Deflated. Had she just seen that?

"You okay?" Ethan asked, blocking her view of the door when he wrapped his arms around her.

She blinked and tried to bring his frowning face into focus. Was he worried about her? Or was he jealous?

"What a lying, filthy hypocrite," Juliet said. "Do you know how many times she's told me not to sleep with Rich? That he's a creep? A lying cheat? And the second I move on, she's already fucking him."

Ethan stood back, looking shocked by the venom in her voice. "Why does it matter who he's sleeping with?"

Juliet raked her hands through her hair and paced around the coffee table. "It's not about him. It's about Alex knowing better and doing it anyway. She knows what he is. She knows he'll hurt her in the end."

"So, you're upset about your friend making poor decisions, not that you know your ex is sleeping with someone else?" Ethan's voice was carefully measured with little emotion conveyed in the tone, like she'd heard him do while reading off test results that meant bad news.

"I don't care about Rich," Juliet said, stepping back into him and wrapping her arms around his neck. "I'm shocked that Alex is his new conquest is all."

Juliet could feel the relief wash over him as he returned her embrace. She was annoyed, both at Ethan's jealousy, and at herself for lying to him. She didn't care who Rich was sleeping with. Not really. But to see him with Alex—to know that he was taking advantage of Alex to get under Juliet's skin—irritated her.

And Alex should know better.

"Alex is old enough to take care of herself."

"Yeah."

She rested her forehead on his shoulder and tried to make sense of the thoughts buzzing around in her head while Ethan rubbed her back and kissed her hair.

"What do you want to do?" he asked after a few minutes.

"I think I need to go to bed."

He sighed. "You don't mean with me, do you?"

Juliet cringed. She'd hoped he'd get the picture and discreetly excuse himself. "Not tonight. Sorry."

He nodded and tilted her chin up so he could kiss her chastely. "Nothing to apologize for." He kissed her again, a whisper across her lips. "I'll call you tomorrow?"

"You better." Juliet forced a smile, and gave him a kiss, trying to convey how sorry she was.

THE NEXT MORNING, JULIET waited for Alex to return. She didn't show up until two o'clock in the afternoon when Juliet had cleaned the entire apartment and was on the sofa folding her laundry.

To her credit, Alex came right in and sat down next to Juliet instead of tip-toeing back to her room like Juliet would have been inclined to do had the tables been turned.

"Okay," Alex said. "Let me have it."

Juliet finished folding a pair of yoga pants and straightened the pile of slippery workout clothes. "I'm not going to let you have it. I'm worried about you."

Alex scooted closer to Juliet. "I'm fine."

"You're sleeping with Rich."

"Yes."

"That's a really bad idea."

Alex sighed and said, "I am not dating him. I don't want to date him. We hooked up last week after you left with Ethan, and again last night. I may never see him again, and I'm okay with that."

Juliet sat back into the cushions, shifting to face her friend, who still wore last night's black dress. "You haven't secretly been pining for him all these years?"

"God no." Alex laughed. "I've thought he was the scum of the earth. Still do, really."

"Then how can you sleep with him?"

She shrugged. "It started as a way to keep him from bothering you, and kind of just snowballed from there."

Juliet sighed and stared at her laundry. Alex had said over and over that she never planned to marry. She wanted to be splendidly single, keeping lovers the way gentlemen in the 19th Century kept mistresses. Juliet thought it sounded like a lonely existence, and she still wasn't entirely sure Alex meant it. Sometimes, Juliet thought Alex hid behind meaningless relationships with men because she was afraid no man could ever love her. But Juliet didn't dare voice that opinion aloud. Alex had a hard enough time with her judgmental grandmother and absentee mother.

"I don't want him to hurt you," Juliet said. "Me, I can handle, but if he did something to you, I might kill him."

Alex threw an arm over Juliet's shoulder. "While I appreciate your loyalty, I don't want you to worry. His gorgeous face and incredible charm have zero effect on me."

Juliet smiled, and wanted to believe her friend, and if it had only been the one encounter, she might have, but seeking Rich out a second time sounded a lot to Juliet like the start of something, even if it was shallow.

When Alex had retreated to her bedroom, Juliet texted Rich that she wasn't impressed with him sleeping with her best friend.

His response: *I'm not impressed with the good doctor, so it looks like we're even.*

When Juliet said that she wasn't trying to make him jealous, he only said to call him when the doctor bored her. He'd wait for her.

Juliet almost threw her phone across the room, but settled on throwing a pair of yoga pants instead, and texted that he was a self-absorbed asshole.

ETHAN HADN'T BEEN JOKING about his schedule. The end of June and beginning of July was when most of his colleagues took their vacations. For two weeks, he worked extra shifts to cover for them. He had never minded working until he dropped, sleeping for a few hours, and then getting back at it the next day. But with the possibility of time with Juliet to tempt him, the schedule chafed like it never had before.

He'd fantasized about inviting Juliet over for dinner one night. He'd make pasta, pour her a glass of wine, and they could finish what they'd started after their date. Realistically though, they hadn't even had time to meet for coffee in the hospital cafeteria.

Even so, something was happening to Ethan that hadn't happened for a long time. He looked forward to her voicemails, and checked his phone more often, hoping for more of the lascivious texts she'd been sending him all week.

That morning, a week after their date, Ethan still hadn't managed to see Juliet face to face. Her teasing texts were driving him so crazy that he thought he might explode if he didn't get to touch her soon. He wanted to kiss her, to feel her legs around his hips with her breasts pressed against his chest. He wanted to hear all the dirty things she'd texted from her soft, warm mouth.

He was in the break room, refilling his coffee mug after an emergency D&C, a woman hemorrhaging with a miscarriage, when Juliet texted.

JULIET: *Are you* still *at work?*

Ethan smiled.

ETHAN: *You sound like my mother.*

JULIET: *I in no way want to remind you of your mother. Ever.*

ETHAN: *That isn't going to be a problem.*

Ethan wasn't expecting a sarcastic response, but Juliet surprised him.

JULIET: *Any chance you can meet me for breakfast at Dino's in an hour?*

Ethan had made his way back to his office and stared at the stack of file folders on his desk. They would take at least two hours to sort through, but he was done seeing patients for the day. There was no reason why he couldn't take a lunch break. It meant one hour less sleep before his next shift started but seeing Juliet would be worth it.

ETHAN: *See you in hour.*

She was there when he arrived, sitting at the small table in the corner he was beginning to think of as theirs. Ethan didn't expect to have a physical reaction upon seeing her, but she wore a pair of clover green scrubs that made her hair look like flame. His stomach dropped when she smiled at him, her green eyes sparkling. He'd never seen someone look radiant in scrubs before, but she might as well have been wearing a ballgown.

He dropped a quick kiss to her lips before taking the seat across from her. "I didn't think you were open on Saturdays," he said.

Juliet poured him a cup of coffee from the carafe on the table. "We had three babies born Thursday. They're all coming in for the forty-eight-hour checkups." Ethan nodded. He knew they did follow up care, but he hadn't ever bothered with the particulars before. He'd assumed it would pale in comparison to the type of care a woman would receive in the hospital, but now he was curious.

After they ordered, Juliet explained they taught the mother how to track the baby's breathing and heart rate and temperature, as well as monitor her fundus. She explained how they called twenty-four hours after discharge to check in and gets the stats on the vitals. Then, at forty-eight hours they came in for an exam, then again at two weeks and six weeks.

"What if a woman hemorrhages in the first twenty-four hours?"

"She's monitoring her bleeding too. She calls us, and we get her into the hospital. If we think something's wrong, we won't send her home at all."

The whole idea of releasing a woman mere hours after birth made Ethan's heart race. There were too many variables—most that resulted in negative outcomes.

"Makes me nervous," he said as he tried to soak the last of his syrup up an already saturated wedge of pancake.

"Well, when you have babies, you can do it your way. I'll do it mine."

Ethan stopped himself from saying that would be hard to do if they were going to have babies together. It was far too soon to have that conversation. And she wouldn't have said it so casually if she weren't referring to work.

"We'll have to agree to disagree for now," he said. Then, when she had pointedly not responded as she sipped her coffee he asked, "What are you doing next weekend?"

"Alex and I usually watch the fireworks from the roof."

He could imagine it. The two them above their apartment, the music from the nightclub thumping in the background. They'd be drinking. In his imagination, Alex had a faceless man beside her, but it was Ethan who was cuddled up next to Juliet, the night just cool enough that she could use him as a chair.

The fantasy was pleasant, and it would do as an alternative, but spending the Fourth on a rooftop was not what he wanted.

"My brother Logan, the one who lives in the country, hosts a big Fourth of July party every year. It's fun, lots of food, games, fireworks. My whole family comes to town, more than even come at Christmas."

He regretted that last part as soon as he said it. Juliet's eyes widened at the words. He'd known she'd be a little hesitant about the family gathering, and while it was probably the largest gathering of the year, it was casual.

Before he could set her mind at ease, she said, "You want me to go with you to a family party?"

"Yes."

"You don't think that'll give the wrong impression?"

"What impression is that?"

A grin spread over Ethan's lips as he watched Juliet squirm. He knew he was putting her on the spot, but the way she chewed the corner of her lip was adorable.

"That things between us are serious."

"Aren't they?"

Juliet paled, and Ethan stifled his chuckle as she sputtered about how they only just started seeing each other.

"It's just a cookout," he said, running his thumb over the soft skin on her palm. "And I want to see you, but this shindig is mandatory, so it's either take you along or not see you at all—and frankly, I don't give a damn if my family thinks we're getting married if it means I can spend more than a few minutes with you at a time."

"Oh God. I can't get married," Juliet said.

That was new. Hadn't she been engaged? "Never?"

She shrugged and didn't meet his eyes as she sighed. "We can't even date past August, so marriage is completely out of the question."

Ethan had not been aware their relationship had an expiration date, and he knew his confusion and annoyance showed on his face when Juliet gave him a half-hearted smile. "Why August?"

"Because that's when school starts back up and we'll both be working at the hospital." She picked at her napkin. "I'd get kicked out of school for dating you."

It made sense, he supposed. Ethan didn't like the idea that they were temporary, but he better understood her initial resistance. For some reason, the potential complication of her doing her practicum at his hospital hadn't ever occurred to him, which only made him more annoyed.

"You should have told me sooner," he said, unable to keep his rising anger out of his voice.

Juliet hooked his hand. "I wasn't sure we would make it past our date last week. Why bring up limitations when you're not even sure you need them?"

He heard his teeth grind together as he prepared to be broken up with, but Juliet surprised him by saying, "I don't want to stop seeing you."

"I don't want to stop seeing you either, but I can't be in a relationship with an expiration date."

"I can't either," Juliet said. She looked nervous and sincere. "That's why I've just been thinking of this as fun, you know."

"Fun?"

Juliet cringed at the flat tone of his voice. "A way for us to blow off some steam over the summer?" The question in her voice made it sound like she wasn't even sure she believed herself, and Ethan latched onto that.

"I don't think of you as fling material," he said.

Juliet's smile turned more satisfied, and hope pushed through the anger. "I didn't mean I don't take you seriously. I do. I just—"

Ethan held up a hand, not wanting or needing to hear her explanations. "How about we just take it one day at a time? Feel things out between now and August?"

Juliet nodded. "I can do that."

"Thank you." He smiled and gripped her hand over the table. "It will be a fantastic summer either way."

Ethan could feel Juliet relaxing again as his words thawed through her panic. "I'll go to your party," she said, "But don't expect me to play nice if one of your relatives starts hounding me about when we're making babies."

Ethan laughed and wiggled his eyebrows. "Just tell them we'll be happy to get started immediately. Maybe they'll leave us alone together."

Juliet turned bright pink, and Ethan laughed even harder as he made it his new mission to make Juliet Hawthorne fall in love with him over the next six weeks.

Chapter Twelve

Juliet's week had been just as busy as Ethan's. She'd picked up a couple extra shifts at the birthing center, and she'd helped Alex fill a big order for a new boutique. It was Friday night before Juliet had a moment to herself, and that was only because Alex had disappeared down into Tokyo Nights and the mother that was due on Wednesday still hadn't gone into labor.

To keep her mind off how Alex was likely downstairs dancing with Rich again, and to make sure there was something for her to eat at Ethan's party, Juliet cooked a pan of *spanakopita*, roasted some vegetables from the farmers market, and just for something fun, made a batch of Gina's grandmother's biscotti.

She hadn't heard from Rich since he'd told her he was waiting for her to break up with Ethan, which still galled her. Just because she didn't plan to stay with Ethan long term did not mean that she was going to run to Rich the second the semester started. She wasn't running to Rich at all. Ever. For anything.

Her nerves picked up as she thought about meeting Ethan's family. They would assume that she and Ethan were more serious than they were, but what could Juliet do about that? Ethan wanted her there, so she would go, even if she suspected he thought they were more serious than they were, despite their short discussion on the duration of their relationship.

To leave him with little doubt that she wanted him for the summer, and to keep things light, Juliet had been suggesting intimacies via text again this week. Juliet wanted Ethan to want her so bad he couldn't think of anything else. Things would be easier that way when it came time to end them.

As she settled down in her room to knit at the end of the night, she received a text from him.

ETHAN: *You're awfully quiet this evening.*

JULIET: *I've been cooking and trying to decide what part of you I'm going to imagine on me tonight, your mouth or your hand.*

The three little dots pulsed and disappeared a few times before he replied.

ETHAN: *I could be heading into surgery. You could be putting people's lives in danger with talk like that.*

JULIET: *Are you heading into surgery?*

ETHAN: *I'm done for the night.*

Juliet uncurled her legs and sat up straighter in her arm chair.

JULIET: *You're off?*

ETHAN: *Just hit the parking garage.*

Juliet's heart pounded. They hadn't planned on seeing each other until tomorrow, but why wait?

JULIET: *Come over.*

The three dots pulsed faded and pulsed again.

ETHAN: *It's midnight.*

Juliet snorted and told him to come over again.

ETHAN: *I'll be there in twenty minutes.*

Twenty minutes later, Juliet buzzed him up, and met him at the door. He wore blue scrubs that made his eyes look even brighter. His hair was greasy and hung in his eyes, which were glued to her breasts. Her nipples had peaked under her pink camisole. Juliet stepped forward and swept his shaggy hair out of his face.

"You need a haircut," she said.

"I need a lot of things." Ethan's voice was gruff as he pulled Juliet against his chest and breathed into her ear, "but I'd like to start with making you pay for your relentless teasing."

"How's that?" Juliet kissed the valley of his collarbone, just exposed by the v-neck in his scrubs. He sighed and sank into her as she kissed her way up his neck.

"I was thinking of torturing you with my mouth," he said. "Or maybe my hand." Ethan ran his hand down her side for emphasis and squeezed her behind through her running shorts.

Juliet raised her chin and Ethan's hot lips came down on hers. His tongue dragged along her bottom lip, and Juliet groaned and leaned against him completely.

"I've missed you," he said between open-mouthed kisses.

"You work too much." Juliet took a careful step backward and pulled him with her.

"Where are we going?" he asked, pausing to nip his way down her neck.

"My bedroom is this way."

When they were safely shut away in the room, Ethan backed Juliet up to the bed until it caught the back of her knees and they toppled over. Ethan squeezed her breasts over her camisole, flicking his fingers over her nipples. "Is this what you wear to bed?"

"Sometimes," Juliet said as ran her hands up inside Ethan's shirt. "Other times I wear nothing."

A sort of growling noise came from Ethan's throat and he pulled the neckline of the camisole down, exposing one of her breasts so he could tease her nipple with his tongue. Juliet arched up into his touch, scraping her nails down his back. Ethan's teeth came down just hard enough to make Juliet squeak. He sat up, pulling his shirt over his head as he went. Juliet's followed his in an arc through the air to land in a heap across her small room.

His lips landed back on hers, urgent and demanding as he pushed her backward onto the bed. Juliet wrapped her legs around his hips bringing the arousal that his scrubs did nothing to hide in line with where she wanted him. Ethan groaned and rocked into her once, then twice before pulling back enough to pull first her bottoms down, then his.

"I thought you were going to tease me."

"You are driving me crazy," he said.

Juliet giggled while Ethan ran his fingertips over her calves and up her thighs. She opened her mouth to tease him some more, but his fingers found a spot between her legs that made her go mute. He prodded again, the pressure just far enough off center to make her pant without being close enough to satisfy.

When Juliet rocked her hips to his rhythm, he rubbed small circles, just nudging her nub at the top of each circuit until Juliet clawed at the quilt beneath her and whimpered. "Ethan, please."

He chuckled and slid one finger into her slick passage. "You're all talk, aren't you?"

"Get over here and find out," Juliet pulled on the wrist of the hand that held her hips down.

"I wasn't expecting to come over. I don't have any condoms."

"Do we need them?"

Ethan stilled, his hands coming to rest over Juliet's stomach. "I always do the first time."

"This is our second."

He pressed his thumb inside her, but did not move, as if to say that was all she was going to get without a condom. "Juliet," his voice was quiet but firm.

"In the drawer, like last time," she motioned to the nightstand and listened to him wrestle with the package so new it was still wrapped in plastic.

Juliet giggled as he cursed and ran her nails over the length of the leg that was still splayed over her. "I am on the pill you know," she said.

"You have too much fun teasing me," Ethan said through clenched teeth as he positioned himself over her.

He teased her back by grinding against her slickness in measured strokes, until Juliet raked her nails down his back and said, "Dear God, what are you waiting for?"

Ethan lined himself up with her entrance, then leaned down to kiss a trail up Juliet's neck. "Now you know how

I've felt lately." His breath tickled her ear like a new leaf in a spring breeze.

Juliet shuddered, and Ethan slipped inside her and started to move. "Shit, Juliet."

"What?" She asked as she moved into his thrusts, but Ethan had closed his eyes and didn't respond. "Concentrating?"

"I lush," he said, and covered her lips with his own. "You feel too good."

Then Juliet was beyond words as his fingers found that spot again. She wrapped her legs tighter, her hands wrapped in his hair as he moved on top of her. The heat from the muggy night had seeped in past the air conditioning and their sweat-slick bodies slid against each other.

Juliet's world shrunk to include only the places where Ethan's body met hers until she exploded in a spectacle of lights and pleasure. Ethan cursed above her, and she felt his climax crash over him as he rode it out, murmuring curses that sounded like prayers.

Instead of collapsing on top of her, Ethan caught Juliet's lips again in a kiss that seared as his tongue met hers, then slowly cooled to soft kisses and whispered affirmations.

"Can we please not wait four years to do that again?" he asked.

Juliet smiled. "We don't even have to wait until morning if you don't want to."

Ethan rested his forehead on hers, sighing as the hand that had tortured her between her legs roamed over the curve of her hip. "I need sleep. And a shower."

"Give me a minute, and the bathroom's all yours."

Juliet pulled on her cotton robe, conscious that Ethan watched her from her bed. She crept into the hallway, making sure the way was clear, but there was no sign of either Alex or Rich.

After freshening up and pulling a clean towel for Ethan out of the hall closet, Juliet returned to her room. Ethan had gathered his clothes and draped them over the back of her arm chair.

"It doesn't look like Alex is here," Juliet held out the towel. "So, feel free to walk around in the buff if you want."

Ethan took the towel and pulled Juliet in to nuzzle her neck. "You like that?"

Juliet stood back and took her time sweeping her eyes over him from top to bottom. His body was solid, with visible muscles in his arms and shoulders and a torso that tapered into trim waist where a line of hair led to athletic legs. "Yeah, I do."

He squeezed her hand and grinned at her over his shoulder as he left, because Juliet made a show of watching him leave.

She straightened the sheets, abandoned her robe, and climbed back into a bed that smelled like spice and sweat and sex. This sated, safe feeling was exactly what she'd wanted from Ethan, and she burrowed into the bed like their lovemaking had infused itself into her sheets.

Juliet didn't even realize that she'd been dozing until Ethan joined her, skin still hot and damp from his shower.

ETHAN WOKE IN AN AIRY, bright room with sun pooling through the windows—so different from his dungeon of a room in his basement. It smelled different too, fresh and green from the line of ferns in front of the south facing windows. It was the soft sigh she made in her sleep that alerted him to her presence, not their legs tangled together or her head on his shoulder—that didn't feel out of place at all.

He stroked the loose long hair that fell down her back and pooled in the crook of his elbow. The memory of the night before played through his mind like a movie. It had been hot. Molten. He'd almost come as soon as he was inside her.

Juliet snuggled in closer to his side, and Ethan's fingers began to roam. He was half in disbelief, half in awe that this was where they were. What had happened to the woman, who, a few weeks ago was afraid to let herself like him? When had she been replaced with this lustful creature?

A surge of pure want shot through him as he remembered her messages, how she'd teased him about licking him, touching him, kissing him—Juliet had never brought up sex specifically, but she'd certainly made sure he'd had it on the brain.

Waking, she arched into his touch as he again traced the fall of her hair down her back. She ran her nose along his jaw, nuzzling into the crook behind his ear. "Morning," she said. Juliet's voice was hoarse and husky, barely above a whisper.

Ethan couldn't help the smile that parted his lips, even as he craned his neck to kiss her. She shifted up, slightly over him to run her tongue over his teeth and into his mouth to greet his tongue briefly before settling her head back down on his shoulder. Ethan wanted to protest, wanted to kiss her more now that they were both awake and he was thoroughly aroused again, but she swirled her hand up and down his chest, and he found that he enjoyed that—enjoyed having her naked chest pressed into his side.

"This is nice," he said after a minute of concentrating of the feel of her hands on him. It was almost too nice. He could get used to waking up with her too easily, and he knew once he did, he'd never want to stop.

A gentle hum was his only response as her fingers dipped lower, under the thin cotton sheet that tented over his arousal. Once beyond that barrier, Juliet lost all pretense and wrapped her fingers around him. Ethan hissed in surprise, then moaned as she stroked him a handful of times. When she disappeared under the sheet, Ethan knew where she was headed, but it didn't prepare him for the feel of her mouth around him. Her wet heat drew him closer and closer as she pulled her tongue and lips over his length.

"Juliet." His throat was so dry he nearly choked.

He felt her lips curl into a smile, then she kissed her way up his chest until she reached his collar bone. She ran her tongue up his neck and through his beard and over his lips. Just as Ethan decided she was the sexiest creature he'd ever seen, she disappeared under the covers again, rolling a condom over his length, then rolling back up along his body and slipping herself onto him in a painfully slow slide.

Ethan watched as she rode him, her palms on his chest, her eyes closed, her bottom lip between her teeth as she concentrated on something deep inside of herself.

"You're so beautiful," he said, his voice winded from the effort of letting her remain in control when all he wanted to do was clamp his hands down on her hips and pump into her.

Juliet's green eyes snapped open and she smiled even as she continued to bite her lip, and she kept smiling as Ethan moved against her, knowing that it would hasten his climax, but hoping it would bring hers sooner as well. Within moments she was grinding into him and moaning louder and louder with each stroke. It felt like the noise was emanating from where she pulsed around him, and Ethan couldn't stop his release.

Juliet collapsed on him in a fit of giggles, which had never happened to him before. She laughed so long and so hard that Ethan found himself laughing as well. "What's so funny?"

"That was amazing," she said as she covered his face, his shoulders, his throat in kisses.

"You are amazing."

Juliet hopped off him and pulled on her robe as she headed for the bathroom, sending a smile back at him over her shoulder. Ethan stretched and smiled up at the ceiling. This thing with Juliet was good. Really good.

When Juliet returned a few minutes later, Ethan hadn't moved. Still clad in her robe, Juliet lay down beside him, resting her head on his shoulder.

"I have a forty-eight-hour follow up at ten."

"What time is it?"

"Eight-thirty."

"I should head out then."

Ethan didn't want to go. He wanted to sleep another few hours and wake up with her again, but he knew he would see her again later in the day. There would be no more weeks' worth of separation if he had anything to say about it.

He rose and pulled on his scrubs as Juliet watched, an appreciative smirk curving over her lips as he dressed. Then she cinched her robe and walked him to the door. Ethan pulled her into his arms by the sash and kissed her softly at first, but the kiss grew in magnitude and depth until he had to pull away, panting.

"I'll pick you up at four-thirty?" he asked, his forehead on hers.

"I'm looking forward to it."

He touched his lips to hers one last time, and as he lifted his head to say goodbye, he spotted someone standing behind Juliet, at the edge of the living room. A tall, dark-haired man wearing only black boxer briefs and a scowl watched them.

And Ethan didn't let his smile falter, because he could see right through Rich. But he did feel a little sorry for Alex.

JULIET SHUT THE DOOR behind Ethan and leaned against it, smiling to herself. She was halfway across the room before she noticed she wasn't alone.

When Juliet raised her eyes, she found Rich frowning at her from the hall threshold, his arms crossed over his chest.

"Have fun?" He asked.

"Yes."

Rich's fists clenched, and the grumpy frown turned sharp and wild as he curled his lip for just a second. His smirk replaced the flash of possessiveness almost immediately.

"What are you doing here?" she asked

"I was sleeping, but you woke me." He crossed the room in smooth, confident strides. Rich stopped only when his body was mere inches away from hers. Juliet had to squelch her cringe. She wanted to go back into her room, snuggle into her pillow, and relish in the lingering smell of Ethan combined with the pleasant soreness between her legs. Sparring with Rich was not on her to-do list.

"What do you want?" she asked, trying to sound bored, like his quiet fury didn't affect her.

Rich closed his eyes and gulped in a deep breath, releasing it slowly through his nose. Juliet watched as his hand raised, reached for her, but did nothing as his fingers trailed down the soft cotton sleeve of her spring green robe, catching in the cuff. "Where's the robe I bought you?"

When she'd been pregnant, there were days she'd been so sick, she could barely get out of bed, but she'd had to for school. Whenever she'd been home that semester, she'd been on the sofa in her pjs, or in bed. It had been such a cold winter and she'd felt so awful, that Rich had gifted her a fluffy clover green robe that she'd worn every day until the days grew so warm she'd roasted in it.

"It's way too hot out."

Rich's frown fell into slack disbelief. "You still have it?"

Juliet shook her head. "I gave it to Goodwill."

His fingers fisted in the cloth at her wrist. "You gave it away?"

Juliet shrugged. "I almost burned it."

"I expected you had," he said, and tugged on her sleeve as he closed the distance between them. Her nose was level with his collarbone. "I'm so sorry Jules. If I could go back and change everything, I would be so much better to you."

Juliet had to crane her neck to see his face, and Rich dipped his head, brushing his nose against hers, not in the proprietary way Ethan had, but more like a tender prelude to a kiss. Juliet forgot she could move away and froze as if any motion on her part would spur more intimacy on his.

"What are you—?"

"Let me make it up to you."

He lowered his lips as if to kiss her, but Juliet caught the smell of Alex's tangy perfume on his skin and backed out of his reach.

"I'm with Ethan," she said.

"And when you aren't with Ethan anymore?"

"Why are you so sure we'll break up?" Rich didn't need to know that she couldn't stay with Ethan.

Rich was back to looking like his usual unruffled self, the anger and jealousy banished behind calm self-assurance. "Because you think Doctors are arrogant asses."

"Not all of them."

Rich shook his head. "It's only a matter of time, Jules."

"And what makes you think I'm going to come running to you when you're sleeping with Alex."

"If it's bothering you that much, I'll break it off."

"I won't sit back and watch my best friend be hurt, but I won't be the reason she gets hurt either."

"It's not like that with Alex," Rich said softly.

Juliet didn't want to know what it was like with Alex. She was done with him. "Do whatever you want. I have to get ready for work." And she slammed the bathroom door behind her.

Chapter Thirteen

E than was more nervous than he wanted to be. He might have left Juliet's apartment wearing a smug smile, but too much time alone in his car ferrying supplies to and from Logan's had seen his confidence wane. What had he been thinking leaving Rich and Juliet alone together barely clothed?

That morning he'd figured she'd blow him off and go to work, but Rich wasn't just any ex-boyfriend. They'd been practically engaged. She'd been carrying his baby. And losing Rich and their child had destroyed Juliet's whole world.

By the time he showered for a second time that day and was headed back over the river to pick Juliet up, he kept checking his phone for her cancellation.

When she answered the door with a smile and an armful of covered dishes, Ethan felt a profound sense of relief, even as he dove for the salad bowl losing its balance on top of a glass casserole dish. When both she and her dishes were buckled securely in his Cruiser, Ethan braved a short kiss before he started the engine. He tried to pull back, but Juliet grabbed a handful of his t-shirt and pushed her tongue past his teeth.

That said something, and Ethan didn't allow the moment to pass, sweeping his tongue against hers until he was certain Juliet knew he had missed her.

After he released her, Juliet settled in her seat with a Cheshire cat grin and asked, "Who am I about to meet?"

Ethan spent the forty-minute drive giving her a brief family history—which cousins were related through whom and what their kids' names were—not that he expected her to remember any of them. But Juliet seemed interested, especially as he talked about his nieces and nephew.

After he'd told her all he could, she said, "Okay, let me see if I've got this straight. Amy, Heather, and Megan are Logan and Vanessa's daughters. Amy is a senior in college, studying education, and Heather is trying to get into nursing school. Megan is the youngest, still in high school, but the most rebellious. Henry and Paige's kids are Emily who just finished eighth grade and likes books. Jason is ten and more interested in Pokémon and Minecraft than playing baseball with his dad."

"Nailed it. You want to try the cousins and their kids now?"

Juliet's eyes widened, and she shook her head. "I'll stick with the direct relations, thank you."

"Fair enough," Ethan said, and they drove a few minutes in silence as he pictured how spectacularly Juliet was going to impress his family.

"So, the only one going into the medical field, so far, is Heather?" Juliet asked.

"Right," Ethan said. "Nursing, like you."

"Not medical school?" Juliet asked.

"Nope," Ethan said.

Then Juliet asked the question he knew she was going to ask but had never himself yet wondered.

"Why not?"

Ethan shrugged.

"You never asked did you."

"It never occurred to me."

"Why?"

"Heather never struck me as the doctor type."

"Because she's a girl?"

"Because she's kind of quiet."

Juliet snorted.

"What?"

"Have you ever thought that maybe she's afraid to want to be a doctor because she doesn't want to disappoint anyone if she fails?"

Ethan frowned at the sun in the distance. "So, she didn't even try?"

"Maybe." Juliet said with a shrug of her shoulder, then added, "I've met a few nurses who did that—and a lot who went with nursing because they thought it was the easier route."

"You don't agree?" He could tell by her tone that she didn't. That many nurses resented doctor's because they thought they worked harder was a conversation he'd over-heard more than once. And it was a conversation he stayed far, far away from.

He could feel Juliet's hard gaze on his right side even as he forced himself to keep his eyes on the road.

"I don't think healthcare is easy. When a person's life could be in your hands, it never is."

That Ethan agreed with.

"Maybe you should talk to her," Ethan said.

"Of course," Juliet said.

They were silent for the rest of the drive, and Ethan could feel Juliet's anxiety grow as they turned off the access road onto Logan's long driveway.

"Are you sure we can't just go back to your place?" she asked as he parked. "I can make it worth your while." She waggled her eyebrows in comical desperation.

"After fireworks, I'm all yours."

"Fine." Juliet sounded like a petulant child but took a fortifying breath and followed him inside.

ETHAN'S BROTHER'S HOUSE was massive. Juliet's parents weren't poor, but she hailed from the land of '70s era split-levels. Logan Harvey's house was a modern country mansion, and it was positively full of people. Juliet was introduced to three cousins, plus wives and kids before the even made it to the kitchen. Logan's wife, Vanessa, was in the kitchen, along with their oldest daughter, Amy. Mother and daughter frosted cupcakes together while a few other women gathered ingredients destined for the grill.

Logan supervised grilling on the deck while Henry shot off parachutes for the kids in the expansive backyard. The younger kids chased down the little army men, shrieking in delight if they got the one with the streamers. There were at least four dogs running around, none of which were Ethan's.

Juliet wanted to meet Camille most. There hadn't been one encounter with him where he hadn't complained about his dog, but Juliet wasn't buying his macho man act. She had a suspicion he loved the dog despite its reportedly small and fluffy appearance. That the dog was coming with his mother, who'd Ethan told her to "take with a grain of salt," Juliet was not thrilled about.

After tailing Ethan for an hour, she'd met most of his family. They'd decided to keep their story simple, telling everyone that they met through work, that they worked in the same field but not together. Not once did it come up that Juliet was a midwife-in-training, nor that she worked at the birth center, probably because Ethan quickly steered the conversation away from them and back onto whatever that relative was up to.

When she couldn't handle the redirection and avoidance anymore, Juliet sneaked inside to see if she could help with the food, she happened upon Ethan's sisters-in-law alone in the kitchen, opening a bottle of wine.

"Can I help with anything?" Juliet asked as they both turned toward her.

"Absolutely not," Vanessa said, and pulled the empty chair at the kitchen island that sat between the two women. "But you should try this wine. I just got it in from France."

"Thanks." The only thing Juliet could make out on the bottle's French label was that it was a Burgundy. "I needed a break from the constant introductions. Your family is gigantic."

Paige held up her wine glass, "You're a kindred spirit already. It's lucky Vanessa always has an obscure bottle of wine we can use as an excuse to get away."

They chatted about Vanessa's job for a few minutes, then they talked about the food and the fireworks and what Paige was doing over the summer when she didn't have to be at school. They asked Juliet about herself, nothing too personal or probing, but she *did* mention her midwifery training to them.

When Paige asked how she'd gotten interested in that, she did something she'd never done before, and told complete strangers her story.

"I was in a bad relationship, and I was pregnant and struggling to make things work and he . . . wasn't. I had a second trimester miscarriage and he wasn't there when I needed him. My family lives in Western Kansas, so the only person who was there for me was my friend Alex. She had just started working at the birthing center, and she got me a job there shortly after. They were all so kind and supportive of what I was going through, and the way they helped women who had similar experiences, or just having a hard pregnancy, was so conscious and sensitive. It was what I'd needed the whole time I was pregnant." Juliet could see pity morph into admiration as she said, "I wanted to be there for other women in a way nobody was for me."

Vanessa filled Juliet's wine glass to the brim while Paige wrapped an arm around her said, "When I had my miscarriage, I'd been spotting off and on for a few days, so we ran some blood tests that showed that yes, we were losing the baby. Then when I started hemorrhaging, we went to the emergency room. When I told them I was miscarrying, they asked me how I knew that's what was happening, like maybe I was making it up. They made me feel like I was an idiot and like the miscarriage was my fault."

Vanessa nodded, then said, "We tried for a boy three times after Megan was born. After the third loss, I told Logan I couldn't do it anymore."

"I'm not sure I *want* do it again," Juliet said. "But at the same time, I want to prove that I can, you know."

Vanessa and Paige told Juliet about their births, Vanessa's all in the hospital with epidurals, but each different as the children she bore. Paige had pre-eclampsia and an emergency c-section with Emily followed by a planned cesarean for Jason.

They were interrupted by laughter and yelling spilling through the bank of windows next to the deck. Outside, Logan cursed and flailed as one of his steaks caught fire. In the background, Juliet could just make out Ethan chasing after a parachute with one of the smaller kids perched on his shoulders.

For a moment, Juliet was jealous that her own family was so small, and that their relationships, by comparison, felt so strained.

Having finished the bottle, Vanessa and Paige rose to move the rest of the food out to the tables lining the deck. They wouldn't allow Juliet to help, saying that next year, if she came, they'd put her to work, so Juliet excused herself to the bathroom. While she had a moment to herself, she texted her sister.

JULIET: *Remember the persistent doctor? He won. I'm at his brother's Fourth party. His family is huge.*

Before she was done washing her hands, Colleen replied.

COLLEEN: *For your first date? Picture?*

Juliet leaned against the wall outside the bathroom to type her message.

JULIET: *More like the third date, I think. Maybe our fourth?*

Then she sent the selfie she'd convinced him to take while they'd eaten their gelato on their first date.

COLLEEN: *He's pretty. Why the rush to meet the family? You aren't knocked up again, are you?*

Juliet responded with an emoji sticking its tongue out.

JULIET: *He's close to his family. He hangs out with his brothers at least once a week.*

COLEEN: *Hmm. Must be nice.*

That stung, but wasn't it why she'd been trying to text Colleen more lately? So they could be closer?

JULIET: *What are you up to tonight?*

COLLEEN: *Hanging out a bar in Boulder.*

JULIET: *Alone?*

COLEEN: *With Friends. And hopefully the guy in the corner who looks like Jamie Dornan from* Once Upon a Time.

Juliet laughed, and was telling her sister to have fun and be careful when Ethan found her.

"So, this is where you've been," Ethan said, standing too close in the dark hallway. "Did we scare you off?"

"No." Juliet wrapped her arms over his shoulders, as he pressed her into the wall. His hand traveled up her sides, over the curves of her breasts and back down again. "Vanessa force fed me a bottle of wine."

Juliet could just see the corners of his lips turn up before he kissed his way up her neck and along her jaw. "She does that," he said between kisses. "Who was on the phone?"

"My sister. She thinks you're pretty."

Ethan pressed his hips to hers, and she could feel his arousal. "You came back here to talk about how pretty I am?"

"Not even close, though I am contemplating seducing you now that you're here," she said, then slipped her hand behind his waistband.

He cursed as Juliet wrapped her fingers around him, then said, "You don't play fair."

"Better for you to learn that now, don't you think?" Juliet grinned, and slid her hand up and down his length a few times before pulling away.

Ethan moaned and rested his forehead on her shoulder. "You're cruel."

"Think of it as a promise." She kissed the tip of his nose.

"You're torturing me."

"I'd rather finish this, but the food's ready. We'd be missed."

"Sinful, teasing woman," Ethan said as Juliet slipped away with a giggle.

TEN MINUTES LATER, Ethan found Juliet on a blanket in the grass, chatting with Heather as they ate. She leaned into his side when he sat down next to her, and he found out the Heather really was interested in health care, but she didn't want to do what her dad did. She wanted to spend time with the people she worked with and was already thinking she'd like to work with geriatric patients.

Ethan listened to the conversation. He'd seen his niece teasing and playful as well as sleepy and surly in recent years, but he realized he'd never spoken with her in any meaningful way. After ten minutes, Juliet already had her talking about her hopes and fears. The attention and sincerity she gave his niece had him wanting to lay Juliet back on the blanket and finish what they'd started in the hallway.

Juliet was telling Heather how she'd known she wanted to be an L&D nurse from her very first OB rotation her sophomore year. Ethan would have been finishing up his residency that year, so he'd missed her then. He wondered if he would have seen her the same way if he'd met her when she was Heather's age, or if he would have seen her as a good kid.

Ethan gave into his gratitude that she was there with him now and set aside the last of his potato salad in favor of burying his nose in Juliet's hair. He placed kisses along the outside of her ear while his fingers played with the end of her long braid. Juliet shot him a naughty look, but otherwise allowed him to continue. Heather wouldn't meet his eye after that, keeping her attention solely on Juliet.

His mother, however, had no qualms about calling him out, "Ethan Matthew, stand up and introduce me to your young lady. And keep your hands to yourself. You're setting a bad example."

Other than her bright red face, Juliet met his mother's disapproving frown with grace. Camille, whom his mother had to release to shake Juliet's hand, danced around Juliet's feet as if she'd been waiting to meet her too. The traitor only allowed Ethan a quick pat on the head before she was back to begging for Juliet's attention.

Of course, Juliet had gotten down on her hands and knees in the grass to play with the tiny dog. Most people scooped her up to their level, but Camille preferred her freedom, and Juliet seemed to know that instinctively. Helen shot Ethan a look that said Juliet was behaving like a child. Ethan gave his mother a slight shake of his head and a broad smile. He could watch them play all day.

His mother, who was not a fan of outdoor parties, was in a pricklier mood than ever, and quickly retreated inside with barely another glance in Juliet's direction. Ethan knew he'd be hearing about that later.

After dinner, they played Frisbee with the teenagers until it got too dark to see, and Juliet surprised Ethan when she turned out to be more competitive, and more talented at the sport than even he was.

Usually, Ethan was one of the guys out lighting the fireworks, but this year he'd begged off, claiming the blanket they'd eaten on earlier. He lay back, and Juliet snuggled into him, resting her head on his shoulder without invitation. Camille curled up by Juliet's feet.

Ethan pulled Juliet closer, kissing her temple, and settled in to enjoy the show. He wanted to tell her she was perfect, but he knew she wasn't ready to hear it, so he kissed her again instead.

AS ETHAN'S CRUISER sped back toward the city, Juliet regretted not napping that afternoon. Of all things, she'd studied instead, reviewing her notes from the last semester so her classes stayed fresh in her mind. Now with the gentle motion of the car, along with the warm weight of Camille curled on her lap, Juliet was having trouble keeping her eyes open. Occasionally she'd see other people's fireworks bursting in the air out of the corner of her eye, but even that was starting not to be enough to keep her awake.

A hand came to rest on her thigh as they slowed to a stop at an intersection. Ethan was smiling at her. He squeezed her knee, patted the dog, then turned back to the road. "I thought the evening was successful, don't you?"

"Your family is great. Gigantic, but nice."

Ethan chuckled. "You only say that because we somehow mostly avoided my mother."

Juliet snorted. "Speak for yourself. She cornered me outside the bathroom."

"When was that?"

"About the same time you were finishing off all the pies."

He flashed her a quick grin that said he wasn't the least big sorry. "What did she say?"

"That she thought it should be a requirement for a midwife to have born a child before telling another woman how to do it."

Juliet watched Ethan cringe. "She does that. I wouldn't take it personally."

"It's okay. I told her I'd never hire a man as my OB for that exact reason."

Ethan laughed, and Juliet couldn't help the grin that spread over her lips as she turned back toward her window, catching three fireworks as they bloomed over the sky to her right. She pet Camille and let her eyes close. Helen would only be a problem between them if they were going to stay together long term, so Juliet was determined not to let Ethan's mom bother her.

What felt like moments later, Ethan shook her shoulder. They were parked in a garage, and he stood at the passenger side door, a sleepy Camille already in his arms.

"We're home," he said.

Juliet stretched and followed him inside. She was vaguely aware of white walls and big windows before she followed him down the stairs.

"I sleep in the basement," was all he said. And when Juliet saw his bedroom, she didn't need to hear anymore. It was dark and cool, and she could imagine it would remain so, even in the middle of the day.

He excused himself to take care of the dog while Juliet got ready for bed. When he returned a few minutes later, he shucked his clothes to the floor and slid under the covers, his hands searching out her body immediately.

"No clothes?" He asked.

"I have a promise to keep."

"You're tired."

"You're not wearing any clothes either."

"I always sleep naked."

Juliet ran her hand up and down his chest, trailing one finger down the line of hair bisecting his abdomen. "Sexy," was all she said before she made sure neither she nor Ethan said anything again for a while.

It was only as she was drifting off with her head on his shoulder, his fingers stroking her hair down her back, that he said, "What was the deal with Rich this morning?"

She'd been wondering when he would ask. Ethan had to have seen Rich before he'd left, but she hadn't intended to bring it up. Standing so close to Rich, him showing just that glimmer of tenderness toward her had rattled her more than she wanted to admit. And smelling Alex's perfume on his skin had made her sick—and not because she was worried about her friend, but because he didn't smell like she'd remembered him—and she'd craved that smell of patchouli and coffee and potted plants for so long.

But the smell that she still considered home wasn't there, and she had to remind herself that looking for home again with Rich—with anyone—was a mistake.

Now, Ethan smelled like grill smoke and fireworks and his bed was comfortable. The way he touched her, with equal parts awe and respect, made her wish that she could stay with him, like this.

He nudged her when she didn't answer right away.

Juliet took a deep breath. "He said we woke him up, and of course had to come out and make an ass out of himself."

"I don't suppose he'd go away if you told him to?"

Juliet snuggled closer into him, nuzzling her nose into his neck. "Hasn't worked yet."

"What did you tell him this morning?"

So that's what he wanted to know. "That I wanted to be with you and that I didn't want to talk to him."

It was more or less true.

Ethan didn't say anything else but pressed his lips to hers in a brief kiss, then stroked her back until she fell asleep in his arms.

Chapter Fourteen

For spending most of her time with a man who didn't cook, Juliet had never been so well fed. Ethan had made her blueberry pancakes the morning after the Fourth of July, but Juliet had seen no other evidence of a culinary inclination in him since then. Instead he took her out for breakfast to Dino's whenever he could, or dinner at the Mediterranean place. He even dropped an egg salad sandwich for her at the birthing center one day, including another box of cookies for the staff.

Their schedules were still tight, but Ethan found as many little ways to insinuate himself into her day as he could. He would come over after a late shift and she would make him dinner at two in the morning. Since she was a vegetarian, Juliet took it upon herself to impress him with meals he might not have even noticed were meat-free. Despite the claim that he would always notice, he ate eggplant parmesan instead of veal, pasta aglioli with artichokes and mushrooms instead of shrimp. He ate pizza with eggplant and broccoli, homemade falafel, and even pad Thai with tofu, clearing his plate each time.

That day, the last Saturday in July, they had accompanied his entire family, including his mother to a Royals game. Juliet had eaten nachos and drunk a beer while she'd watched

Ethan down three hot dogs in a row. He'd bought her a Royals shirt, since she was the only one in the whole group without one. She'd worn it to make him smile, because try as she might, Juliet could not drum up much enthusiasm for the game going on in front of her.

Ethan did his best to explain what was happening, and Juliet enjoyed the crowd's reactions to good and bad plays, but she was more interested in watching the family around her. Amy and Heather conspired together. Megan brought her boyfriend along. Jason hadn't stopped bothering the poor boy about Pokémon since the boyfriend said, when asked, he'd played the games when he was younger. As soon as they sat down, Emily had pulled out a book, that going by the cover, looked to be a YA romance. She appeared to be ignoring the game and everyone around her, but Juliet caught her sneaking peeks at how Ethan played with the end of Juliet's braid or the way he leaned into her to explain a play.

Vanessa knit on a sock, and Juliet wished she'd thought to bring her baby hats. Logan sat with his arm over the back of Vanessa's seat, his gaze often distracted from the game by the boy sitting next to his youngest daughter. It wasn't a protective look in his eye though. He looked more curious than judgmental. Ethan explained that it was a rule of Logan's that any new boyfriend had to make it through a baseball game or two with the family before he could take one of his girls out. Juliet thought it sounded strict, but Ethan only shrugged, like he thought it was a good idea.

Paige sat to Juliet's left, with Henry on her other side. The couple held hands off and on throughout the game, though Paige kept dropping her husband's hand when she jumped to her feet to cheer or complain, depending on the situation.

Ethan had warned Juliet on the drive to the stadium that Paige was a voracious baseball fan. She had been one of the student assistant managers for Henry's college baseball team. It was how she and Henry had met. Juliet thought it was fun watching the seemingly mild-mannered English teacher let loose on the umpire.

Henry, who Juliet was surprised to find was the loudest and most brash of the bunch, kept watching her much in the same way Logan watched the new boyfriend. Something in his eye made her nervous. Partially because she could almost see the inappropriate jokes he wanted to crack at Ethan lurking just beneath the surface, but also because it hadn't occurred to her until then that she was going through her own hazing, just like Megan's boyfriend.

Helen sat in the row behind them as if she needed to be able to keep her sights on all of them at the same time. Indeed, Juliet felt the woman's eyes on her often, and did her best not to be ruffled, but it made every action feel like a performance. Juliet tried not to care that Ethan's mother didn't like her, but the more time she spent with the rest of his family, the more it bothered her.

The day before, Juliet had woken up at Ethan's place. He'd been at work until after midnight, but he'd asked her to meet him at his place. They'd eaten pizza in bed and made love sleepy and slow. Ethan had fallen asleep immediately afterward. Upon waking, Juliet had let him sleep and had taken Camille with her out into Ethan's backyard. The morning had been warm, and Camille had run up and down the length of the yard. Juliet hadn't needed to be at work until ten, so she'd decided to do a short yoga practice before going back inside.

She'd thrown on one of Ethan's med school t-shirts and a pair of running shorts she'd left at his place. Juliet had tied the shirt in a knot at her waist to keep the loose fabric from impeding her poses. She'd been inverted, her left leg raised in the air in three-legged dog with the shirt riding up her abdomen when the back door had slammed, and a sharp female voice had said, "What on earth are you doing?"

Juliet had been so startled, she'd crumpled into a tangled heap on the grass. Camille had bounded for her and had jumped into Juliet's lap and tried to lick her face. "Camille and I were just doing a little yoga to greet the morning."

It had been the wrong thing to say, Juliet had known that. It had made her sound like a new age kook, and that was not the way she was going to win over Ethan's mother. But the contrarian part of her hadn't cared. That had been exactly what she had been doing, and if Mrs. Harvey hadn't like it, there was nothing Juliet could do about it.

"Do you really think that's appropriate given your attire?"

Juliet had looked down. Her shorts had been short, but covered everything, and sure the shirt had been riding up, but it had still covered her breasts. Then she'd looked to Ethan's privacy fence. Nobody could have seen her, and she hadn't known what to say, so she'd only shrugged.

Helen had said something to herself about Ethan being a typical man but was interrupted when had Ethan stuck his head out the door and asked if his mother had been planning to join them for breakfast. Helen had followed him back inside, and Juliet had finished the sequence she'd been in the middle of, then stolen into the shower. When she'd cracked the door in the hallway to let the steam out, she'd heard Mrs. Harvey's voice drifting down the hallway from the kitchen.

"You're too blinded by a pretty face and flexible body to see that she isn't good enough for you."

"I think you're wrong, Mom," Ethan had said.

"She's too young and too much of a flake to stick with you through the hard times."

"You've barely spent any time with her."

"All I needed to see was that hideous tattoo to tell me what I already knew, and that's that this girl isn't what you're looking for. You're wasting your time with her."

Juliet had moved the towel aside to gaze down at the sun and moon tattoo her hip. The male moon was cradling the female sun. The tattoo was whimsical, and sure, a little hippy dippy, but so was she. She'd had it done when she was eighteen, a representation of how she and Rich had orbited each other for three years but were finally going to reside in the same place. Despite that, Juliet still liked her one and only tattoo. These days she felt it represented the peace and balance she struggled for.

And she'd been able to hear the smile in Ethan's voice when he'd said, "I like the tattoo, personally."

Juliet had made it a point to make a bunch of noise as she'd dressed, and the voices had quieted. When she'd finally emerged, Helen had gone, and Ethan hadn't mentioned the conversation, but had greeted Juliet with a bagel and a kiss.

Juliet had wanted him to bring it up so she could defend herself to him. Then she'd remembered that she'd only be around for a couple more weeks and felt like a fraud. Juliet knew that when she walked away at the start of her semester, she was going to hurt him, whether he had already agreed to it or not. The truth was, Juliet was going to hurt too.

She liked the hectic routine they'd built up, staying up all hours of the night, eating, talking, and having sex, then grabbing sleep whenever they could. She liked how he would massage her feet and ankles as they sat on the sofa sharing a bottle of wine. She liked the stories he told about his childhood, about his adventures in the mountains when he was in medical school.

His stories helped Juliet see how little she'd been living the past few years. Yes, she was proud of what she'd accomplished, but she wanted to go hiking and rafting in the Rockies. She hadn't been skiing since high school. But also knew that before she had any of that, she needed security, to be able support herself—which meant she needed to finish school and find a job as a midwife. Focusing on that made it easier to ignore that she wanted to do all of that with Ethan.

As they rode back to Ethan's house after the baseball game, Juliet acknowledged that one of the perks of keeping odd hours and spending half her nights at Ethan's was that it made it easier to avoid Alex. Juliet wasn't sure how to act around her best friend anymore. Alex kept insisting that whatever was going on with Rich was just fun, but Juliet had seen Rich's shaving kit in the bathroom multiple mornings in a row. While she'd avoided another run in with him, the walls were thin. Juliet could hear them in the bedroom, laughing over coffee in the morning, and sneaking into Alex's room after they thought Juliet was asleep. Something more was going on than either of them would admit to.

When they finally made it through traffic and back to Ethan's house after the baseball game, he surprised her by heading straight to the fridge. "How can you still be hungry after all those hot dogs?" Juliet asked, busy greeting Camille.

"It's almost dinner time," he said, and when Juliet looked at her watch it was after six. Then she looked up when she heard him shaking something crinkly. It was a plastic bag full of chopped vegetables in a marinade.

"When did you do that?" she asked, crossing into the kitchen to peer over his shoulder. Four giant portobello mushroom caps sat marinating in another plastic bag. They'd left for the game from her apartment, and he'd come over right after work.

"I might have come home for a minute last night before going to your place," he said, like it was no big deal. When Juliet only looked at him, stunned, he shrugged. "I wanted to surprise you."

"By cooking vegetarian food?"

He leaned in and placed a quick peck on her lips. "Don't look so surprised," he said and took off for the back door.

Juliet and Camille followed him out on the deck. It was small, and needed a few potted plants to make it homey, but Ethan had a grill and a bistro table, as well as two Adirondack chairs overlooking his yard. Though enclosed by a privacy fence, Ethan's backyard got plenty of sunlight because the neighborhood was too new for there to be many trees. Long and narrow, the space was perfect for a vegetable garden, maybe even a couple of apple trees in the back. All the yard did now was provide a place for Camille to run. She galloped the length of the fence and back while Ethan prepared his grill.

"But you don't eat vegetarian food."

Ethan chuckled. Attractive creases formed at the corner of his eyes when he laughed, and Juliet took a moment to appreciate how delicious looking he'd become to her over the last few weeks. She constantly craved her hands in his hair, actively missed the feel of his bearded chin rasping over her neck. Her new favorite game was running her fingertips over the muscles in his arms, to see how long it would take him to guess what was on her mind.

Before, Juliet hadn't believed she was capable of this level of infatuation with anyone other than Rich. She knew she shouldn't allow herself the indulgence, because missing him after August would cause a gaping hole in her chest if she kept up like this, but as the semester loomed ever closer, she couldn't bring herself to give him up early.

"I'm not giving up meat," he assured her. "But I wanted to make you dinner for a change, and it's perfect grilling weather."

Juliet had to agree, it had been a steady eighty-five degrees all day, and not as humid as it usually was in late July. There was a slight breeze, and the deck was in the shade of the house making it pleasantly cool.

"You're cute when you're trying to impress me," she said and pulled one of the Adirondack chairs around to face the grill.

Ethan flashed her a naughty smile and disappeared inside. When he came back, it was with two wine glasses and a bottle of Juliet's favorite wine, a sauvignon blanc that Rich used to buy for her. It was pricey enough that Juliet never bought any for herself.

"You really are trying to impress me," she said as he handed her the first glass. When Ethan poured one for himself and clinked his glass against hers, Juliet asked, "Is it a special occasion?"

Ethan knelt next to her. His wine glass disappeared next to his feet as one hand skimmed over the smooth skin of her legs while the other came to rest on her neck, beneath her braid.

"It has been two months since we found each other again," he said. "I think that's worth celebrating."

Ethan kissed her then, and it was all Juliet could do to keep up the pretense of enjoying it while panic seized every nerve inside her. The glaze to his eyes had been far more than infatuation, and the soft way he kissed her was too tender, too much like love. She'd told him. She'd told him this was temporary.

Tears pricked at the corner of her eyes. This wasn't supposed to happen. She wasn't supposed to fall in love with him. The thought was both unexpected and unwelcome, so Juliet did what she'd done with him for the last two months. She turned the kiss heated and made Ethan forget all about tenderness and talking and the heating grill.

They didn't even make it inside.

ETHAN WAS STUNNED. He'd barely unzipped his shorts before Juliet had pulled him on top of her on the deck. He thought he'd appreciated the running shorts Juliet was wearing earlier in the day. He hadn't been able to keep his eyes off her long, toned legs, but when he pulled down her elastic waistband and was inside her with zero effort, he decided elastic waistbands were his favorite inventions ever.

Their coupling was hard and hot and way too loud for being outside in broad daylight, even if he did have the luxury of a privacy fence. Ethan couldn't help it. He'd expected Juliet to reject his show at romance. He'd been pushing the last couple of weeks, trying to test her boundaries by bringing her around his family more often, by not saying a word when she served him eggplant and pretended it could stand in for meat, by giving her every tender look and touch he'd wanted to give her.

Ethan had known he'd fallen in love with Juliet the moment he spotted Rich in Juliet's living room on the Fourth of July and realized how many ways he could lose her. It had been a delicate balance, displaying how much he wanted her in his life without spooking her, but she was kissing him like she'd never get enough of him. Since Ethan knew he would never get enough of her, he let himself get lost in the intensity, the words he wanted to say with every thrust.

Ethan didn't try to staunch her cries. He wore them like a badge of honor until he felt her clamp down around him as her words became unintelligible and he'd given into his desire with a few loud grunts of his own.

When he stilled on top of her, Juliet was beset with a fit of giggles, a state he strove for each time they were together.

He buried his face in the space between her neck and shoulder, inhaling her scent as he let out a hearty laugh. The words he wanted to say to her almost escaped, but Ethan kissed her to silence himself.

Then he grilled for her. There was no shortage of appreciative groans as they ate, and halfway through the second bottle of wine, Ethan was contemplating a second round, this time in his bed, when Juliet surprised him. They'd been laughing about a story he'd told of Henry "accidentally" dropping his towel in front of Paige one day after practice in college when Juliet sobered, and fiddling with the hem of her shorts, asked. "So, why aren't you married?"

Ethan jerked, slopping expensive white wine over his knuckles. Nobody had ever asked him that. Everyone either already knew about Amanda, or just assumed he was married to his job. Ethan went with the neutral response, "Haven't found the right woman, I suppose."

Juliet snorted. "Please. Your parents got married young. Your brothers got married young. You can't tell me you weren't on the same path once upon a time."

Ethan fidgeted in his chair. They were lounging in the Adirondack chairs, gazing up at what they could see of the sky over the city lights. Ethan searched out the North Star in the too bright sky, but he felt Juliet's eyes on him. Without looking at her, he said, "Amanda and I went to med school together. We lived together for three years. I asked her to marry me on graduation day."

"And she said no?" Ethan was gratified by the note of incredulousness in Juliet's voice.

Nodding, Ethan said, "She said no. She'd accepted an internship on the east coast, with a promise of a prestigious fellowship to follow. Her career was more important to her than I was."

"Did she actually say that?" Juliet asked.

Ethan shrugged. "Not in so many words, but she made it clear that moving back to Kansas with me had never been an option. I had no idea she'd felt that way."

Juliet was quiet for a long time, and he could almost hear her thinking. He'd finished medical school nearly ten years before. Ethan could practically feel her realizing he'd only had casual relationships since then. Not because he was too busy with work, but because he hadn't been able to stomach the potential rejection. But then again, his buddy that *had* gotten engaged on graduation day had just told Ethan a few days ago that he was getting divorced.

"I'm so sorry, Ethan," she said, laying a long-fingered hand on his elbow. "You deserve better than that."

Ethan shrugged again. Because he didn't want to talk about it, he asked, "Why haven't you tied the knot with Rich already?"

Juliet pulled her hand back and shuffled her feet against the deck, tucking her empty glass under her chair. "You know why."

"You've had four years to move on, and yet he's still around."

Juliet sat up, both her cheeks and the top of her chest flushing red. "He's with Alex. I haven't seen him in weeks."

Jealousy clanged through Ethan's veins so loud he could almost hear it reverberating like a gong. He set his own wine glass aside and leaned toward her, propping his elbows on his knees. "Do you still love him?"

Her bare foot knocked into his knee with enough force to pitch him forward so he was kneeling at her feet. Her toenails were painted a shade of emerald green that looked positively edible, but when she raised her right foot to kick him again, Ethan scrambled to his feet. He put his chair between them as Juliet enumerated on what an ass Ethan was.

She didn't pay him any attention as she ranted how she'd been sleeping with Ethan for weeks as she paced her side of the deck throwing her hands in the air, repeating that he had a lot of nerve asking her such a stupid question.

"Why is it a stupid question?" Ethan asked.

Juliet stomped across the deck until they were nose to nose. "Because of course I still love Rich." She raised both hands to Ethan's chest and pushed. He stumbled back a step before steadying and grabbing her wrists before she could push him again. Juliet struggled to free herself and tears dripped down her cheeks. "He gave me everything I needed to become me," she said. "He supported me. He encouraged me. He loved me so hard, and I gave him everything. I gave him everything, but it was never enough. *I* was never enough."

Juliet's tears transformed into sobs as she melted against Ethan and cried into his neck. He released her wrists and wrapped his arms around her waist. All Ethan could muster was a quiet shushing as she balled his t-shirt in her fists.

After a few minutes her sobs quieted to silent weeping. "You are perfect," Ethan said when he thought Juliet might hear him.

A snort of a laugh ricocheted from her chest to her shoulders and back down again. Ethan held her tighter.

"You are."

She rolled her forehead back and forth over his shoulder. He couldn't tell if she was shaking her head or trying to regroup.

"I just cried all over you about losing another man."

"You lost your family, Juliet. Not just him. You're allowed to mourn that."

Finally, Juliet shifted and leaned back enough to meet his eyes. "Gina wouldn't speak to me for months because of you."

"I'm glad you guys figured things out," Ethan said.

"Only because Rich finally told her where he'd been."

"I hope she froze him out for a while, too."

A feeble giggle escaped her throat. "No, but they were eating dinner and she started throwing things at him, her silverware, her bread, her full water glass."

Ethan couldn't help the laugh that swelled in his chest, and soon he and Juliet were laughing together.

When Juliet sobered, she said into his neck, "I don't want anything to do with Rich anymore."

Ethan buried his nose in Juliet's hair. She smelled like she'd been in the sun all day. "I know. I'm sorry."

"I'm sorry your old girlfriend didn't love you."

Ethan sighed. He'd thought the same thing to himself so many times. He'd decided long ago that he'd done nothing wrong. He'd offered himself and been rejected. Amanda was off living her life someplace else, and he'd moved back home to be close to his family. He wasn't sorry he hadn't followed

Amanda to the coast, not that she'd offered, but he did want what his brothers had. Ethan wanted a wife and kids, and he wanted them with Juliet.

Chapter Fifteen

After the first weekend in August, all traces of Rich had disappeared from Juliet and Alex's apartment. His shaving kit no longer languished on the back of the toilet. There was no third bath towel flung over the shower curtain, and no extra coffee cup by the sink in the mornings. Alex said nothing to Juliet, and Juliet was thankful, because it only made her think about how Ethan's things would be conspicuously absent soon also.

Juliet dreaded the conversation looming in front of her. The more time she spent with Ethan, the more the two of them together made sense. Guilt gnawed at Juliet for leading him into something that could never be. And yet, even as the semester loomed, Juliet found herself putting off the inevitable.

Maybe that was why she'd allowed him to talk her into going away with him for a weekend before school started. He'd rented a cabin near the Lake of the Ozarks, only a three-hour drive where the fishing was supposed to be fantastic. While Juliet could have cared less about the fishing, she thought the seclusion sounded lovely.

When Juliet had said, "I can't let you pay for something like that," Ethan had only told her that it was already booked, and it wouldn't cost any different whether she came or not, so she might as well go. And because Juliet thought they deserved one last hurrah, she agreed to tag along.

They left Friday afternoon, a week before her classes were meant to start. The drive down was easy. A light, cool rain followed them south. The view was unspectacular as they drove past farm after farm, but as they neared the lake, woods sprouted. What Ethan hadn't told her was that their cabin was a tree house with a giant jacuzzi tub, a fireplace, a gigantic log-framed bed, and a deck that overlooked a wooded path with direct access to the water.

Juliet tossed her overnight bag onto the bed. "You got us the honeymoon suite, I see."

Ethan tossed his bag alongside hers. "All I asked for was a cabin with a king-sized bed."

The tub was directly next to the bed, instead of tucked into the bathroom like a tub normally would be. "Why would they do that?" she asked.

Ethan wrapped his arms around her waist from behind. "Maybe it's supposed to be romantic?"

Juliet snorted but leaned back into his embrace, he was warm, and Juliet was damp from the rain. The sun was already nearly set, and the air was chilled "Light a fire and pour some wine, and it would be very romantic."

He kissed her neck. "I'm on it."

They drank the wine while Juliet cooked her favorite pasta dish. They ate on the sofa in front of the fire, laughing and teasing before making their way to the bed. Ethan spent more time than usual pleasuring her with his hands and mouth until she was such a mess of desire that his every caress made her moan. And when she finally came around him, she practically screamed his name as Ethan roared his own release.

A few minutes later, as she lay curled in his arms, the dizziness from too much wine just starting to hit her, he asked, "Did I manage to pull off romantic?"

"Hmmm," Juliet ran a lazy finger down the line of hair bisecting his abdomen. "You don't have to try very hard at being romantic." He didn't. Aside from his regrettable propensity toward steak, Juliet thought he was perfect. He was trying so hard to show her how well he could love, that more than once, Juliet had wondered why she was going to end it with him when they got back home.

She'd rehearsed what she would say to him, and even thinking it made her heartbeat tick up. She knew he wouldn't take it well, that he was invested in them even though she'd told him not to be. But she'd been right there with him for the dinners and the sex and the late-night conversations—and they'd only talked about when their relationship would end the one time. Juliet suspected he hadn't taken that conversation seriously.

Ethan's chest rumbled as he chuckled. "Glad it looks effortless. Half the time I'm worried you'll decide I'm not worth the trouble."

That Ethan had voiced that fear broke her heart—that what she had to do would only reinforce the underlying insecurity he'd carried around ever since his medical school girlfriend had denied his proposal.

But she needed him to know that it wasn't the same. That Juliet didn't have great aspirations, and she didn't think she was better than him or the life he wanted. Juliet felt the opposite. She needed to prove to him—to herself—that she was his equal. That she could successfully provide for herself doing what she loved. Midwifery was what she had been born to do, just like he'd always been meant to be a doctor—and there was no way she was ever going back to the place she'd been in after she lost the baby, lost Rich, lost everything. Juliet never, ever wanted to have to build herself back up from the bottom like that again. If she failed everything else, she would at least have a career to fall back on. Juliet would be able to take refuge in taking care of others instead of only taking care of herself.

"You're too good to me," was all she said.

He ran the hand that wasn't wrapped around her shoulders over her hip and around to cup the roundest part of her bottom. Juliet had always thought she was too thin, too many muscles and not enough curves, but Ethan disagreed. He'd never said anything, but he found any excuse he could to touch the curve of her hip or hold the fullness of her breasts.

"You'll forgive me if I respectfully disagree."

"If you talked to patients as pretty as you talk to me, you could start your own practice," she said, barely able to hold in her giggle.

Ethan groaned, and his grip on her ass hardened playfully. "Not you too. Next thing I know, you'll be angling for a job."

They'd made it somewhat of a joke between themselves that Ethan would never go into private practice, while Juliet hoped to start a homebirth midwife service someday. Neither one wanted to work in a typical doctor's office.

"In your dreams," she said, then sighed and gave in to the pull of the wine, dragging her into sleep.

ETHAN WOKE WITH A JUMP, one hand already reaching for his bedside table, groping for his phone. He could tell, without opening his eyes all the way that the sun was up, which meant he was either late for work, or that he'd missed a call. Instead of his bedside table, Ethan's knuckles grazed a wood paneled wall. He was conscious of Juliet cuddled into his left side, and while the wall made no sense, she did, and she almost always forgot to take her watch off before bed. Ethan hauled her left wrist in front of his eyes. It was after nine, and somewhere in the back of his mind he knew it was the second Saturday of the month. He should have been at work an hour ago, but as he settled Juliet's arms back around his chest, the rest of the room came into focus and Ethan remembered that he was on vacation.

He was on vacation with Juliet.

And she was naked in his bed.

She didn't always sleep in the nude. Sometimes she'd throw on one of his t-shirts, and while he appreciated how the fabric just covered everything but her long, shapely legs, nothing beat having direct access to her sensitive skin.

Juliet stirred as he ran his hands up over her waist and back down her hips over her thigh to her knee and back again. She made the whimpering noise in her throat that meant he was waking her up, but when he continued to run his hands over her, she rocked into him until she pinned him on his back and was astride him before she even fully opened her eyes.

Ethan crunched upward, taking one of her nipples into his mouth. She sucked in a breath through her teeth, and he decided it was one of the sexiest things she did. He ignored the burning in his abs as he pumped up into her.

Juliet was so wet and hot around him, he needed her like he needed air. That she gave herself to him as freely as she breathed humbled him. She was the most precious gift he'd ever been given.

He knew she was still skittish around the idea of commitment. Ethan couldn't blame her after having Rich as a partner. But the whole point of this weekend getaway had been for Ethan to make Juliet fall irrevocably in love with him, because he didn't want to go on without her.

The next four months would be the tricky part. Keeping their relationship hidden would probably be best, just in case. But Ethan also knew he could keep them from ever having to work together. Even if it meant working opposite shifts for four months, they would make it work. Four months wasn't long.

And after that. At Christmas time, when she had her certification, he saw himself proposing in front of the giant Christmas tree he was going to put in his picture window this year. Ethan never usually bought a tree, but this year seemed like a year for new traditions.

Juliet gasped as he nipped her breast, then pushed him down, her nails digging into his shoulders as she leaned in to give him a scorching kiss. Ethan slipped his thumb between them, hitting the spot at her apex he'd learned she liked best.

Her curse turned into a moan that vibrated all the way down her spine and around him. He bucked, and Juliet lost control as her moans grew louder. Ethan's climax came hard and sudden and almost involuntary. Juliet was overcome with giggles, and Ethan couldn't help but laugh as he hugged her close.

She lay in his arms for few minutes before she said, her words muffled into his shoulder, "I can't believe one of us isn't hurrying off to catch a baby."

Ethan's hands traveled the length of her velvet smooth back of their own accord. "Perhaps we'll happen upon a laboring woman stuck on the trails."

"Shut your mouth," Juliet said.

"Just think how lucky she'd be. A doctor and a midwife stumbling across her in her time of need."

"In my experience, having both a doctor and a midwife at a birth only leads to hostility." Juliet's tone was light, but Ethan heard more than she said. Now that he knew her better, he saw how much she loved what she did, and how it gave her purpose. He'd seen the glow on her face after she'd worked a birth. After her breakdown on his deck a couple weeks ago, he knew that her drive to become a CNM was in part to prove her own worth. That part of her had broken that day he'd slept with her but shouldn't have. And to have to continue to fight for legitimacy among supposed colleagues, he knew would always bother her. While they still disagreed on a few of the finer points of maternal and fetal care, his attitude toward midwives had come a long way in the last few weeks.

"I'm sorry it does," he said.

Juliet just said, "I know."

ETHAN MADE JULIET WAFFLES for breakfast. If he had packed a waffle iron, or the cabin had one hidden in its meager stash of dishes, Juliet did not want to know. The waffles were heavenly, light and sweet, and she covered hers in maple syrup and raspberries with a side of similarly dressed Greek yogurt. Ethan unapologetically cooked himself bacon, and despite the cabin stinking of pork fat, they lingered over their coffee until nearly noon.

They spent the afternoon on the trails, hiking the wooded hills that surrounded the water and the streams that meandered off the lake. As the sun set, they hauled the fishing gear from the back of the Cruiser, and Ethan caught fish after fish from the river while Juliet read on her eReader.

"I'm a little afraid of how good at this you are," Juliet said as Ethan landed his fourth fish.

He laughed, whether at her or the fish flopping at the end of his line she wasn't sure. "It's not usually this easy," he said. "They must stock this stream daily."

Then Juliet averted her eyes and plugged her ears while Ethan took a knife to the poor fish. She didn't want to know what he did to it, but he put whatever parts he was keeping in a cooler.

"Are you seriously going to eat that?" she asked when he cast his line again.

"That's dinner, love."

"Hell, no it's not."

"I'll fry you some hush puppies."

"I'm not eating anything that's been in oil with whatever the fuck's in your cooler."

Ethan propped his pole on the shore and knelt in front of her. "Am I upsetting you?"

Juliet took a deep inhale and exhale through her nose, "I just can't."

"I know," he said, tracing the line of her jaw with his fishy smelling fingers. "Do you want to head out?"

Juliet peered into the fading light. "I am getting hungry."

"Then let's go." Ethan stood up and reeled in his line without one complaint.

"I don't want you to not do things you like because of me," she said as guilt overtook her revulsion. "This is your vacation."

Ethan knelt in front of her again, kissing her briefly on the way down. "This is our vacation," he said. "And as much as I enjoy fishing, I want to make sure we're both enjoying ourselves."

Juliet set her eReader in her lap and cupped his bearded chin in her hands. "It's been a very peaceful evening, and then you have to keep murdering fishes."

He grinned and kissed her hand. "Then let's go back to the cabin."

When they returned, Ethan cooked dinner as promised. He fried up hushpuppies and sautéed some greens and mushroom and onions as per Juliet's instructions, before frying up his fish for himself. Juliet had to admit that she didn't mind the fish so much when he was popping fresh hush puppies into her mouth and topping off her beer while she finished her book.

Juliet allowed herself to enjoy the easy domesticity of it all, even entertained how easy it would be to live with Ethan. He was so cheerful and easy going, she almost didn't recognize him as the intense misogynist she'd known four years ago.

But as Saturday faded into Sunday and they spent another day hiking farther into the woods and lazing about the cabin, Juliet became more and more conscious of how quickly their time together was ending. Each caress, each kiss was bittersweet. And when Ethan backed her onto the bed Sunday night and peeled her clothes off as slowly as he could manage, it really felt to Juliet like maybe they weren't after their own pleasure, but simultaneously making love and saying goodbye. She had tears in her eyes by the end of it, and Ethan kissed them away, saying only, "It's okay. I feel it too."

Chapter Sixteen

Taking Juliet away for the weekend was one of the best ideas he'd ever had. As Ethan drove them home Monday morning, he was soaring. He couldn't help it. After last night, he had no doubt that he'd accomplished his mission. The three days away together had been what she'd needed to admit her feelings for him to herself. And tonight, when they got back to his place, they'd make it official.

They were a little over halfway home. Ethan had been enjoying the quiet ride, daydreaming about a bacon cheeseburger, but knew Juliet wouldn't eat fast food, so he was suffering in silence when Juliet said, "So school starts again next week."

School meant her work at the med center birthing center would begin, something they hadn't spoken about since that breakfast back in June. Ethan's contented bliss seeped away as he caught Juliet wringing her fingers out of the corner of his eye.

"It does," was all Ethan could bring himself to say. His heartbeat was as heavy as a sledgehammer on an anvil. His surety that he was going to marry this woman had shifted just a quickly into the certainty that he was about to be dumped.

Neither one said anything for a long time, and the tension in the car rose to uncomfortable heights. Ethan could feel his whole manner change, instead of the idiotic grin he'd been wearing all weekend, he now ground his teeth together so hard his jaw ached, and his knuckles were white on the steering wheel. Juliet's posture was stiff beside him, and she rolled the colorful braided bracelets around her wrist like she always did when she was nervous.

"I'm going to be working at your hospital."

"You are."

She cleared her throat. "Did you know that the first rule in the nurses' practicum handbook states that it is forbidden to form a romantic attachment to any hospital staff, and that any discovery of such an attachment is grounds for expulsion from the program."

"I was aware of something along those lines." She'd said as much in June.

"It means that if someone finds out about us, I won't get to finish my CNM."

Ethan wrung his hands around the steering wheel. "Our *attachment* is established. That's different. Surely they can make allowances for—"

"They'd make me change practicums," she cut him off.

"So, change. Find another program."

"The only other program is at my birthing center."

"And?" That sounded perfect. She could work there as a nurse and do her practicum with the midwives she already knew, and they could stay together.

"I'd have to quit my job to do my practicum there. And I can't afford not to work."

"Surely they could find a way-"

"You don't think I've already asked?" Her voice raised in both volume and pitch.

"And you want me to say, 'Oh well, I guess we better break up?'"

Ethan kept his eyes on the road during the long silence that followed. He tried not to notice Juliet fiddling with her bracelets out of the corner of his eye. He heard her sniff but would not turn his head to see if she was crying, but he could hear it in her voice when she said, "It was always the only option."

The heel of his hand met the ring of the steering wheel. "Damn it, Juliet. No, it's not." He barely recognized his own voice. It was strained and hard, and not at all the soft joy he usually used with Juliet. "We could be discreet. I can make it so we never work together. I have that power."

In a voice he could barely hear over the wind from the road and the rushing of blood in his own ears, Juliet said, "I can't risk it."

"What can't you risk, exactly?"

"You would never have risked your career like you're asking me to," she said.

"I'm asking you to find another way."

"There is no other way."

Ethan had pulled the Cruiser over to the shoulder before he'd realized he done it. He turned the vehicle off and faced her. She did indeed have tears running down her cheeks, but she was still telling him she wasn't going to continue their relationship.

"You're telling me this summer has meant so little to you that you can walk away, just like that?"

"No."

"But?"

"But it could only ever be temporary, don't you see that?"

"I never saw us that way. I knew we'd have to be careful this semester, but what's four months?"

"Someone would find out."

"No one is going to be following you to my house for dinner."

"Someone would see us out somewhere."

"So, we stay in and study instead. I'm good at that. I could help you."

"And someone we know would still post pictures of us on Facebook or on Instagram and the wrong person will see. I can't risk it, Ethan. Don't you understand how much I need this?"

"Don't you understand how much I need you?"

"You don't need me."

"I love you."

Juliet stared at him for a solid minute. "You don't mean that."

Ethan wondered what sort of self-delusion she needed to employ to get her to that conclusion, but he only growled out, "The hell I don't."

ETHAN WAS ANGRY.

Juliet had expected as much, but she hadn't prepared herself for the force of it. And she her temper rose in return.

Did he realize he'd been panting like an angry bull when he'd told her he loved her?

Probably not. At least he'd had the presence of mind to pull over.

Just for something to say, and because she had never wanted to hurt him, she said, "I'm sorry."

Ethan snorted, and Juliet imagined him pawing the ground with one of his sneaker-clad feet.

"I tell you that I love you and you say you're sorry?"

"Well, you don't sound very happy about it." Her voice was sharper than she meant it to be.

"That's because I'm not right now."

He had his seatbelt buckled and the car pulled back onto the road before Juliet could think of what to say.

She hadn't meant to do this here and now. Not this way. Part of her had been hoping that Ethan had a solution better than "let's hide." Did he really think that would cut it after he sent all those ridiculous gifts to the birthing center? After they'd gone to all his favorite restaurants and run into his colleagues? Did he really think no one would remember?

Yes, it was a stupid, sexist, archaic rule, but Juliet was bound by it nonetheless. She didn't want to lose Ethan, but she truly had no other choice.

A grim sort of numbness settled over her as they drove without speaking. It was one thing to know she was going to have to break up with Ethan and another to do it.

It had been a good summer, better than she'd imagined it would be when she'd given herself permission to start the affair. An ache was already starting to form in her chest at the thought of moving forward without him.

When they reached the outskirts of Kansas City, Ethan still hadn't even so much as looked at her. Juliet felt like she couldn't say anything, not anymore. He'd just taken her for a gorgeous, romantic weekend away, and she'd repaid him by breaking up with him on the drive home. He was probably thinking all sorts of horrible things about her.

Every single one of them was completely warranted.

Ethan was silent until he pulled into a space in front of her building. Juliet sat with her hand on the door handle for a minute, waiting for him to say something, and had just decided it was best for her to leave when he said, "You know my mother told me this would happen."

"What?" Juliet had only had the three run-ins with Ethan's mother, but the conversation she'd overheard between Ethan and Helen about how Juliet wasn't good enough for him came back to her. She'd known since she overheard them that Helen was right. Juliet wasn't good enough. She never had been.

"Right after Fourth of July she told me that I shouldn't get serious about you. That you were too young to stick around. That your job would be more important to you than I was, than a family would be."

Juliet cracked her door open. Didn't he understand that she couldn't have a family if she didn't have a job first? "It's nothing to do with either of those things, but if that's what you need to think, that's fine."

"Then why?"

Juliet faced him. Ethan's knuckles were white around the steering wheel. "Because I have worked too damn hard to risk it. I need to have my certification and my career at least somewhat established before I can be in a serious relationship again—for my own sanity."

The hard glint in Ethan's eyes turned steely. She could see the words he wanted to say, that he at least, had been in a serious relationship with her, but said, "I'm not Rich."

"I never thought you were."

"I could take care of you," he said. "You wouldn't have to work. And if you wanted to, I could find you a job. I could call Logan tomorrow and you'd have a full-time job at his clinic. Hell, I'll start my own damn clinic, and you can be my nurse." A half smile crossed his face, as if he were imagining the domesticity of it.

"I'm not a nurse. I'm a midwife. And in December, if you still want to hire me, you'll have to condescend to work with a midwife, not some pretty assistant you also get to bed."

Juliet got out of the Cruiser and slammed her door shut, enjoying the crunching sound the old metal always made as it latched. That was why it was best to break things off now. Ethan didn't want her. He didn't want Juliet as she came. He wanted the version he could put in his pocket and get out when it was convenient for him. She'd almost forgotten about that side of him. He was good at hiding it.

When she went around the back to pull her duffle bag out of the piles of Ethan's fishing gear, Ethan twisted in his seat to watch her.

"My mom was my dad's nurse," he said.

Juliet had to disentangle the handle on her bag from one of Ethan's fishing rods. "I'm glad that worked out for them, but that's not me, and you know it."

"I don't want this to be it," he said.

Juliet shrugged, not quite meeting his eye. "I don't either."

"I'll speak to your program director. I'll guarantee it won't be problem."

Juliet didn't mean to cringe, but she couldn't help it. "That would only make things worse."

"So that's it then?"

She hoisted her bag over her shoulder and nodded. "I guess so."

Only as she closed the rear door did Juliet meet his gaze, and the turmoil there nearly undid her. She didn't want to hurt him, but she couldn't do what he asked. She only wished he could understand why.

"I'm sorry," she said again before she closed the door, and raced inside.

Once she had shut the apartment door behind her, Juliet leaned against the wood and buried her head in her hands as the reality of what had just happened washed over her.

Juliet had just broken up with Ethan.

Good Ethan. Loyal Ethan. Strong, stubborn, opinionated Ethan who ate meat and loved fishing but also researched vegetarian options at every restaurant he took her to, and who rubbed her feet even after he'd worked a twelve hour shift himself. And oh, God, he did love her. He wasn't just saying that.

A sob lodged itself in her throat for a second, then two, and just when Juliet thought she was going to suffocate because of it, it broke through with such force, she dropped to the floor.

Juliet wasn't sure when Alex took her into her arms, or how long she coached her to breathe before Juliet stopped crying, but when the tears stopped, Alex was holding her, telling her that everything was going to be alright.

Chapter Seventeen

E than hadn't thought for weeks.

He functioned. He ate. He slept. He worked out a little more than usual. He ran the ward, performed surgery, but it was all on autopilot. Food had no taste. Sleep provided little rest. Even delivering babies failed to move him in the usual way, as if he were watching a television in the living room from down the hall.

For six weeks, Ethan preferred living that way. He knew he was surly and growled when spoken to, but it was better to feel nothing or annoyance than it was to fall into the yawning pit of despair he tumbled into every time he thought of Juliet.

He hadn't considered that he might have already fallen until he had gone three Sunday nights without anyone asking where Juliet was or how she was doing. Juliet had only come to Logan's for baseball twice, but when Juliet hadn't come with him the week after their trip, it had been clear that everyone had expected her to be there. Rather than address the matter, he'd told them she'd been called into work.

Ethan used the same excuse the next week, which was true, he'd seen her name on the rotation. By the third week, his mom had figured it out, and told everyone that all of Juliet's things had disappeared from Ethan's house. When Henry had tried to ask what had happened, Ethan had barked out that he didn't want to talk about it.

When everyone was still walking on their tiptoes around him three weeks later, he wondered if maybe he should talk to someone.

He'd been avoiding talking to anyone at all, but his family didn't deserve the anger that he meant for Juliet. For a moment, he'd considered calling Cynthia, finding out if she she'd been seeing anyone, but the idea of another woman had turned his stomach sour.

By some miracle, or his astute avoidance of the birthing center wing, Ethan had not run into Juliet once. He told himself that not seeing her was a good thing, but there were days when nothing but the possibility of glimpsing her in the hall held his imagination.

Ethan missed Juliet with a longing so fierce it felt like it was eating him alive. If he sat still with it too long, his grief might devour him whole, but he was exhausted with trying to outrun it. That was how he'd ended up at Tokyo Nights by himself on a Thursday night. He needed to be near where she was.

As he watched the laughing couples dance, Ethan remembered what is was like to have Juliet's hands on his hips, her lips close to his ear as they tried to talk over the music. The memories were strangely calming.

Halfway through his second beer, someone took the empty stool beside him and said, "Buy me a drink?"

He knew before he looked that it was Alex. He motioned to the bartender, and tried not to look surprised when Alex, whom he remembered being a tequila drinker, ordered only a soda with lime. Her answer to his questioning gaze was a tired smile, and he thought maybe she looked a little green.

"So, Doc, what brings you to this neck of the woods?"

Ethan motioned to the dance floor with his beer bottle. "I miss her."

Alex nodded.

"She's not—"

"No," Alex didn't let him finish his question. "She's babysitting for Gina tonight."

"Good," he said, trying not to feel disappointed. Ethan didn't know what he would say to Juiet if her did see her. More than likely he would make a fool of himself. "What about you? How have you been, Alex?"

Alex collapsed against the bar with her head down, took a deep breath in, and said, "Do you really want to know?"

"I wouldn't have asked otherwise. "

Alex took a sip of her drink, squared her shoulders and said, "It's good I ran into you." Alex let out a forced laugh. "I mean, who better to talk to when you've just found out that you're knocked up than a lady doctor, right?"

Ethan gulped so hard on his beer the swallow hurt. "You're pregnant?"

"Just found out," she nodded. "I'd been feeling pretty gross for the last couple of weeks, but I just figured it was from working too hard with all my Christmas orders rolling in, but then I threw up out of the blue and wondered." She sighed again. "So, I took a test and here I am."

"In a bar?"

"It was too quiet upstairs," she said, and downed her soda water like it was a shot. "And I can't keep it."

Ethan didn't say anything as his stomach dropped. He knew better than to offer opinions or advice in these situations. He did wish that, out of all the times he'd called Alex for advice on impressing Juliet, he'd thought to ask her about herself, then at least he might be able to offer less sterile comfort as she sorted out what she was going to do. But he could be a doctor, like she'd asked him to be.

Alex said, "There's no chance the test was wrong I guess?"

"Positive results are usually accurate. And you've been feeling sick?"

"Kind of seasick."

"Anything else?"

"Bloated, sore boobs, but I just thought my period was coming."

"Have you missed a cycle?"

She shook her head. "I do the birth control where I only get one period every three months."

Ethan nodded. He hated that brand just for this reason. "And you've been taking your pills?"

"Religiously, which is why I don't understand how this happened."

"If you've been on any antibiotics or left your pills in a hot car they can fail."

Alex pushed her glasses to her forehead and rubbed her eyes. "This is so not fair."

"You should get it confirmed with your doctor and find out how far along you are, especially if you're going to terminate."

Alex squeaked dropped her head onto the bar again, and Ethan noticed the bartender eyeing them.

"I need Juliet," Alex said.

"You should call her."

"No." Alex grew even paler and tears filled the corners of her eyes. "Things have been weird between us for months, and this would only make things worse. You have to promise me you won't tell her about this. Ever. She can never know."

"She loves you like a sister," Ethan said, placing a hand on Alex's shoulder. "She'd want to know."

She shuddered beneath his grip, and hastily wiped her eyes beneath her glasses. "I am the worst best friend in the history of the universe."

"Why?" Ethan asked, but the answer occurred to him even as he asked the question. "It's Rich's baby?"

Alex nodded and swiped at her cheeks with her wrist. "I am such an idiot."

Ethan ignored her self-recrimination and his rising anger at the destruction Rich always left in his wake and tried to be helpful. "I thought you two were square on the Rich situation."

"You weren't there after her miscarriage. Losing that baby nearly killed her, and she hadn't really been happy again until you came along. If I tell her that I'm pregnant and that Rich is the father, she might throttle me, especially with how she's been lately. I can't have his baby when she couldn't have hers. I won't do that to her."

Ethan's mind snagged on the words *not with how she's been lately* and forgot about Alex and her dilemma. The rising panic his chest needed to know about Juliet. "How has she been lately?"

Alex let out a defeated laugh. "There have been a few times over the last few years where I have wanted to shake Juliet out of her pseudo-peaceful, gentle, hippy-dippy yoga instructor persona. I wanted her to get angry, to scream, to throw tantrums and stop hiding behind work and school. Now all she does is stomp around the apartment snapping at me and cleaning so violently I'm afraid she'd going to snap the broom in two."

"She's making herself miserable," Ethan said, his sympathy for the Juliet waning. If she was angry, she only had herself to blame.

Alex gave him a knowing smile. "She cried for two days, you know. And when she found the box you left in the hallway with her toothbrush, she cried another two days."

Ethan gritted his teeth. "I'm sorry to hear that. I don't want her to be in pain, but I still think we could have found another way."

Alex played with the straw in her drink, pushing the lime down into the ice. "And if she could be convinced to give it a try?"

Ethan had to down the last of his beer before he answered. Reconciliation was not something he had let himself consider. In a place in his heart that he wouldn't acknowledge yet, he did have hope that maybe come December he and Juliet might be able to work things out, but his practical side said there would be too much distance by then. Too much hurt.

"I don't see that happening."

"But, hypothetically. Would you be interested?"

Ethan shook his head. "Juliet wanted to be done. We're done. There's no going back."

Alex deflated a little. "Fine."

"You should still tell her. She'll be there for you, whatever you decide."

Alex only shook her head, and Ethan took the opportunity to signal for his tab.

"If you need anything, call me. And if your insurance doesn't cover the procedure, don't come to the med center. It will cost you about three times as much as Planned Parenthood."

"Thanks, Doc." Alex stood and pushed in her chair.

"You should tell her," he said again as he signed for the bill. "She'd want to know."

THE ONLY TIME JULIET wasn't angry these days was after her Monday night yoga class. Even then, she was only satisfied after she'd pushed herself, and her students, to the point of exhaustion. While a few of her more advanced students had taken to raving about how good they felt afterward, Juliet noticed that her attendance had dwindled over the past few weeks. Some of the women had sat out a set of postures, either reclining in child's pose, or panting in *savasana*. She didn't blame them; Juliet's course was meant to be beginner friendly. It had not been since school had started.

Juliet's home practice had been similarly grueling. Yoga had helped her moved past Rich, so she'd thought it might help alleviate how much she missed Ethan. Aside from the pleasant ache of sore muscles and the temporary calm that stole over her from conscious breathing, Juliet lived in a fury she had not expected.

She wasn't even entirely sure what she was angry about.

School was going well. Her practicum was engaging enough to keep her mind occupied while she worked. Juliet was under the supervision of another midwife, working with three specific patients who were due before graduation. She would still see patients as they came in for their monthly visits and attend births that occurred while she was on shift, but for these three women, she would be called in to attend the birth as the primary midwife on duty. It was both exhilarating and terrifying, but halfway through the semester Juliet was excelling in the program.

She still had her regular shifts at the birthing center, which were strange. She and Alex were genial, or even almost cheerful with each other at work, but they were barely speaking at home. Juliet was either working or studying, and Alex had been working almost non-stop to fill orders for her jewelry in time for Christmas. Alex hadn't asked for Juliet's help packaging all her new pieces. Juliet hadn't offered to help, even though she'd heard Alex up past midnight most nights.

It was easy to blame their hectic schedules on why they weren't getting along. They were both tired and frazzled and taking it out on one another. A few days before, Juliet had been trying to organize some of Alex's bead containers, which were spread out all over the living room. Alex, who had stayed home from work for the past two days, stomped out of her room looking sickly and pale.

"Do you have to make so much fucking noise?" she had asked. Then, noticing that Juliet had moved all her totes into the corner, Alex had stomped past and pulled the heavy plastic box from Juliet's hands and had replaced it on the coffee table. "Just leave them alone. Do you have to meddle in everything that isn't your business?"

"I'm sick of living in a jewelry factory. I want to be able to sit on the sofa without having to move a whole warehouse full of beads first."

"Get used to it," Alex had said. "It's going to be that way until Christmas."

"I can't live like this anymore." Juliet had motioned to the cluttered surfaces all over the apartment.

"Then find someplace else to live," Alex had said. "Especially if you're going to keep being rude and ragey all the time."

"Fine then." Juliet had thrown up her hands stomped into her bedroom. "I'll be gone by graduation."

Juliet had fumed all night, then not seen Alex for three more days. She'd had a text from Alex saying that she wasn't feeling well, and she hadn't mean what she'd said. Juliet had also apologized for being irritable, but instead of getting together and talking it out, Alex had made an impromptu visit to her grandmother's. Alex had grown up with her grandmother in southeast Kansas and had claimed she had vacation time she needed to take before the end of the year. She had been gone five days already, and Juliet didn't know when she was coming back.

To cure her loneliness, Juliet called her sister. They had been talking more recently, mostly via text, but some phone calls made it past voicemail. This one did not. Colleen either wasn't up yet, or already stuck in traffic for her commute downtown.

After the beep, Juliet said, "Hey, it's me. I just got home from work at the hospital. I led my first water birth, and I know you think it's disgusting, but it was so peaceful. It was a little girl and she was so alert and hungry from the start. I helped them figure out how to nurse, and while I'm still not sure I'll ever get used to grabbing another woman's boob, the moment when the newborn latches on is magical. And because I know you'll ask, there were zero Dr. X sightings tonight, which left me in a much better state of mind than the three in one shift from two days ago. And no, I didn't talk to him. Just saw him from afar. Anyway, I'm off the next thirty-six hours, then I'm back on day shifts for a while. Call me."

Next, Juliet texted Gina that she was going to sleep and shower, and then she'd be over to help with the boys, and to text her two hours before she needed to leave, just in case she slept through her alarm. Anytime Juliet had more than twenty-four hours off, she would volunteer to babysit for Gina, and Gina would usually find some excuse to take her up on it.

Juliet avoided being at the apartment whenever she could. When she was there and awake, she wandered around as if she was searching for something she couldn't find. Her hand would absently lift any object it alighted upon into her line of vision, sigh, then replace it. It had taken her five weeks to realize she was searching for that little piece of her she'd left in Ethan's Cruiser that day in August. As much as she told herself she was never going to find it again, that didn't keep her body from searching it out.

For weeks, Juliet had caught only glimpses of him, always walking away from her or disappearing around a corner, as if his white coat turned him into a specter that was always just out of reach. More probably, he was avoiding her on purpose, catching sight of her and then turning around and heading the other way. She wouldn't blame him for it.

When Juliet finally did catch him standing still, it was in the break room for the main maternity ward. She'd had a patient transferred there the day before and was checking in on her. Snagging coffee from the closest break room was meant to be expedient, but she opened the door and there he was, leaning against the counter next to the refrigerator, a cup of coffee in one hand, a stack of papers in the other. A half-eaten bagel sat on the counter beside him.

Juliet almost backed out the door on tiptoe like she would she'd come upon a hibernating bear unaware, but decided she had no reason to hide. Ethan stood only a few paces from the coffee pot but stayed absorbed in whatever he was reading as she approached.

The coffee was still steaming when Juliet poured it into the chipped pink mug she'd found in the cabinet. She took a sip and winced. Before she could think about it, she said, "I thought I taught you how to make the good coffee."

Juliet felt the moment his eyes landed on her, even though she kept her cowardly eyes on her mug. His gaze felt hot on her skin. Her scalp tingled as she sipped the horrid excuse for coffee, but she willed herself to act casual, even though she was panicking on the inside. She hadn't meant to speak to him, but the words came out as if they recognized him, like this was any other morning three or four months ago.

As she lowered her mug from her lips, Juliet allowed her eyes to find his. She'd forgotten how blue they were, even when they were hard and unforgiving.

"Elsie made the coffee."

"That would explain it then." Juliet tried for a friendly smile, but Ethan held his glare.

He stood to his full height, setting his file on the counter next to the bagel. Juliet could see the tired lines he had under his eyes. His beard needed a trim, and her traitorous fingers wanted to scratch along his jawline. She wondered if his hair was too long under his surgical cap, and then wondered just how much he'd been working.

"Have you been here all night?" she hadn't seen him the night before, but she'd known he was on the ward when she'd come in with her transfer patient. He'd been on stand-by in case the woman needed a c-section.

Either something about the question or maybe just his exhaustion affected him, and he allowed his glare to slip, his eyes darting to her lips, lower, than back up. "I have a sched-uled surgery at ten. It was easier to stay."

"Are you sure you're up for that?"

"I slept."

She knew that was all the explanation she was going to get. Juliet tried to take another sip of the coffee, but it smelled a little too much like the fish Ethan liked to catch and turned around to dump it down the sink instead.

Ethan surprised her by sliding closer to her along the counter, almost close enough to touch. "How's your patient?"

Juliet checked her braid, making sure that the hair was secure in each link before answering. "Still tired but recovering well. I'm glad she went with the epidural in the end."

Ethan stepped into her personal space, and Juliet had to force herself not to back up. "I didn't think you believed in epidurals."

If that was the way he wanted to play, Juliet was up for it. She turned so that they were nearly nose to nose. If Juliet inhaled too deeply, their chests would meet. "I never said that."

Ethan rolled his shoulders and angled his head and looked like nothing more than a playground bully. "We've had this discussion more than once."

Juliet straightened her back. "Then you should remember that I said I don't believe epidurals are usually necessary. When they help a mother rest, and regain her strength, and push her baby out, I think they're an invaluable resource, which you would know if you took my work seriously at all."

She hadn't realized she'd been jabbing him in the chest with an accusatory finger until his hand wrapped around her wrist. The warmth of his touch jolted through her. Then he said her name, and she met his eyes again. The hardness was gone, replaced with a startled shock that Juliet knew was mirrored on her face. Was that what she'd been angry about all this time?

Ethan didn't let go of her wrist. He didn't move or speak. His eyes searched hers, as if it had only just occurred to him that she was hurting too.

"Let go of me," she said.

Ethan released his fingers, holding both hands up as he backed away. "I'm sorry."

Juliet breathed audibly through her nose. "Yeah," she said. "Me too."

Chapter Eighteen

Ethan stood in front of his bathroom mirror. It had been a day since his encounter with Juliet. He'd showered and spent most of his day off sleeping. As he took in his unkempt beard, and the hair that was too long in the back, he thought a trip to the barber was probably on the agenda for the afternoon.

He leaned in closer to examine the new growth that was creeping up his cheeks when he saw them. Three faint, yellowish bruises on the left side of his chest, just below his collarbone. Juliet would be horrified if she knew she'd marked him. She hadn't even known she'd been emphasizing her words with sharp jabs from her long fingers until he stopped her.

It hadn't hurt. He'd only grabbed her wrist to make her aware of what she was doing. The moment he'd touched her, his arms had almost folded her into him, as if his body knew where she belonged.

The way she'd been glaring at him, though. As if she really believed he didn't respect her. And the way she'd disappeared, he guessed she'd regretted giving him that glimpse into her. Ethan wanted to know how long she'd felt that way. Was it because he hadn't wanted to break up, or had she felt that way since the beginning?

He absently rubbed the bruises over his chest as he tried to remember if she'd ever said or done anything that suggested he didn't flat out worship her and couldn't think of anything. The conversation he had with Alex the morning he'd driven her to the clinic the week before replayed in his mind, and he felt only some of his indignance return.

"Distract me," Alex had said when Ethan's reassurances that it would be a simple and safe procedure had done nothing to calm her nerves.

"I'd juggle, but I'm driving," he'd said.

She'd called and asked him to take her to her appointment a few days after they'd run into each other at Tokyo Nights. She hadn't trusted anyone else to do it without asking a million questions, she'd said, effectively cutting off any inquiries of his own Ethan had about Alex's decision. Being alone with Alex had made him anxious. It should have been Juliet in his seat. If Alex hadn't been so stubborn, it would have been.

"You could tell me what happened between you and Juliet" she'd said.

"Don't you know that already?"

Alex had shrugged. "I only know that she never meant for you to be more than a distraction, but she's been devastated. She hasn't been up for details."

Ethan's temper had sparked then. A distraction? He'd practically begged her to give them a chance, to let him prove to her that he was worth the risk, and all she'd ever wanted him for was sex? No wonder her texts had been so hot and heavy from the start. He wanted to hound Alex for exactly what Juliet had said about him, but he'd known better to ask that of her on this day. Maybe not ever.

"Her fear of getting expelled was greater than her desire to stay with me. Pretty simple."

"Hmm," Alex had drummed her hands on her thighs. "That's basically what she said. She's terrified she won't finish."

Because Ethan finally wanted to talk to someone about it, he'd said, "I was thinking about asking her to marry me."

"Bullshit," Alex had said, but her head had whipped around so fast Ethan could have sworn he'd heard her neck pop.

"Not immediately." Ethan had kept his eyes on the road, but he had felt Alex reevaluating him. "I was thinking at Christmas time. After she'd graduated."

"Holy shit, you're serious."

"Of course I am."

"Does she know this?"

Ethan shook his head. "Does it make a difference? We're over."

"It might," Alex had said. "Going forward."

Ethan hadn't felt like talking about it after that. He couldn't face the prospect of hoping to reunite with Juliet once she was done with school. "Why don't we talk about something less painful. How about religion, maybe politics? Both would be preferable."

"You don't want to talk to me about politics today. If there are protestors outside this place today, I'm going to lose it on them." She'd drummed her hands on her legs again for a minute, then said, "But you should know, that Juliet really needs to graduate. After everything she's been through, Juliet needs this victory. Don't hold that against her."

Ethan had only nodded. He understood but that didn't make it hurt any less.

Back in his bathroom, he stared at himself in the mirror, beard trimmers on and poised, but he was too lost in his thoughts to use them.

On one level, Ethan knew exactly why Juliet didn't want to endanger her degree. As much as he didn't want to be apart from her, as much as he wished she had approached it so that they could still be friends at least, in the past few days, he'd been stuck on the part where Juliet had started seeing him with the knowledge that their relationship would never go anywhere.

He'd known she'd been nervous about starting a relationship with him because of school, but they'd agreed to take it one day at a time. In his mind, that did not mean diving into a relationship and then bailing on a deadline. She had met his family, endeared herself to his brothers, been adopted by his sisters-in-law. Juliet had completely twined herself into his veins and had never once mentioned that she was after nothing more than a good time with an expiration date.

The anger that had been simmering just below the surface had dissipated since their conversation in the break room. Juliet's fears had shone on his fury, and it evaporated it like a desert sun over a shallow puddle. Juliet was afraid to trust him, but he could help her through that. And perhaps, if he was very careful with her, he could spend the next few weeks convincing Juliet they could pick up again in December.

IT WAS ANOTHER WEEK before Juliet saw Ethan again. She told herself she wouldn't look for him in the hallways, but she saw him in every white coat, every set of blue scrubs. Juliet wasn't even sure why she was looking for him. She was infuriated with him. After last week, it had never been clearer to Juliet that the reason he thought they should stay together over the semester was because it wouldn't bother him if she never completed her CNM.

He didn't care if she ever became a midwife.

Which meant, as much as he claimed to love her, he didn't understand her at all. And Juliet hated him for it. She hated Ethan for making her think it was safe to want him, to want to be wanted by him. It made her feel like she'd been nothing more to him than an accessory.

But then Juliet would remember him dancing with her because she enjoyed it. She remembered him clumsily chopping sweet peppers and marinating mushrooms to make her dinner. She remembered the cabin and the waffles and the way his broad chest looked in the firelight, and all she could think about was how much she missed him.

When she did see Ethan again, he sneaked up on her doing paperwork late at night in the birthing center break room. He helped himself to a seat at her table, even though there were two empty ones, and said, "They don't even give you an office?"

Juliet gave herself a chance to take him in. He'd trimmed his beard, and while his hair looked shorter than he usually kept it, it still hung in limp strands over his forehead like he'd been awake too long without a shower.

"Did you have one when you were an intern?"

"No. Not until I was a third-year resident." He craned his neck to peek at what she was working on.

Juliet flipped her folder closed so he couldn't read the file. "You might not have noticed, but I'm bottom of the totem pole around here."

Ethan only chuckled as he stood and poured himself a cup of coffee, then topped hers off without asking. Juliet flipped her file open so she didn't have to look at him. She was afraid of what she would see if she met his eyes.

He was acting so differently than he had the week before. He'd been cold, distant, bordering on rude until she'd pecked at him like an angry hen. This week he was at ease, casual and warm, the way he had been when they'd been together. She could feel his eyes on her, like when he would watch her read the newspaper on her phone over breakfast. There had always been a tenderness in his gaze that she couldn't quite own up to, so she'd kept reading until he looked away.

"What's got you worried?" He asked after a few minutes.

"What makes you think I'm worried?"

She was worried about this patient. Her blood pressure had been steadily climbing in a way that concerned Juliet, and she'd been reviewing her file in search of other red flags.

When Juliet looked up. The tenderness wasn't there, but a half-smile curled over his lips and his blue eyes sparked with amusement as he reached across the table.

"You always chew the corner of your lip when you worry." His thumb caressed left side of her bottom lip, which she still had partway clenched between her teeth.

Juliet should have reared back and smacked his hand away, she knew she should have, but his touch had immobilized her body.

Ethan ran his thumb across her lip again, and she had to suppress a shudder as pleasure shot down her spine. Then his hand cupped her cheek, and her name fell from his lips in a mixture of desire and despair.

Juliet leaned into his hand and closed her eyes, giving herself just a moment to enjoy being close to him.

"God, I have missed you so much," he said.

"Ethan," Juliet said, but she didn't know if it was a plea or a warning. She couldn't feel much other than the slamming of blood through her veins.

He took it for a plea, and leaned across the tiny table, saying her name again. Then his lips were on hers. The kiss was soft, tentative at first, but when Juliet pushed into him, he nearly upended the table to be nearer to her. Before she knew it, she was wrapped in his arms and pressed against his chest. She met his tongue with hers, the taste of him like coming home. The feel of his shoulders under her hands made her drunk with pleasure, so she kept drinking him in like they were in private, like anyone couldn't just walk in the door and—

"Ethan, no." Juliet pushed out of his embrace and backed herself all the way into the refrigerator.

His hands fell limp at his sides. "I'm sorry," he said.

Juliet gulped in a breath of air and buried her face in her hands in hopes of quelling the tears burning in her eyes. She would not cry or have a panic attack in front of him. Not today.

"I'm sorry," he said again.

Juliet breathed a few deep breaths, then scrubbed her eyes, before saying. "You're better than this. You're so much better than this. Don't you see what a difficult position you're putting me in?"

He furrowed his brow for a moment, perplexed.

"You have all of the power. You're a senior member of the staff, a mentor to someone like me. You're supposed to help me, not put me in danger if being expelled. Don't you see how awful that is?"

Ethan's face turned pink, then red. His voice was low when he said, "You're accusing me of abusing my position?"

"No."

"Sounded like it to me."

"I'm telling you how it could affect me. I'm telling you why it should be in your code of conduct not to date students instead of mine not to date doctors."

Tears again pricked at the back of her eyes when he only stared at her, jaw clenched, hands fisted.

"Someone could have walked in that door and seen you kissing me, and it wouldn't matter what your intentions were or that we're not together. I would be gone, my whole career ruined, and you'd get a pat on the back at Dino's for being the guy that nailed the redhead."

Ethan took one cautious step forward, and then another when Juliet did nothing to stop him. When he stood in front of her, he hooked his index finger around hers, not noticing that she didn't engage. "We could get through all of that though. I don't care what anyone says, as long as we can be together."

Once upon a time, Juliet would have melted at those beautiful words. To hear that she was worthy, to know that someone wanted her enough to fight for her. Wasn't that all she'd ever wanted from Rich?

But instead of melting, Juliet stood straight, lifting her chin and meeting Ethan's eyes.

"We wouldn't be together," Juliet said.

"We could make it work," he said, cupping her chin in his palms. "You know we could."

Juliet shook her head, denying herself the pleasure of getting lost in his touch again. "I would never forgive you for taking this away from me."

"Juliet." This time he said her name like a prayer.

"Please, Ethan." Juliet covered his hands with her own. "Just let me go."

He was the one chewing the inside of his cheek now, looking at her like he was watching his whole life slip away, and Juliet realized that he still loved her, and it broke her heart.

When he pulled back and turned away, the tears Juliet hadn't wanted to shed finally fell. She swiped at them as she gathered her papers and was sniffling them away when her supervisor burst into the room.

Felicity's eyes cut between Ethan and Juliet before she said, "Dr. Harvey," and nodded in his direction. "Juliet, Laura's hit transition."

Juliet pasted on a smile, tamping down all her frustration with Ethan. She didn't have to deal with the fury at how little her career mattered to him. He had no say in what kind of work she did, and never would. "Then we better hurry," she said, the smile making her cheeks ache.

She didn't spare Ethan a second glance as she followed Felicity out the door, but Felicity wasn't fooled. "What was going on in there?"

Juliet shrugged. "We were arguing about the merits of midwifery. He's not a fan." It wasn't a complete lie.

Felicity nodded, but swept Juliet over with a critical eye. "Dr. Harvey likes surgery, but he also likes to date pretty nurses that are too young for him."

Juliet must have look stricken enough that Felicity took it for surprise. The woman, who was a few years older than Ethan said, "Rumor has it he was dating some young nurse over the summer, and then Leslie, who also works at Planned Parenthood said she saw him bring the blonde who works at the birthing center in for a D&C a couple of weeks ago."

Juliet stopped walking. There were a couple of blonde nurses who worked at the birthing center, but they were all older and married or hadn't taken any time off recently No, there was only one blonde at the birthing center who fit the bill, and she certainly wasn't a nurse.

Rage like Juliet had never known burned in her. She was going to kill Alex. And then Ethan, and then Alex again.

"You okay?" Felicity asked.

Juliet forced herself to nod and start walking again even though her limbs felt numb. "Just putting two and two together."

"Oh, that's right, you probably know who I'm talking about."

"Yeah."

"Right," Felicity said as they reached Laura's suite. "Moral of the story, stay away from Dr. Harvey."

"Not a problem," Juliet said. And she meant it, wishing she'd slapped him across the face when she'd had a chance.

THE ONLY SHIFT THAT had taken more fortitude for Juliet to work through had been the day she'd lost the baby. This night had been far less eventful, Laura's son had been born only twenty minutes after Juliet and Felicity arrived at the suite, and Juliet attended to the aftercare. By the time Juliet had been on her way out the door, a migraine had bloomed behind her eyes and her jaw ached from gritting her teeth so hard.

In a free moment, Juliet had texted Alex. She didn't care that it was four o'clock in the morning and that Alex would be asleep. She didn't care that all she typed was *We need to talk,* with no explanation. Alex was smart, she would know what Juliet meant.

Alex had slept with Ethan. And not only slept with him but gotten pregnant by him. It had barely been three months since Ethan and Juliet had broken up—and it had been a couple weeks since Alex had "been sick," since she'd gone home to spend time with her grandmother. It couldn't have been long after Ethan and Juliet had split before he hopped in bed with Alex. A couple days, maybe a week at most.

How could he? How could he tell her that he loved her and then screw her best friend? Juliet thought he had been different. She'd thought he had been better than Rich, that Ethan was a good man. But it turned out that he was the same. Worse, even.

And Alex. At least with Rich she'd been up front about the affair. She'd even apologized to Juliet after it was over, admitting that it had been a horrible idea, and a bad friendship move. And Juliet had forgiven her. Had she already started sleeping with Ethan? Had she kept it secret because she was trying to save Juliet's feelings or because Alex and Ethan were serious?

And if they were, what the hell was Ethan doing kissing her in the damn break room?

When Juliet finally made it to her beat up Toyota in the parking garage, it was only to notice that Ethan's Cruiser was parked next to her car. She hadn't seen the man himself until it was too late to avoid him.

"Have breakfast with me," he said as she pushed passed him to unlock her door.

"No," Juliet said without looking at him.

His hand came to rest on her shoulder, "Juliet, please."

She swiped his hand off her shoulder, allowing every ounce of the revulsion she felt to show on her face. "Don't touch me." And when he opened his mouth she said, "Don't talk to me, either."

Ethan backed off, but he didn't stop talking. "I know you're upset, but—"

"I am so far beyond upset you should be grateful I am not a violent person, because I am tempted to run you over with my car."

"Whoa. Hey. What happened?"

"Were you ever going to tell me about Alex and Planned Parenthood, or were you just gonna pretend that never happened?"

Ethan's open concern fell into a frustrated frown. "That's Alex's story to tell."

Juliet snorted and tossed her purse onto the passenger seat. "Men are only ever pro-choice when it's convenient for them."

Ethan started to protest, but Juliet ducked inside her car and locked the doors. He pressed his palms against her window, his eyes pleading with her to listen to him, but she put her car in gear and backed out of her space, barely giving him time to avoid having his feet run over.

Alex had already left for work when Juliet got back to the apartment. Juliet showered, forced herself to eat, then slept fitfully until she heard Alex come through the door.

"I'm home!" Alex called. "And I brought falafel!"

Juliet's headache had barely abated, and her exhaustion and despair were not feigned as she allowed her bedroom door frame to hold her up.

Alex stopped in the hall entry, the bag of Mediterranean food from Juliet's favorite restaurant in her hand. "Ah, honey," her shoulders sagged, and the falafel fell to the floor. "I am so sorry." And Alex moved forward as if to embrace Juliet, but Juliet pressed her palm to Alex's chest to stop her.

"How could you?"

Juliet couldn't keep the tears out of her voice, and Alex welled up as she backed away a few steps.

"I'm so sorry," she said again.

"You should have told me," Juliet said. "You both should have told me."

"I didn't know you and Ethan even were speaking until today," Alex said.

Juliet's tears turned to sobs. Because they were both trying to hide it from her. Juliet barely heard Alex say, "But you're right, I should have come to you right away."

Alex let Juliet cry for a few minutes, huddled against the hall wall with her arms around her knees. Alex sat across from her, sniffling and wiping at her silent tears. "You were just so upset about leaving Ethan. I didn't want to add to it."

On one level, Juliet knew she should be more charitable to her friend. Alex must have been having a rough time of it too. The hormone fluctuations alone must have been difficult, but to be facing all of it virtually alone had to have been a burden. The charitable, sympathetic side of Juliet's personality had gone on hiatus the second she realized her best friend had been sleeping with the man she loved. The man who claimed to love her—Juliet, not Alex.

That Juliet realized she loved him during all this only added to her sense of betrayal. Why did everyone she loved just not care?

"Then why couldn't you just keep your pants on?" Juliet asked.

"I never wanted to hurt you."

"You knew how I felt."

Alex nodded gravely. "I know. I was stupid, and it hurts knowing I betrayed you in the worst way."

"But why him?" Juliet's voice cracked, but she had to know. She had to know if she could ever trust Alex again, could ever look at her again with her heart breaking.

Fresh tears formed in Alex's eyes. "I was lonely, and he was there. I guess I fell a little under his spell, just like you did."

Juliet remembered all of the little kindnesses that made Ethan so endearing: running after parachutes with his five-year-old cousin on his shoulders, doting on his mother's dog, teasing his sisters-in-law, calling Alex to learn Juliet's favorite restaurants. Right. Calling Alex.

Anger and jealousy burned inside Juliet, and she stood abruptly. "I can't do this. I don't want Ethan anymore. You can have him."

Juliet shut herself in her room. She could hear Alex talking to her from the other side of her door, but Juliet put her headphones in and turned up her music so loud that all she could hear over it was Alex banging on the door. Eventually the knocks subsided, and Juliet fell into a restless sleep.

The next morning, Juliet packed a bag of clothes, and all her textbooks, and showed up at Gina's door unable to hold herself together. She succumbed to her despair on Gina's living room floor.

Chapter Nineteen

I t had been five days since Juliet had nearly run him over, and she still hadn't returned any of his calls. Alex told him Juliet had probably deleted his texts without reading them. It's what she'd always done to Rich when she'd been pissed at him.

Ethan had called Alex each day to see if either one had received word from Juliet and to strategize about ways to get through to her. He didn't want to piss Juliet off anymore, but he needed to feel like he was doing something. He could not allow Juliet to go the rest of her life thinking that he'd slept with her best friend.

He tried to think about what his dad would say in this situation. The idea of sitting down in front of his staunchly pro-life father and explaining that he'd taken a friend to get an abortion was no less terrifying now that his father had passed. His father would have considered driving Alex only slightly less of a sin than if Ethan had performed the procedure himself. Not that he hadn't done them in the past, but it wasn't a regular part of his work at the hospital. Ethan and his father had only ever had one conversation about the subject when Ethan had first announced he was going to become an OB-GYN. It hadn't been a living room or dinner table talk. It had been a *come into my office and have a scotch* type of talk.

Ethan had sat down across from his father. His dad had taken the chair Ethan now had behind his desk.

"What worries me about this discipline, is that you're going to learn a set of procedures that are easily abused this day in age."

"You mean D&C's?"

"Yes." His father's reply was clipped, almost spoken over Ethan's words, as if uttering the name could summon unwanted fetuses the same way you could call up demons in fairy tales. "Have you thought about how you're going to handle that diplomatically."

Ethan hadn't, not seriously anyway, but he nodded all the same. He wanted to go into this field to help women. He was intrigued by the high-risk cases, the ones where a woman wanted her child so badly that she gambled with her own life to bring it into the world. He wanted to tip the scale in the mother's favor and allow her the joy of having the family she wanted. That was the answer he'd given his father. He wanted to take on this job to save women and their babies. It had appeased the Harvey patriarch in the moment. But as Ethan had grown into his practice, he'd come to understand that sometimes, helping a woman wasn't always the same thing as making sure she carried to term. Sometimes it was the opposite. And when it came to something like that, the decision had only ever been agonizing on all sides.

While Ethan had never had *that* conversation with his dad, it was something he wished he could talk to him about now. If he could ask his dad for advice now, that's how he would frame the conversation about Alex: being there for a friend who felt trapped and alone and sad. Then Ethan would venture into the meat of it and explain how the woman he loved thought he'd slept with her best friend and gotten her pregnant. Then the pregnancy had been terminated—all within weeks of the break up. Would someone removed from the situation understand?

Ethan heard the reply in his father's voice. "How did you let things get so bad? If you care about this young woman, you need to make it right for her sake. She doesn't deserve to suffer."

"But she's not talking to me," Ethan would say. "She's not answering my calls. Not responding to my texts. How can I make it right if I can't get through to her?"

"You find a way," his father would say. "If this is the woman for you, then you find a way to make sure she hears you."

Ethan wrapped his knuckles on his desk, coming back to reality. It was the day before Thanksgiving, and he had to figure out a way to tell Juliet he hadn't betrayed her.

He pulled out his phone. He was crawling out of his skin for word from Juliet, but he called Alex first.

Alex answered after the second ring.

"Anything?"

"Nothing." Alex sounded just as despondent as he felt.

"I'm going over there," he said.

Alex tried to talk him out of it by reminding him that Gina had slammed the door in her face when she'd tried to talk to Juliet in person. He insisted and had to threaten to lift Gina's address from her hospital records before Alex relented.

"You are going to get me into so much trouble," Alex said before she hung up.

Ethan did not care. He liked Alex. She was a good friend to Juliet, the awkwardness with the Rich situation notwithstanding, but he could not allow Juliet to think that he'd touched Alex for another minute.

Ethan pulled up outside the colorful midtown Victorian and sighed, running his hands over his face and through his freshly washed hair. His heart thumped against his ribs. He was going to demand she listen to him.

With a deep breath, Ethan launched himself out of the Cruiser and up the walk. He could hear a baby crying inside as he waited for someone to answer the door. The man who answered was about his age, but taller with the sandy hair and the fading tan of a man who spent a lot of his time outdoors. Ethan did not recognize him. The only hope that he had the right house was that the baby with tear-stained cheeks on his hip could be about the same age as the one he'd delivered in May.

When the man gave Ethan an expectant look, Ethan said, "I'm looking for Juliet Hawthorne."

The man still said nothing.

"I'm Ethan Harvey—"

"I know who you are, Dr. Harvey," he said. "I'll ask Juliet if she wants to speak to you. Wait here."

Ethan caught a glimpse of hardwood floors and leather furniture with brightly colored blocks spilled over a red Persian rug as Gina's husband retreated inside. He heard nothing for a minute, then a few pounding footsteps later, a strikingly beautiful, slender woman with dark hair was shaking a finger in his face.

"How dare you come here. She came here to get away from you, you selfish, lying bastard!"

Ethan backed away as she advanced on him until he was teetering on the edge of the porch steps.

"Gina," he said, doing his best to remain calm when his instincts were telling him to scream his innocence. "I need to see Juliet."

"No."

"If I could only talk—"

"No."

"It's a misunderstanding—"

Gina surged forward once again, and Ethan was forced to retreat down one of the steps, putting himself at Gina's eye level. "You don't get to make excuses. Not to Juliet. Not to me." She continued insulting him in language he hoped her children could not overhear.

Outrage ballooned, and Ethan couldn't hold in his anger. "I drove Alex to the clinic," he shouted over Gina's objections. "That's it. I never touched her."

Gina's teeth clacked as she shut her mouth. Ethan realized his hands were in the air and he'd stepped up onto the porch, forcing Gina to back up this time. He dropped his hands, hoping he didn't look like a threat.

"You can go now, Dr. Harvey," Gina said, turning on her heel. "I'll pass your message along to Juliet." The door slammed behind her.

LIKE A COWARD, JULIET hid in the kitchen while Gina confronted Ethan—not that Gina had given her much choice. The second Colin had told them who was at the door, Gina was out of the gate like a raging bull. She came back five minutes later, less overtly angry, but still huffing every few minutes.

"What did he want?" Juliet asked after Gina hadn't said anything.

"To tell you that he never slept with Alex in person I suppose." Gina said it as if it was well-known fact. Then she huffed again. "The nerve of him coming here though. As if you didn't come here specifically to get away from him. I'm starting to understand what you mean about him not respecting your decisions."

Over the past few days, Juliet and Gina had a few heart-to-hearts about how Ethan made Juliet feel like she was the most cherished woman in the world until her occupation came up. Ethan's low opinions of midwives always made Juliet feel inadequate, while feeling her desire for a career wasn't enough for him.

"What do you mean he never slept with Alex?" Juliet asked.

Gina, who had been drying dishes in her fury, sighed, and tossed the wet towel in the little kitchen hamper. "Did you actually think he did?"

"I—" but Juliet couldn't finish her sentence. Someone had seen them together at the clinic. "Why else would he have been there with her?"

Gina sighed again. "There are some messages on your phone that you should see."

Gina had been screening Juliet's phone since Juliet had moved in, passing along anything work related, and shielding her from anything else.

Juliet collapsed into a kitchen chair, the smell of baking apples rising around her as the pie she and Gina had made together baked in preparation for the next day's feast. The scent was comforting, reminding Juliet how she and Colleen had overseen the Thanksgiving pies as teenagers, baking both apple and pumpkin. At least, that's what she told herself as she'd suppressed memories of Ethan sampling some of every pie at Fourth of July. It was better to think of Colleen than Ethan.

When Gina handed over Juliet's phone, the screen showed the text thread from Alex for the last week. "Perhaps if they're both denying it so vehemently, there's some truth to it," Gina said, before leaving Juliet in peace.

Juliet read the oldest messages first, most of which asked Juliet to open her door, to talk to Alex, to come home. And when it appeared that Alex had given up on Juliet responding, she'd sent a text telling Juliet to listen to her voicemail.

Alex had left her three voicemails.

"I think you're being really stupid," she started. *"If you would just pick up your goddamn phone or stop deleting my messages or whatever, you'd know how stupid you're being."*

The next one said, *"Juliet, I'm sorry. I don't think you're being stupid. You have every right to be upset. And I fully expect you to be pissed as hell at me once we get this sorted out, but don't be mad at Ethan. He doesn't deserve it. He was just try-*

ing to be a friend—and I really needed a friend." Alex's voice sounded near tears when she hung up.

In the third voicemail Alex said, *"Just so we're clear, I never slept with Ethan. He was my ride to and from the clinic. That's all."*

There were more texts of Alex trying for normalcy, asking her about her day, or when she was coming home. She reiterated a few more times that she didn't sleep with Ethan—that she would never sleep with Ethan.

At the end of them, Juliet still didn't understand. If Alex and Ethan didn't . . . she couldn't quite bring herself to finish that thought, then why hadn't Alex come to her when she found herself pregnant. And as Juliet scrolled through Alex's messages a second time, the answer came to her.

JULIET: *Rich was the father.*

Alex's *Yes* took less than a minute to arrive and was quickly followed by a string of apologies.

At least she was being honest now. Juliet appreciated that and texted her back.

JULIET: *I need some time.*

Alex didn't reply.

Juliet excused herself to her bedroom to try to wrap her head around what she'd just learned. She'd been so wrapped up in her own grief and sense of betrayal that it hadn't even occurred to her that Rich could have been the father. Alex had tried to protect Juliet from knowing anything about it.

God, Juliet was the worst friend in the world. She'd been so consumed with Ethan that she hadn't noticed what Alex was going through. But Juliet would have been there for her. They could have talked out what Alex wanted to do together. She could have at least been the one to take Alex to the clinic, and to take care of her afterwards.

Juliet should have realized what was going on. Pregnancy was her specialty, and she'd completely missed it in Alex.

As she stared at the ceiling, Juliet found that she really didn't care who Alex had gotten pregnant by. She was glad it wasn't Ethan, but even if it had been, Juliet would have liked the chance to support her friend. Alex had done so much for her over the past four years, thinking of her alone and scared, and most probably heartbroken since it was Rich they were talking about after all, made Juliet heartsick for her friend. Juliet would do her best to make it up to her friend after the holiday.

Her phone buzzed in her hand. She flipped over onto her belly to read the text from Ethan. Barely enough time had passed for him to drive home. Butterflies erupted in Juliet's stomach as she opened the message.

ETHAN: *My mom just asked me if you were coming to Henry's for dinner tomorrow.*

That was not the message Juliet expected.

JULIET: *Why? We're not together. And she doesn't like me.*

ETHAN: *Because she knows I want you there.*

Juliet felt tears spring to her eyes. She wanted to be there with him, but she knew if she dwelled on the feeling, she'd feel heartbroken all over again.

JULIET: *Thanks for being there for Alex. It should have been me.*

ETHAN: *I agree. We only hurt you more trying to protect you. I'm sorry.*

A teardrop landed on her screen, and Juliet had to turn it off to clean it. By the time she had it turned back on, Ethan had sent another text.

ETHAN: *I'm on vacation through mid-December so I won't be around the hospital to bother you. Congratulations, Juliet.*

Disappointment settled in her chest, but it was for the best. She thanked him and buoyed herself to check all the messages he'd sent her over the past few days. Most of them proclaimed his innocence, a few asked her to call him. The last one he'd sent yesterday read only *I miss you,* and Juliet spent the next fifteen minutes reminiscing about the things she liked most about him: his love for his family, the way he slept with one arm over his head, the vulnerability when he'd confessed that his greatest fear was losing a mother.

She loved him, but she had chosen her career over him, and it was time to forgive herself for making that choice.

Her phone buzzed again, and Juliet expected another text from Ethan, but it was from her sister instead.

COLLEEN: *I know you've got a deal worked out at your birthing center for a job after you graduate, but I saw this and thought you might be interested. Bonus, it's like two hours from me. *Hint hint**

There was a link to a job listing for a traveling midwife to serve a network of three rural hospitals in the middle of ski country. Intrigued, Juliet spent the rest of the afternoon sifting through Colorado job listings.

After dinner, Juliet explained to Gina what she'd learned while they washed the dishes. Gina grew quieter the more she heard, and when Juliet finally got around to how Rich had been the sperm donor, not Ethan, Gina set down her dish towel and stared out the kitchen window without speaking.

After nearly a full minute of silence, Gina said, "He's going to be so disappointed."

"About Alex terminating the pregnancy?"

Gina nodded, then shrugged. "About everything."

Juliet didn't know what to say. As far as she was concerned, Rich didn't have a say in Alex's decision—especially since he'd been using her to get to Juliet. The opinion must have shown on Juliet's face, because Gina pursed her lips.

"I know my brother has hurt you. When it comes to women, he's just like our dad. He doesn't see it yet, but you can bet the second he does, he'll change his tune. When you two moved in together, I thought maybe he'd already figured it out."

Juliet harrumphed, but Gina narrowed her eyes until Juliet motioned for her to go on.

"Did you know that during your last year of nursing school, right before you got pregnant, he was terrified you were going to leave him after you graduated?"

Juliet shook her head, too surprised to speak.

"He thought you were going to get some amazing nursing job in a different city and take off. After you guys announced the baby, I wondered if maybe he'd done something, tampered with your birth control or something. I even asked him, but he said it was a divine accident." Gina worried her bottom lip. "When you lost the baby. When you left. I've never seen him so devastated. He was a mess for months."

Juliet wanted to comment about how that hadn't stopped him from seeing the girl he'd cheated on her with. It hadn't stopped them from moving in together, but she waited for Gina to finish.

"I asked him why, if he was so afraid of losing you, why did he start seeing someone else, and the only reason he could give me was that was what he'd always done when he was stressed. I told him it made him an asshole, and he didn't argue, but he has always been sorry, Juliet. Always. And when he says you're the only woman he's ever loved, I believe him. He wanted to marry you. He wanted that baby. He wanted to be a father. So yeah, when he finds out that he missed his chance at fatherhood again, he's going to be disappointed. But more than that, when he figures out how much you like this Ethan guy, he's going to be devastated."

Juliet wasn't sure what to address first, so she said, "If he felt that way, feels that way, why then, when I was pregnant, did I feel so alone?"

Gina pulled Juliet into a hug, and only then did Juliet realize she was crying again. She'd barely stopped crying for a week.

"I'm sorry," she said. "I didn't know." Gina tightened her arms around Juliet's shoulders. "You'll always be my sister, no matter what my stupid brother does."

When Rich showed up for Thanksgiving Dinner the next day, it wasn't a surprise. Their mother was on the east coast now, and Rich had finals coming up, so he never travelled far. Despite the kids needing a lot of adult attention, the day was fun. It reminded Juliet of before, when the four of them would go out for movies and ice cream or stay in and drink too much wine and play cards.

After the kids were in bed, they had just finished a hand of cards when Juliet took a deep breath and said, "I applied for a job in Colorado yesterday."

Shocked silence met her announcement.

"What about your birthing center?" Rich asked. "I thought you were going to work there."

"That was the plan originally." Juliet played with the straw in her water glass, "And I love it there. But I've worked there for four years. This other job would be something I haven't done before, traveling and working with hospitals that have no birth center but want to develop a program. How amazing would that be to help start?"

The more she talked about it, the more excited Juliet became about the possibility. If she didn't get the job, she would be happy to stay and work at her birthing center, but now that the idea of leaving Kansas City had occurred to her, Juliet couldn't let go of it. With everything that had happened in the last few months, maybe it was time to move on. So, sitting there, on the receiving end of doubtful looks from three of her oldest friends, Juliet decided that she'd apply for a few of the other open positions she'd found within a couple hours of Denver.

Being closer to Colleen and to her parents felt like the right thing to do.

Gina and Collin retreated to their bedroom just after ten. Juliet remained at the table returning a happy Thanksgiving text to her sister, too invigorated by her decision to go to bed. Rich disappeared, then returned a few minutes later with a bottle of Juliet's favorite wine.

"Shall we?" He asked.

Juliet grinned and nodded. "But someplace more comfortable."

Rich grabbed the corkscrew, made a teasing comment about his bedroom, but then led Juliet by the hand to the sunroom. Gina and Colin's house was built into the side of a hill, so both the basement and the main level had exterior doors. Gina kept the room stocked with big leafy ferns and flowering plants. There was a set of cushioned wicker furniture in one corner, and Rich pulled Juliet down next to him on the loveseat. He switched on a string of Christmas lights and opened the bottle of wine while Juliet looked up at the full moon, just visible through the tops of the trees.

The wine was clean and crisp and dry and almost reminded her of apples. The last time she'd had it had been at the cabin with Ethan.

"You're not really going to move away to the middle of nowhere are you?" Rich asked.

"You know, I think I am," she said.

"I'll miss you."

"We haven't seen each other in months."

Rich nodded, and Juliet thought he was probably already a little drunk, he and Colin had opened a bottle of Scotch earlier. "And I've missed you," he said, then scooted closer, laying an arm around her shoulder. She allowed it, because right now, in his sister's house, Rich was harmless.

"What have you been up to?' she asked.

Rich told her about his semester, about the girls who had crushes on him and the woman he dated for a few weeks after Alex. He told her about how he was planning the summer's month-long trip to Italy for his students, where they would go, and how they would earn their credit hours.

"We never got to go to Italy," Rich said. "You should come with me."

"I'm not going with you to Italy."

"Ah, Jules," Rich nuzzled her neck. "You're always such a spoilsport."

"Am I?"

He ran his nose from her ear to her collarbone and back, and Juliet would be lying if she said she didn't shiver. "You work too hard."

Juliet scoffed. "If I remember correctly, the reason we never went to Italy was because you were too busy teaching summer school."

"I didn't have tenure then."

"You got tenure?"

"This year."

"Congratulations."

They were quiet for a long time, watching out the windows as the moon moved through the trees, Juliet's head on Rich's shoulder.

"If I asked you to stay, would you?" he asked.

Juliet shook her head, deciding then that she was moving to Colorado after she graduated. She would find a job when she got there if she didn't get the one she wanted. The idea made her feel lighter than she had in months.

"Will you ever forgive me?"

"I want to," she said.

"We could start over, and actually get married this time. We could visit my grandmother in Italy for our honeymoon. We could conceive our baby on a day trip to the countryside while we trespass in a vineyard and make love on a checkered tablecloth."

Juliet giggled. "You're such a romantic at heart, you'll make me forget why we broke up."

"I never wanted to break up."

"Don't be ridiculous."

"I'm serious."

"Even after you found me in bed with Ethan, you still thought we could work it out?"

Rich sat up straight and tilted her chin up. "Jules, I still think we can work it out."

"Why?" It was the only word in her head.

"I love you," he said. "I have since that ridiculous dance at your high school."

Juliet smiled as she remembered how dazzled she'd been by him. "I definitely fell in love with you that day."

Rich grinned and touched his lips to hers in a soft, warm kiss, then leaned back just far enough to look into her eyes. When Juliet didn't shrink back, he captured her lips again in a kiss that any other time in her life would have made her toes curl. She wanted to allow the familiarity of Rich's touch wash over her and draw her into a place where only physical touch mattered, but as he dipped his tongue past her lips, instead of the usual thrill in her stomach, Juliet just remembered that not long ago, he had been kissing Alex like this, and another girl after that.

And Juliet burst into tears.

She'd never spontaneously cried before, but it felt as if the grief inside her had burned to the point of ignition. And now she burned with it.

Rich didn't hesitate to fold her into his arms, rubbing her back and shushing her until she calmed to a sniffle. Even then, he didn't ask what was wrong. He waited for her to sigh wipe her tears on the back of her hand.

"Did you know that Alex had an abortion a few weeks ago?" she asked as she pulled free of his embrace.

Rich shook his head, but she could almost hear him counting back the weeks, doing the math in his head from the last time they were together. He didn't even need to ask. "She never told me she was pregnant."

"She never told me either."

Rich squeezed Juliet's hand. "Is that why you're staying with Gina?"

Juliet shrugged. "She didn't want to tell me that she was choosing not to have your baby, when she knew how badly I wanted the one we lost." Her voice broke on the last words, tears springing to her eyes again.

Rich whispered, "Ah, Jules," and tried to embrace her again, but she stopped him with a hand to his chest.

"But what Alex doesn't know is that I was so desperately clinging to that pregnancy because I had to feel like I was good enough for something. I wasn't getting along with my family. They weren't happy with my choice to move, my choice to go to nursing school, to move in with you, and they let me know it. You were cheating on me, and part of me believed that if I could be an amazing girlfriend, be the best mother, that maybe I would finally be good enough for you, or for them or for someone. And then, I couldn't even keep our baby alive. I couldn't even do that right."

Rich seemed to sense that trying to touch her was a bad idea and kept his hands to himself as he repeated her name, "Juliet," like he was saying penance.

"Why wasn't I ever good enough?" Juliet asked through her tears, and Rich hugged her so hard, she could barely breathe.

"You have always been perfect," he said in his ear, his voice rough. "I was the idiot, Jules. I was so afraid of you leaving me, I went out and made it happen. I'm so sorry. For the cheating, for the lonely pregnancy, for losing the baby, for making you feel this way. I am so sorry, *amore mia. Sei il grande amore della mia vita.*"

Juliet laughed through her tears. "No fair speaking Italian."

"It's true."

With a sigh, Juliet sat back and tried to remember what she'd learned from living with him all those years ago. She was pretty sure he'd said she was the greatest love of his life, or at least the love of his life. Juliet said, "I'm in love with Ethan."

To his credit, Rich listened while Juliet explained the whole misunderstanding with Alex over who the father of her baby was and why Juliet was staying with Gina, even though she knew he must still be reeling from the fact that Alex had been pregnant at all.

When she finished, he asked, "Are you going to tell him how you feel?"

Juliet sat up straight and said. "I think it's something I just have to live with until I can move on, and I'm okay with that. Moving will help."

"And nothing I can say will change your mind about leaving?"

Juliet finished the last of her wine, and said, "I'm wondering if I beg really hard, maybe my sister will let me live with her while I look for my own place. What do you think?"

And Rich said, "I bet she'll only make you beg a little bit."

Chapter Twenty

For the past week, Ethan had been staying at Will's cabin in the mountains. It was where he usually stayed when he came to Colorado in the summer, but since he'd chosen to skip his normal vacation in favor of spending more time with Juliet, he found himself with three weeks of unused vacation at the end of the year and a director who insisted he used them. Since Ethan's med school friend, Will, was going through a divorce and wanted to piss off his soon-to-be-ex-wife by taking a vacation just before Christmas, Ethan had decided to join him and make sure Will didn't go too crazy.

Ethan and Amanda had spent most of what little time they'd had off in med school with Will and Heather. While Ethan, Amanda, and Will had all been OB track, Heather was in pediatrics. She loved kids, had wanted a family, and had married Will as soon as they'd graduated—just like Ethan had planned to do with Amanda. Their son, Aiden, had been born three years ago—a reminder that Ethan could have, and probably should have had kids of his own by now. That had always been his plan, and he'd always been jealous of Will for fulfilling Ethan's personal goals.

After this past week, Ethan was no longer jealous of Will. His friend was a mess.

He held it together well during the day while they were on the slopes, but once the sun went down and the whiskey came out, Ethan heard all about Will's marital troubles.

Ethan supposed they were the usual sort, though he had no practical experience. Will and Heather hadn't spent enough time together and they hadn't communicated when they had seen each other. Then, somewhere along the way, Heather had started sleeping in the guest room and had stopped doing any of the housework. Will had to wash the laundry so Aiden had clean clothes to wear to daycare.

One weekend she'd gone away to a Zen meditation retreat. And though she'd made all the childcare arrangements for Aiden with her mother, the only notice she'd given Will was a text from the guest room before she'd left, saying she would be gone for three days and when her mother would be by to watch the baby.

When she'd come back, she'd told Will she wanted a divorce, and he still wasn't entirely sure what had happened. While Will seemed to miss Heather, he also hadn't seemed inclined to do a damn thing to save his marriage.

After he'd had a few shots of whiskey, Will would mutter, "A fucking meditation retreat," into his glass.

Ethan did his best to be supportive, and while it hardly seemed appropriate in the moment, he wanted to ask his friend if it had ever occurred to him to help with the laundry. Before he could stop it from happening, he thought about how Juliet would narrow her sharp green eyes at him and hiss like a cat if he expected her to just have his laundry done when he needed it after they were married.

Ethan gasped aloud when the thought hit, like it had punched him in the gut. Did he still think they had any possibility? The last time he'd seen Juliet, she'd almost run him over in her fury. While they had cleared up the misunderstanding about Alex, things with Juliet felt far from settled. If anything, they felt over. He'd said congratulations and good luck, and she'd said, *Thanks.*

There was no encouragement in that thanks. There was no intimacy in it either. It was how you responded to an acquaintance or a colleague, not a lover. And yet, Ethan could not move on from her. When he was awake, he wondered if she was still at Gina's or if she and Alex had reconciled. He wondered if she was hanging Christmas lights from her tropical plants instead of getting a proper tree. He wondered if she missed him as much as he still missed her. He wondered if she dreamed about him.

The longing for her was so intense that on the night Ethan suggested he and Will hit up a local bar instead of staying home and moping, Ethan regretted it immediately. The place was crawling with tourists and vacationers. Will found a couple of girls in their twenties who were impressed by their doctorates. While the blonde was practically sitting in Will's lap, Ethan wound up listening to the brunette girl's complaints about her mother and how she wasn't living up to her full potential working as a ski pro. Ethan shared his mother's distaste for his beard and his schedule, which made the girl laugh.

When she said, "Well, I like your beard," and then tried touch his jaw, Ethan gently pushed on her wrist and shook his head. The brunette had to be about Juliet's age, but she seemed so much younger. He excused himself, and when he came back from the bathroom, he sat at the bar instead of re-joining Will and the girls at the table. No longer in the mood for drinking, Ethan ordered a Coke.

The bartender smiled as she placed the glass in front of him and said, "You're the first guy all week to turn her down."

Ethan shrugged.

"Your friend is looking pretty comfortable, though."

Looking over his shoulder, he saw Will and the blonde laughing together, their noses practically touching. Ethan sighed. "He's getting divorced."

The bartender's smile turned up a notch, and Ethan noticed that she was pretty, with curly black hair, pale, freckled skin and sharp eyes that reminded him of Juliet. She could be Juliet's black-haired older sister.

"What about you?" she asked.

"Not on the market," he said, hoping sounding surly would make her go away.

Instead, she held up her left hand. A gigantic diamond sparkled there. "Married twelve years," she said. "And have four amazing, pain in the ass kids."

Ethan chuckled despite himself and said, "Congratula-tions."

She settled a couple tabs, and Will, rather than leave the blonde's side, sent him a text saying he'd see Ethan in the morning. Ethan waved to Will as he left, and then the bar-tender was back in front of him with another coke.

"I'm Marney," she said, holding out her hand.

"Ethan," he said, shaking her hand. "Nice to meet you."

Then, Marney rested her elbows on the bar in front of him. "So, Ethan. What's your story? Why aren't you available?"

Ethan told her everything—things he hadn't even discussed with his brothers or with Will. He told her about his fantastic summer, about Juliet's choosing school over him, about her accusing him of abusing his position when he kissed her at the hospital. He finished with the most recent drama.

Marney blinked at him. "Wow. You guys are a train wreck."

Ethan chuckled and shook his head. That was an apt description if he'd ever heard one. When he looked back up, Marney was tapping a finger to her bottom lip in thought.

"So now that she's done with school, you're planning to head back home and fix things with her? That's why you're off the market?"

"Exactly."

"What's your game plan?" Marney asked.

Ethan hesitated, other than sending her flowers on graduation day, he didn't have one. He was hoping that was enough of a starting place.

"Ah," Marney said. "You have no idea, do you?"

"Not really."

Marney tapped her lip again. "What do you want out of a relationship with Juliet?"

That was easy. "I want to marry her. I want a family with her. She's everything I've ever wanted."

"Which is?"

Ethan told Marney how Juliet made him laugh, how she challenged him, how she was brilliant, and professional. How she would make the perfect partner.

"You respect her, but you're embarrassed that she's a midwife?" Marney asked.

Ethan felt his jaw move, but no words come out for a moment before he said, "I never said that."

Marney smiled in a way that said he didn't need to.

"I'm not embarrassed, exactly," he said. "I just..." but Ethan didn't have an alternative word. "Midwives are valuable," he said instead. "They have a place, but I don't think they should replace doctors."

"Ah," Marney said, still giving him that sly smile that said she heard more than what he'd said. "And does Juliet want marriage and a family and all that?"

"She was going to do all of that with Rich."

"That was years ago. It could be that what she wants has changed. Maybe she just wants to be a midwife without being made to feel second class to his holiness the OB-GYN."

Ethan did not know Marney well enough for her to talk to him like that.

"I don't act like that."

"You shouldn't," Marney said, but already Ethan was remembering the scene in the hospital when he'd told Juliet she would survive being kicked out of her program because he would take care of her. He would make her *his* nurse, and he buried his head in his hands. He'd known it had been a mistake after he'd said it, but the drama of the thing with Alex had overshadowed that entire conversation.

He shouldn't have said anything of the sort. He shouldn't have wanted Juliet to suffer that humiliation, but oh how he *had* wanted it. Ethan had wanted all hindrance to their relationship gone. If he was being honest with himself, it had been his greatest fantasy, possibly even the source of his crush, to make Juliet his nurse and work and live with her beauty and her talent.

But that wasn't what Juliet wanted, and he'd been trying to box her in since the beginning.

"Maybe you should start by asking Juliet what she wants," Marney said, setting his bill down in front of him.

Ethan wasn't even sure he responded, his mind was working so quickly.

For the next two weeks, Ethan tried to take his mind off how much Juliet's rejection was going to hurt, but he knew he had to try.

JULIET STAYED AT GINA'S on Black Friday, arriving back at the apartment she shared with Alex Saturday morning. Alex wasn't due back from her grandmother's house until late. Juliet spent the day cleaning the apartment from top to bottom and tending to her neglected plants. She was sweaty, covered in dirt and grime, and standing on a bar stool hanging Christmas lights in the living room windows when Alex opened the door.

She dropped her bag on the sofa and said, "You're home."

Juliet abandoned the lights, letting them sway half hung to clink against the glass as she scrambled off her stool. Alex let out an "oomph" as Juliet latched her arms around the shorter woman and pulled her in for a tight hug. It only took a second before Alex's arms banded around Juliet's back.

"I'm so sorry," they said at the same time. Then their words came in quick succession, both needing to get out all the apologies they'd kept inside over the last few days.

"I should have told you right away," Alex said.

"I should have known," Juliet said. "I was so wrapped up in being miserable that I didn't even notice what you were going through."

"I didn't want to make things worse. But the whole thing was screwed up from the start." Tears welled in Alex's eyes. "I never should have slept with Rich. That was the first mistake."

Juliet pulled back from the hug, her arms still resting on Alex's shoulders. "You can sleep with whoever you want. Even if you had slept with Ethan, I should have put you first."

Alex laughed as tears spilled over her eyes. "First off, I would never, in a million years sleep with Ethan. I learned my lesson with Rich." She wiped her tears, and Juliet let her arms fall to her sides. "Besides, you're still in love with him. I might have been stupid enough to sleep with Rich, but I'm not that stupid."

Juliet's own tears started then. "I'm so sorry I wasn't there when you needed me."

Alex nodded, and took a deep breath, and did something Juliet had never seen her do—not over a man, not over her deadbeat mother, not even over burnt garlic bread—she bawled. And Juliet held her until she was spent, like she should have been doing since the beginning.

RETURNING TO WORK THE week before Christmas was a relief. As much as he'd enjoyed hiking and skiing and catching up on medical journals in front of the fire, he missed the practice. He missed the hard cases where the child's life was uncertain, and the emergency cases where the mother's life could be in danger. Helping to make it right was soothing. His first night back, when he went from a normal, successful vaginal birth into an emergency c-section, he could almost believe he was happy—if he didn't think about Juliet.

His second day back was Juliet's graduation, and he sent her a large bouquet of multicolored roses. All day, he waited for her call, but he hadn't heard from her by the time he went to work that evening, so his mood was already dour when he showed up for his shift. All the nurses were talking about was fitting in Christmas preparations for their families around their shifts, and Ethan did his rounds resenting the fact that all he had to do was buy a few gift cards for his nieces and a video game for his nephew. Maybe he'd get Camille something fancy to chew on.

He set the emergency c-section from the night before up with a lactation specialist. He took a few minutes to chat with Ann and her husband about their holiday plans. He'd been trying harder lately not to be so clinical all the time. He left Ann and her husband with matching grins a few minutes later and noted that her feet were still a little swollen. She'd been on a lot of fluids, so he wasn't worried. Ethan made a note to monitor the situation over the next couple of days.

Ethan had grabbed a cup of coffee and was reviewing a progressing case with the lead nurse on duty when an alarm sounded from the Ann's room. It was likely a malfunction. Ethan had only been in there ten minutes before and she'd been fine.

A nurse was already there, trying to coax the woman's husband away from the bed, his newborn clutched in his arms.

"What happened?" Ethan asked, approaching the patient, who was non-responsive. Her alarm blaring that she had no pulse.

He worked, even as more support staff arrived. Someone removed the frantic husband from the room while the first nurse said via the husband that the new mother had been uncomfortable, but in good spirits. The baby had woken them, and she'd been trying to nurse the baby, then sort of gasped and gone limp. The husband had grabbed the baby and the had alarms started going off, and that's when Ethan had arrived.

He worked on her too long. The nurses around him had all stepped back from the bed, but still, Ethan worked. He saw nothing but a woman he needed to revive. He'd never lost a mother before, and he wasn't going to start tonight.

Finally, someone placed a hand on his bicep. Ethan looked up to see Elsie's sad eyes. "There's nothing more you can do, Dr. Harvey."

Ethan closed his eyes and stepped back from the bed. Elsie was right. It had been too long with no response, and he checked his watch, his whole body numb. He couldn't feel his lips as he said, "Three-forty-eight," not quite believing it himself, as he turned from the room, allowing the staff to do their job while he had to face the sorrowful reality of doing his.

A man had just lost his wife. A child, only a day old, had just lost her mother, and Ethan was supposed to be the person who made it all make sense for them. While he suspected a blood clot, he had no real explanation. No excuse for how he'd missed it. No explanation for why the man's wife had died on Ethan's watch. He could only relate to the man that he was sorry she hadn't made it and offer his condolences.

Ethan had one of the nurses get the husband a coffee and then sat him down and explained to the man how something like that could happen even in a hospital, then left him with a nurse and a social worker.

Unable to do anything else, Ethan sat in his office, in the dark, in the middle of the night, shaking. Now he understood why his father had always kept a bottle of scotch locked in his bottom drawer. It wasn't because of the era he hailed from, but so he could recover from shifts like this and rally himself to complete the accompanying paperwork.

Ethan knew, as he watched his hand twitch on his desk calendar, that he wouldn't trust himself to do more surgery tonight. The only other night he'd ever felt this way had been the night his father died. And this wasn't the same. His father passing away after a quick, fierce battle with cancer had been nowhere near the same thing as a woman dying from a preventable, if unpredictable, condition on his watch. He'd known his father was going to die. Ethan had been gathered around the hospital bed with his brothers and his mother when it had happened. It hadn't made the loss any easier, but it had made it final. Being there had driven home that the most important person in his life was really and truly gone.

But this poor man was supposed to be celebrating new life—and it was Ethan's fault he was having to now plan a funeral.

Ethan had known it was unrealistic to think he'd never lose a mother, especially since he sought out high risk cases, but having it happen was so much worse than reading the maternal death rates. Knowing the odds hadn't stopped him from imagining he could live his whole life, practice his whole career never once losing a mother. And now that fantasy was gone. His record was tarnished.

Ethan scrubbed his eyes with his fingers, ignoring the wetness that marred his cheek and soaked his beard. When his door opened and closed, Ethan scrubbed his eyes again, thinking he must be dreaming, or hallucinating. Juliet stood with her hands behind her back, leaning against his office door. She wore the pink scrubs he always imagined her in.

Feeling foolish for disbelieving his eyes, he said her name aloud.

And then she moved, not through the desk like the phantom he expected her to be, but around it.

"I just heard," she said as she stopped at his side. He watched as she gripped his hands and knelt in front of him. "I'm so sorry."

Chapter Twenty-One

The only light in Ethan's office came from the street lamps filtering through the blinds on the wall adjacent to his desk. Ethan was hunched over in his office chair, his elbows on his knees. He looked small and young and scared. When he raised his eyes to hers, Juliet let out a strangled gasp and pulled her hands out of his limp grip to wipe the tears from his face. "Oh, Ethan. What are you doing here all on your own?"

He didn't say anything as he wrapped his arms around her waist and squeezed. There was no space to spare between them as Ethan buried his nose in her neck, and no room for Juliet to breathe as he tightened his embrace around her ribs. Juliet, who's arms wound over his shoulders, ran one hand up and down his spine while she tangled the other in his over-long hair, massaging the scalp at the base of his neck. Ethan did not shudder and sob the way Juliet wanted to do, but wept silently, soaking the shoulder of her scrub top.

His grip loosened after a few minutes, and Juliet inhaled through her nose, and with it came a flood of his clean citrus and pine scent, the combination that ironically reminded her of a health food store bath and body section. He smelled like oranges and tea tree oil wrapped in crisp eucalyptus.

"How are you here?" he asked into her neck, and Juliet couldn't stop the shiver that shook down her spine.

"I came with a birthing center patient. She's got her epidural and is sleeping a little bit. I went in search of coffee and heard the news. When Elsie said you were still here, I wanted to make sure you were okay."

"I lost a mother."

"I know, honey. I'm sorry."

"Childbirth is supposed to be safe for women. That's why we do what we do. I should have spotted the clot, and now..." Ethan's voice grew thick with unshed tears as he spoke. "I've given a family bad news so many times, but rushing into that hospital room where there was nothing I could do. . ."

"It's not your fault," Juliet said.

"I should have caught that clot."

"Even if you did, there's no guarantee you could have changed anything."

Ethan's hands bunched the fabric around her waist. "You should get back to your patient."

"Charlie's here, and the hospital nurses, and Dr. Taylor. They won't even notice I'm gone."

Ethan held her for long minutes in silence. Then, clearing his throat, he asked, "Did you get my flowers?"

Juliet pulled away just far enough to look at him again. "I did. Thank you. They're beautiful."

A hint of a smile played on his lips for a second before they slipped back into a mournful slash separating his mustache from his beard.

Perhaps it was desire, or maybe it was recklessness, or the lingering effects of admitting to herself that she loved him. Maybe she couldn't stand to see him look so disheartened, but Juliet would decide on an excuse later. Right now, she wanted to kiss Ethan.

He was hesitant when she first placed her lips on his, but as she nipped his bottom lip, life bloomed in him again. He slipped his tongue past her lips, making Juliet go limp and hot all over. His fingers had bunched up her top enough to slide his left hand easily beneath it and over the small of her back. His right hand dipped below her waistband, automatically finding the place where he knew a perpetual knot of muscle lived, and Juliet moaned and arched into the massage.

"I've missed you so much," he said against her lips, then slid out of his chair and maneuvered her on her back behind his desk. His touch wasn't gentle as his fingers roamed to her front, pushing her shirt up and pulling the cups of her bra down. He took her nipple between his teeth. The sharp sting straddled the line between pleasure and pain and Juliet bit her lip to stifle her reaction.

Ethan ground his hips into hers and Juliet gasped. His touch was more desperate than she'd known in the past, but Juliet didn't care. He needed her, and she needed to be here for him now. She had enough presence of mind to whisper, "We shouldn't do this here."

Ethan pressed his erection right into her core. "I know," he said, but neither one of them stopped.

Juliet reached between them, working her hand beneath his waistband until she had his familiar length cupped in her palm. He cursed as she stroked him.

Ethan was shimmying her pants down her hips before Juliet thought of protection. They'd stopped using condoms before, but it had been months since they'd been together. Instead of asking if he had protection, Juliet just managed to gasp out, "I haven't been with anyone since you."

"Me either," he said, and sheathed himself inside her. It was Juliet's turn to curse.

The pace they set was not forgiving. Grief and regret and desire had Juliet's legs wrapped around Ethan's hips, urging him to go harder, to go faster.

"You are so perfect," he said as Juliet rotated her hips against his, little moans escaping despite her best effort to keep quiet until his rhythm shifted slightly, and an orgasm overtook her almost without warning.

Ethan clamped his lips over hers to muffle her cries, taking advantage of the deeper angle to find his own release.

He kissed a trail down her neck before settling his weight on top of her. Juliet played with his hair as they caught their breath. She'd missed the coarse thickness between her fingers.

The silence drew out, and more because she felt she needed to say something than because she was worried he might have the wrong idea, she said, "I didn't come here for this."

"I know." He rolled to the side, and Juliet realized how undignified they looked. Her shirt was still up, her bra pulled down. Both of them were still in socked feet, scrub bottoms hanging off one ankle.

Juliet hurried to right herself. Ethan did the same and said, "I don't make a habit of this." As if he was afraid Juliet thought he often bedded nurses in his office.

"I know," she said, ducking to slide her feet back in the tennis shoes she didn't remember kicking off.

The air grew thick between them. Juliet had only meant to check on him and make sure he wasn't devastated, but she'd had no real plan. She hadn't realized that this might happen. She only knew that pull to see him, to go to him after tragedy was too strong for her to deny.

When the silence remained, and they both still sat on the blue carpet, staring at their shoes, Juliet wanted to cry. Not for the dead mother, her devastated husband and poor child that would never know her, but for herself. This was not how she wanted things to turn out with Ethan. She'd wanted to see him, to tell him that she and Alex had worked things out. She wanted to apologize for nearly running him over and ask him how his vacation was. Fucking on his office floor had not been on her list of to-dos, and she felt dirty and more than a little ashamed of herself.

No. If there was any chance for them, they would both have to be better than this, and as much as she admitted that she was in love with him, the same thought that had sustained her over the last few months, especially the last three weeks, was that they just weren't right for each other. If anything, this encounter proved that. People who loved each other didn't use one another.

Bolstered, Juliet pushed to her feet, saying, "I should go," at the same time Ethan said, "Have dinner with me tonight."

Juliet paused. Ethan still sat on the floor next to his desk chair, a high-backed dark leather monstrosity that had probably cost his father a fortune but was so scuffed and worn now it deserved to be scrapped. Ethan would most likely keep it until he died. His elbows rested on his bent knees. He gazed up at her with sad eyes and a determined expression.

"You want to go to dinner with me?" she asked.

"This wasn't how I wanted to start things between us again." He motioned to the floor. "We're more than this." Ethan wrung the fingers of one hand around the wrist of the other, like it was sore. "I want to sleep, shower this awful day off me, and then I want to take the woman I love out to dinner. Someplace nice, where we can talk."

Juliet couldn't say anything. She physically felt as if her tongue were stuck to the roof of her mouth. Part of her had wanted to hear nothing but this since August—had wanted him to fight for her in August. A bigger part of her was tired of not being heard.

Ethan pushed off the floor and wrapped one hand around her waist, the other cupped her cheek. "Please, Juliet. Let me in again." He brushed his lips against hers, then held her.

"I can't tonight," she said into his cheek.

"Tomorrow then."

Juliet shook her head, butterflies welling in her stomach and fluttering up into her chest as she leaned back enough to look into his eyes. "I have a flight to Denver tonight."

Ethan frowned, but said, "You're going to see your sister."

"And spend Christmas with my parents."

"When you get back."

Juliet shook her head again and felt Ethan tense as he realized what she was going to say next.

"I'm not coming back."

His hold on her tightened, pressing her into his chest.

"What?" His voice broke.

"I'm spending Christmas in Goodland, then my sister is going to help me move into my new place."

"In Denver?"

Juliet didn't miss the anger and outrage in his voice. He'd never been good at hiding his emotions outside of the operating room.

"It's a little town about an hour and a half outside of Denver. I found a cottage on a mountain. I'm going to have to get an SUV, and I'm a little terrified of bears, but I got the job I wanted, and I start the second week of January.

"You're leaving?"

Juliet pushed against his chest, and he dropped his arms, shock written all over his face.

"I'm helping start a midwifery program in connection with three different rural hospitals. I'm going to train a team to do home births safely since not everyone can get to the hospital in time, especially in the winter."

Juliet trailed off as Ethan's stance changed from shocked and confused to betrayed and angry. His fists clenched, and his jawline went rigid as his chest heaved with his heavy breaths.

"You're going to live in the middle of nowhere, by yourself, so you can put yourself in danger to deliver country babies during snowstorms?"

"If I have to."

"Why has no one talked you out of this?" His voice rose with every word, and Juliet crossed her arms, taking a defensive stance.

"Everybody else has been supportive so far." Juliet let the implication that his lack of support was not appreciated hang in the air.

For a solid minute, he stared at her. He opened his mouth a few times but stopped himself. When he finally said, "You can't go," Juliet couldn't hold in her disdainful snort.

"I don't need your permission. I'm already going."

Then she left, slamming his office door behind her. Ethan didn't follow.

Juliet checked her phone as she as left the hospital hours later. Ethan hadn't left her any messages. The only reason Juliet got any sleep at all was because she'd been teetering on the edge of exhaustion for weeks. What sleep she did get was fitful. She dreamed that Ethan was in her bed, touching her, rubbing her, telling her that he loved her. But when Alex knocked on her door and told her to get her butt in motion, Juliet was alone, and there was still no word from Ethan.

Chapter Twenty-Two

"I can't believe you had sex in his office," Alex said for at least the fifth time on the way to the airport.

Juliet bristled at the glee in Alex's voice. "I'm glad you're excited about it."

"What I want to know is why aren't you?"

"Did you not hear the rest of the story?"

Alex took one hand off the wheel to brush off Juliet's disgust. "Yeah, yeah, yeah, Lover Boy's gone all territorial because you're leaving, and the only way he knows how to deal with it is to revert to a caveman. But *you've* been pining after him for weeks."

Juliet crossed her arms over her chest. She had not been pining. It had seemed natural, after she and Alex had made up to at least try to clear the air with Ethan. But, he'd been on vacation, and Juliet had tried to respect that. Not calling him had been agony. She'd thought school would keep her plenty busy, but it mostly kept her exhausted and longing for the easy comfort of waking up in Ethan's arms.

"I've not been pining," Juliet said aloud.

Alex snorted.

"He tried to tell me I couldn't go," Juliet said. She still could not believe his audacity. She had been so excited to see him and to talk to him and share her news. While she'd known he'd be sad to see her go, she'd hoped that maybe they could settle into a place where he could be happy for her.

Perhaps it was foolish to hope that they could at least be friends, because today had been a disaster.

"But you didn't listen to him," Alex said like that was all that needed saying.

"And where did he get the idea that we were going to just pick up where we left off in August?" Juliet asked. "We never even talked about that."

"It makes sense. The only thing keeping you apart was school. That's over. Why not?"

"That is not the only reason," Juliet said.

"You're not still mad at him because of me?"

"Of course not."

Things had been better since Thanksgiving, but Juliet was still relieved to be leaving. She and Alex had been so close for so long, maybe they needed a little time now to grow separately.

Packing up her suitcase to leave their little apartment had felt more like growing up than leaving her parent's house at eighteen had.

"Then why?" Alex asked.

"He doesn't think I can do my job."

"He just doesn't want you to do your job in Colorado."

"Then he doesn't think I *should* do my job."

"I'm confused. Isn't watching you work one of the things that got his attention in the first place?"

"As a nurse," Juliet said. "As his nurse."

"He wants to hire you?"

Juliet explained his parents and how he and his brothers idolized their father, and how their mother had been their father's nurse for years. "Ethan wants what his parents had, what his brothers have, and I'm just the warm body he wants to fill the role."

"One, I think you're wrong about the warm body part. And two, you guys jumped each other's bones the second you were alone together. That says something." Alex sighed after she spoke.

"Huh-uh. No. It was not romantic. It was desperate and sad and completely inappropriate."

"But it still happened."

Juliet stared at her hands in her lap. Tears welled. She did not want to cry in front of Alex. She needed to be alone before she gave into her grief and frustration. She needed to be away from Ethan, away from Rich, away from Kansas City and all the bad memories. Even away from Alex.

"Do you really regret it?" Alex asked.

Juliet shook her head. Seeing him, holding him, kissing him had been exquisite, but now she felt the pain of losing Ethan all over again coupled with the shame she felt in going in to comfort him and taking her own frustrations out on him instead. "It's not who I want to be."

"Then who do you want to be, Juliet Hawthorne?" Alex patted Juliet's knee.

"I'm hoping the answer to that is in Colorado."

It was after midnight when Juliet's plane landed in Denver. That didn't stop Colleen from greeting Juliet with a more enthusiastic hug then Juliet had ever remembered them sharing. Colleen was shorter and curvier than Juliet, but they shared the same green eyes and freckled noses. Colleen's blonde bun tickled Juliet's nose throughout their hug, and it was annoying and fantastic all at the same time.

"I'm so glad you're finally here," her sister said as she led her out to the parking garage, babbling the whole way about the lineup of activities she had planned for the week—mainly shopping, for Christmas and for Juliet's new place. "Of course, I still have work until Friday, but I figure you can take the time to explore or you know," Colleen's eyes examined Juliet in the dim light of the parking garage, "sleep."

"Do I look that bad?"

Colleen shrugged. "It's the middle of the night, what do I know?"

It was a thirty-minute drive to Colleen's apartment from the airport. Colleen didn't need Juliet for conversation, starting with her critique of the creepy charger statue just outside the airport, and ending with a thorough description of the guy she met over Thanksgiving weekend, stopping not quite far enough outside the bedroom door of that encounter for Juliet's comfort.

"But listen to me," Colleen said, glancing quickly enough at Juliet that the blonde curls escaping from her bun bounced in the moonlight. "Here I am going on and on about Devon and I haven't even asked about Ethan. Did you guys get a chance to say goodbye?"

Juliet snorted, and pretended to pick a piece of lint off her glove.

"I haven't been around you enough to know what that means," Colleen said. "Is that good, bad? It's bad right? Did he do something stupid, or did you?"

"We both did."

Colleen was silent, and Juliet kept her eyes on the passing streetlights.

After a minute of quiet, Colleen tapped the steering wheel. "Okay, I can't handle the suspense. You can't say something like that and then not spill. What happened?"

Juliet gave her sister a brief explanation of what had transpired almost twenty-four hours ago.

"Um, wow," Colleen said when Juliet finished. "So, you slept with him without telling him you were leaving, and then you didn't even tell him goodbye?"

"*That's* what you took away from that story? That I screwed him over?"

"Didn't you?"

Juliet crossed her arms and huffed, remembering why she and her sister had barely spoken for years. "I didn't go there to sleep with him," Juliet said. "I went there because I care about him, and I knew he would be upset."

"So, you made him think you were emotionally and physically available, and the second you get his hopes up, you dash them in the worst way. It's kind of cruel is all I'm saying."

Juliet straightened in her seat. "Did you miss the part about him telling me I wasn't allowed to leave?"

"No." The nonchalance in Colleen's voice made Juliet want to hit something, and she took deep breaths in and out through her nose to calm her temper as Colleen kept speaking. "But I'm guessing he was shocked and didn't mean it that way. He's never been the most articulate guy, right?"

"Right," Juliet said as Colleen turned into a parking lot outside a shabby looking building in Lakewood.

"I'm sorry," Colleen said as she cut the engine and put a hand that looked almost identical to Juliet's, thin and long-fingered on her shoulder. "I know you're hurting too. You gonna be okay?"

Juliet attempted, and failed, to smile. "I will be."

By the time Juliet was tucked into the hide-a-bed in Colleen's living room, Juliet couldn't turn her tears off, but like she'd found Ethan the day before, she couldn't sob and shudder, only weep silently.

JULIET HADN'T CALLED, not even to let him know she was safely settled in. Of course, not clarifying that he didn't want her to go because he wanted to marry her instead of telling her she flat out couldn't go probably didn't put him on Juliet's list of people to stay in touch with. Ethan had tried to call her once, just after the new year, but her line had been disconnected. Now he had no way to contact her at all. Ethan hadn't quite got up the courage to ask Alex yet, hence why he was on the rowing machine again after a twenty-four-hour shift at the hospital. He should be dead on his feet, but he'd been host to a sort of raw, anxious energy that wouldn't let him rest since Juliet left.

On top of missing Juliet, his hours at the hospital were plagued with worry over the patients under his care. He was double and triple checking every symptom. He was being such a hard ass, that nurses had started switching their shifts to try to avoid him.

Ethan didn't care. He wasn't going to lose anyone else.

When he showed up to Logan's for the super bowl party the first weekend of February, Ethan did not want to be there. He smiled for his cousins and listened to the story of Logan's office manager's daughter's college search, but he was so worn out that all he really wanted was a beer and to watch the game in peace.

He wound up sitting in the back row behind his niece and two of her friends, who were playing with their phones and alternating between whispering and giggling. Something about one of the apps they kept scrolling through nagged at him until he recognized Instagram. Juliet posted on Instagram.

He'd downloaded the app over the summer and followed her, but he hadn't opened it in months. When he opened the app now, Juliet was smiling back at him. She was almost naked—from the waist up anyway. She wore a sports bra and posed between two similarly clad women, one of whom was heavily pregnant. The caption invited him to skip the super bowl and join them for a night of yoga and meditation followed by refreshments (prenatal modifications included).

The next photo showed a dusky, snowy, mountain scene, and the one after that the same scene in shining daylight. There was a picture of her old heap of a car stuck in the snow, just after a photo of a new pair of mittens she'd knit herself. The photos alternated between knitting, mountain scenes, and yoga selfies. Two or three were selfies of herself at coffee shops or bakeries, or bars as she found places she liked in her new hometown. Ethan lost track of how long he'd been scrolling when he came across a photo of her standing in front of her mirror in a black pencil skirt and flowy yellow blouse with a wide smile on her face. The caption read, *My first day as a CNM for Ski Valley Health. Don't worry, the scrubs are in my bag, just in case. #firstday #midwivesdoitbetter*

Further down there were pictures of her new house as she settled in, and shots of herself in Denver. There was one gorgeous photo of Juliet and her sister with their heads together, both grinning like they'd just done something mischievous. Colleen's features were softer than Juliet's, and her face-framing blonde curls almost made her look angelic, but the sisters shared the same discerning green eyes. Her gaze so sharp, it was like Juliet could watch him through the phone, and he felt that same pull just behind his navel that he felt every time she walked into a room.

He had just run a thumb over the little heart to like the photo when Paige said over his shoulder, "Ah, ah, ah, Facebook stalking the ex is not allowed."

Then Paige plunked into the chair next to his, slopping some of the white wine in her glass over the rim.

"It's not Facebook," Ethan said, locking his phone and sliding it into his pocket.

"Same principal," Paige giggled. "Have you talked to her since she left?"

"She doesn't want to talk to me," he said.

Paige tsked. "Now how do you know that if you haven't asked?"

Ethan raised his eyebrows at his sister-in-law. "Have you spoken with her?"

"We trade emails every couple of weeks."

His eyebrows rose higher.

"What?" Paige asked and took a prim sip of her wine. "Just because you two broke up doesn't mean we did."

Ethan allowed silence to fall between them as he turned his attention to the game, but he could still feel Paige watching him. "Come on," she nudged him with her elbow. "Ask me."

"It's nonc of my business," Ethan said. It's what he'd been telling himself about not knowing her number. If she'd wanted him to know, she would have texted him when she changed it.

"You're allowed to still care about her, you know."

Of course, he knew. But he wanted to stop. Ethan wanted to toss his feelings for Juliet into a forgotten room, turn the light off and lock the door behind him. But he couldn't. He'd done his best to tamp down his worry and hurt over the last few weeks but seeing that Instagram feed had resurrected all his fears and anger and anxiety over her moving. Seeing her car stalled in snow past her wheel wells had made him want to curse. If the photo caption hadn't been lighthearted, he might be halfway to Colorado already.

"How is she?" He asked.

Paige smiled at him, and he thought the sadness he couldn't keep from his eyes reflected in the turn of her lips. "She's happy in some ways. She likes her job, and she's found a small yoga studio to work with."

"But?"

"She's lonely," Paige's smile turned brighter. "She hasn't said as much, but she misses you."

Ethan must have looked skeptical, because Paige's grin turned feline. "She asked about you. Said she was worried about you."

A dry laugh escaped his lips. Why would Juliet be worried about him. More like she felt guilty for leaving the way she did.

"I told her you were grumpier than usual, and she said she was thinking about getting a dog."

Ethan wished he had the ability to raise just one eyebrow, he would do it right now if he could. "This was the same conversation?"

Paige continued as if his half of the current conversation didn't matter. "And I couldn't help thinking that you have a dog."

Too late, Ethan realized he was caught in a trap, one he should have spotted the second Paige sat down. "It's mom's dog," he said.

Paige's dubious look told him how flimsy an excuse that was. The dog hadn't been his mom's for almost two years.

"Juliet fell in love with Camille," Paige said. "From how much she talked about her the couple times we got together, I almost thought she liked the dog more than she liked you."

Ethan couldn't help the bark of a laugh. Paige wasn't wrong, Juliet had adopted Camille, saying repeatedly how she'd never imagined she'd like having a little dog. Juliet had taken over feeding her, had brought her new toys, had started letting her sleep on his bed, something Ethan had never allowed before, but which he was now powerless to put an end to.

"I think Camille liked Juliet better than me too."

Paige nudged him again and waggled her eyebrows, "So maybe you should take her for a visit."

This time, Ethan's laugh had no buoyancy, but fell out of his lips like a stone to the floor. "I can't afford to take any time off right now."

Until that moment, Paige's tone had been light and teasing, but her eyes narrowed, and she set her wine glass on the floor. "For fuck's sake, Ethan. You've been miserable with missing Juliet, and you're going to choose your job over her?"

"She chose her job over me," he said. And when Paige's scowl deepened, he added, "I haven't been miserable."

"Take a look around," Paige gestured. The room was nearly empty, despite the game still playing on the projector, and those few who were left, his brothers and Vanessa, were crowded in the front row of seats with their heads together. "Me sitting down next to you was a signal for the rest of the guests to clear out to the living room for a while." Then she called the others over.

When Ethan looked confusedly between the four of them, Logan sat down on his other side. "We think you should go to Colorado," he said.

Ethan opened his mouth to object, but Henry said, "You can be an OB-GYN anywhere, and Juliet is in Colorado."

"No brainer," Vanessa said.

"You guys want to get rid of me that bad?" He didn't know what else to say. He didn't think he'd been outwardly behaving badly enough to warrant an intervention, but that was exactly what was happening. Though it felt more like his family was kicking him out.

"If you're going to continue being a surly, grumpy ass all the time, then yes," Henry said.

"And we think you will be until you make things right with Juliet," Paige said.

"And if she doesn't want me either?"

"Then you'll be all set up to start over," Logan patted Ethan on the shoulder with one hand and grabbed Vanessa's hand with the other. "And we'll finally have an excuse to go skiing every year."

Ethan let them talk for another few minutes, promising to give the idea some thought. Truthfully, he hadn't thought of the possibility. Moving had never been in the cards, his family was here, but when his mother pulled him aside just after the game ended, Ethan ran out of excuses.

"What are you going to do?" she asked him. She didn't have to explain herself.

Ethan shook his head. "I'll have to give it some more thought."

"Do you want my advice?"

"You've always given it whether I wanted it or not."

That earned him an amused grin. Then his mother laid a hand on his shoulder. "You're not a coward. You never have been. And I think if you don't take this chance, you'll always regret it."

"But you don't like Juliet," he said.

"It doesn't matter how I feel about her. It matters how you feel, and I hate seeing you so miserable when you deserve to be happy."

"You think Juliet will make me happy?"

"You loved living in Colorado before."

Ethan smiled for the first time all night. "Yeah. I did."

"Then you should go. We're not going anywhere. We'll always be here when you need us." She patted his cheek and walked away.

Driving home and getting ready for bed happened in a blur. Ethan didn't remember any of it as he puzzled out what his family had said. He vacillated between disbelief that he had been so noticeably unpleasant and outrage that they thought him moving away was a better solution than him sticking it out and getting over it, which had been his plan since Christmas, even if it was slow going.

He came back to himself as he sat down on his bed, and Camille followed him, settling down into her spot at the foot of the bed on what had been Juliet's side. Instead of plugging his phone in, Ethan opened Instagram and snapped a grainy photo of a sad and sleepy looking poodle. He captioned it, "She misses you."

It was the only photo on his feed, and he only had one follower, so there was no question who it was Camille missed.

Then Ethan plugged his phone in, turned out the lamp, and spent the night tossing from one side to the other as he tried to remind himself that his family wasn't kicking him out of town because they didn't like him.

In the morning, groggy and irritable from his intermittent sleep, Ethan picked up his phone to find a notification from Instagram. Juliet had liked his photo and commented, "I miss her too."

Chapter Twenty-Three

J uliet's car was stalled in the snow again. She was supposed to go shopping for an SUV with her sister in Denver over the weekend, but that was no help to her now. How was she supposed to make it to her client's house when she couldn't get out of her own driveway?

So far, the snow hadn't been bad. Though she lived in ski country, she lived far enough down the mountain that the roads were normally cleared quickly. But it had snowed ten inches overnight and her neighbor with the snow blower, was off on a snowboarding trip. Until her car got stuck, Juliet had been relieved. Dirk was nice, but he wasn't shy about voicing his ulterior motives.

During her first six weeks in Colorado, Juliet had never felt so free, nor so lonely. She'd never been someplace before where she knew literally no one. True her sister was in Denver, but that was almost two hours away. This was the kind of town where everyone knew everyone else and a good number of the people in the surrounding tiny towns. Which made it even more awkward, because everyone seemed to know who she was before she introduced herself, making it more difficult for Juliet to remember who she had and had not met yet.

She'd made a few new friends at the little yoga studio she was teaching at. Still, that was only one class per week, and there hadn't been time for more than a coffee date or two with the couple of women she'd clicked with there.

Juliet had also gotten to know a couple of local doctors, both general practice clinicians, but those were professional relationships. She had yet to speak with either of them about anything outside of work, even if Dr. Stevens, who did have the silver fox thing going for him, had given her more than a few meaningful glances. Juliet had ignored the looks. She was through dating doctors, especially ones she worked with.

While she technically worked out of the hospital that was forty-five minutes away in the next county, and was part-nered with a doctor there, she mostly drove to where her patients were, whether at home or at their local doctor's office to consult. Her main duty was to aid with labor and delivery. She'd already attended four births, and she was only getting started.

But work only took up so much of her day. She'd found the local coffee shop slash bakery and the local bar. She'd found the library and the hardware store. But when she couldn't go out with yoga friends, hanging out at the bar or the cafe by herself only seemed to bring her the kind of attention she didn't want. The dating pool in the area must be very, very small, because she had never been hit on this much in Kansas City. To avoid having to awkwardly decline strangers, Juliet was knitting herself a new winter wardrobe, because there were four majorly cute yarn shops within an hour of her new home.

Cursing, Juliet trudged back up to her garage to the re-trieve the snow shovel and attempted to clear a path for her little Toyota. The road didn't look much better than her dri-veway. She wasn't sure how far the snow plows would have made it that morning, and Juliet did not have a lot of time, but she had to try.

When Juliet had first moved, she'd had to get a new phone from a company that offered coverage in this rural area, because a working phone was essential, and her old one had shut down completely. A few minutes ago, Juliet had been drinking her coffee, checking to see if Ethan had posted anymore photos of Camille on Instagram when a call from one of the doctors she worked with, not the silver fox, had come in. One of his patients, whom Juliet knew through yoga was in labor with her first child and home by herself. Her husband was at work on the mountain at the ski resort. Could Juliet bring her to the hospital?

Juliet had agreed, thrown together her birth kit just in case, and come outside to find the mountain of snow in her driveway. Until that moment, she'd felt good about turning down her dad's offer to help her buy a car, but right now, she didn't have any time to spare. Giving up on digging herself out, Juliet scrolled through her phone, wondering who she could call. Did she know anyone in town well enough? Near-ly everyone drove a four-wheel drive of some sort, and now Juliet knew why. But the person Juliet knew best was the one in labor.

Just as she was about to toss her phone into the snow in frustration, she heard an engine coming down the street, and she hopped through the snow drifts until she was approximately where she guessed the curb was, waving her arms in the air, hoping the passerby was neither a psycho, nor in the hurry to get somewhere else.

ETHAN'S TRIP TO SEE Juliet had been fraught with setbacks. He'd followed a snowstorm all the way across Kansas, until they'd closed I-70 at Hays and Ethan had to try three almost full hotels before he found one that would allow Camille to stay with him overnight. After a restless night's sleep, Ethan was back on the road again by five am, when they opened the barricade. He's sped across the plains where the roads had been mostly clear until he got into the mountains. Juliet's town, which was only about twenty miles from Will's cabin, hadn't seen a snow plow when he pulled in just after eleven.

His GPS was spotty, but he managed to find her neighborhood, a series of small cottages separated by enough pine trees and space to make them feel isolated. He'd been counting the numbers on the mailboxes, expecting hers to be one or two cabins away when he rounded a curve and saw a woman decked out in winter gear waving her arms and running toward the car.

As he pulled over and parked, he realized that it was Juliet running toward him. Camille bounced and yapped in excitement, bounding across the passenger seat into Ethan's lap as Juliet crossed over to the driver side window.

She was talking before Ethan even had the window rolled down all the way. He'd been expecting her to ask a lot of questions, and frankly, to be a little pissed off, but she immediately launched into a story about how she was stuck in the snow and she was a midwife and she had a patient in labor. She wasn't looking at him but gesturing to her stuck car in the driveway a few yards ahead, and even Camille's excited yapping didn't derail her from her begging.

"She's only twenty minutes away," she was saying as her eyes finally shifted toward his. "And I know it's a lot to ask, but if you could just help me—" Her eyes grew wide and her words gave way to a confused scowl, but Ethan couldn't help but beam.

"Ethan?" she asked.

"Hey, Juliet."

She rested her hands on the open window. "What are you doing here?"

"We came to see you," Ethan said as Camille yapped and launched herself at Juliet. Ethan had to stop her from bounding out the window.

"Hey Camille," Juliet said, scratching the dog behind the ears. "You're a long way from home."

He watched Camille lick Juliet's face while Juliet tried to nuzzle the dog over the side of the truck, then he said, "So, you need a ride?"

Juliet stiffened and went pale, as if she'd forgotten all about her patient. "Holy shit, Shelby!"

Without another word, Juliet ran back toward her house, tossed a snow shovel in the front door and ran back toward the Cruiser with an old Samsonite suitcase bouncing against her legs.

"What's that?" He asked as she tossed it in the back.

"My go bag."

"Your what?"

"Pitocin, oxygen, gloves, chord clamp—my home birth kit, just in case."

"Right." Ethan was skeptical there was enough in the suitcase to make a difference, but he didn't push it. "Where are we going?"

He followed Juliet's directions, watching out of the corner of his eye as she checked her watched every time they hit a stop sign, but said nothing.

"How far is the hospital?" He asked.

"About thirty minutes away. I've already wasted so much time."

"I'm sure she's fine."

"But it's her first baby and she's home by herself. She shouldn't have to do this alone."

Ethan wondered if she was remembering her own loss, and how she'd had to handle so much of it alone.

"No, she shouldn't," Ethan said.

Neither one spoke again outside driving instructions until they were pulling up into the long driveway that wound up the side of the mountain to a large cabin Ethan could just make out through the trees. Juliet said, "I don't suppose it's too much to hope that you're here for a weekend on the slopes?"

Ethan had kept his fear that this was a gigantic mistake at bay until then, but her words confirmed his suspicions that despite liking and occasionally commenting on each other's Instagram shots, she did not want to see him. Juliet would probably rather ignore what was left between them than face it. But since his entire reason for coming was to convince her that he was there for her, he did his best to grin and say, "We can go skiing if you like."

He just caught Juliet shooting him a dubious frown out of the corner of his eye as they pulled up to what was not just a large cabin, but an enormous rustic-built house jutting out of the side of the mountain, with two whole walls of windows facing the peaks to the south. A pull in his gut that he'd only felt twice before, once when he was doing his first OB rounds in medical school, and once when he saw Juliet in action for the first time, he felt now as he looked up at the big house and slipped a leash on Camille.

"You go on," he said. "I'll be in—" he was going to say, he'd be in after the dog did her business, but Juliet was already trudging up the front steps to bang on the door. Juliet waited there longer than he anticipated, and he could just make out a dark-haired woman doubled over at the door. "Hurry up, Camille, we're working against the clock."

After being stuck in the car all morning, it didn't take Camille long, and though she pulled at her leash to explore in the trees, Ethan scooped her up and followed Juliet in the house in case the laboring woman needed help getting down the stairs. What he found was a heavily pregnant woman with black hair and olive skin laboring in a fluffy, powder blue bathrobe bent over the back of an expensive looking dove gray sofa.

Juliet's suitcase lay thrown open on the floor, and Juliet was on her knees beside the woman, gloves already on, doppler held to the woman's exposed belly.

Ethan tied Camille's leash to the table by the door, the marble top more than heavy enough to keep the dog out of their way. When he turned around again, Juliet was just lowering the back of the woman's robe, tucking the garment around her so that she was covered as her contraction ended.

Still leaning on the sofa, the woman said, "I don't think I can get dressed." The words were almost a sob.

Juliet rubbed the woman's back and smiled. "You're doing great, Shelby. But I think it's a little late to put clothes on."

Shelby's head cranked to the side and Ethan could see panic streak through her. "What?"

Juliet kept smiling and massaging the woman's lower back, "You're fully dilated, Shelby. Your baby's going to be here soon."

While Juliet's voice was all confidence and serenity, Ethan felt Shelby's panic pass out of her and right into him. His chest constricted, and he had trouble breathing. As if she could feel it happen, Juliet met his eyes and held, soothing him with only her demeanor. "Are you ready for your first home birth, Dr. Harvey?"

Shelby noticed Ethan for the first time and her hands automatically tried to pull her robe closed, but another contraction started, and it was clear that Juliet was right, Shelby was beyond caring that a strange man was in her home while she stood, nearly naked in her living room. Juliet stood with Shelby, speaking quietly until the contraction subsided, and Shelby looked back to Ethan again. "You're a doctor?"

Ethan nodded. This was the pregnant woman from the yoga photo on Juliet's Instagram. Ethan had spent more time than he cared to admit staring at that picture in the last few weeks. Shelby was easy to recognize now.

Juliet answered for him. "He's an OB, Shelby. A colleague of mine, who also happens to have a car that can drive through anything. He was kind enough to rescue me after my Toyota got stuck. So, lucky you, you get an OB and a midwife, seeing to your every need."

When another contraction hit, Juliet beckoned to Ethan and said as he neared, "I think this is where this is going to happen. Will you find some blankets and towels, nothing too nice if you can manage it, and I'll call the hospital and her husband to let them know what's going on. We don't have very long. "

Ethan nodded and started down the hall, looking for a linen closet and Juliet hollered after him, "And don't forget a mixing bowl for the placenta!"

He shook his head. This was crazy. They should be at the hospital, but despite his unease, Ethan agreed it was better to have the baby here where they could control the environment than in the car in the snow. That didn't stop Ethan from being terrified that something would go wrong, even when he returned with an armload of older looking blankets and scruffy towels and Juliet was again checking the baby's heart rate with the doppler, he could only think of all the ways this could go wrong and all the tools he didn't have to fix it.

"Did my husband say how far away he was?" Shelby asked.

"He'll be here soon, Shelby. Twenty minutes."

"Will he make it?" She asked and scrunched her face as another contraction came on.

"Breathe, Shelby. Breathe into the rushes. Vocalize if you need to. There you go, it's just like in yoga isn't it?"

Amazingly, the corners of Shelby's mouth picked up into a small smile and her shoulders relaxed as she took deep, hearty breathes in through her nose and gave a deep throaty moan as she exhaled out through her mouth.

"That's it," Juliet said. "That's it exactly." Juliet took the blankets from Ethan and started spreading them out on the floor between the back of the couch and the stairway. "She's a yoga instructor too," Juliet explained.

"Smart," Ethan said as he pushed an oriental runner rug to the side and straightened the corner of the blanket.

Juliet scooted a towel under Shelby's feet between contractions, explaining that it was so Shelby didn't slip on the hardwood if her water broke. Then she sat back and let her labor, offering encouragement, and checking her watch to time the contractions.

Ethan felt entirely useless. Everything he usually relied on monitors to read out, Juliet was keeping track of in her head.

Shelby had three more contractions standing behind the sofa, rocking her hips in time with her breath, and while Ethan wanted to ask her to lay down on the floor and rest, Juliet seemed content to let her stand. The gravity should help the baby descend, but as he thought it, he noticed a change in Shelby's stance, and the tail end of her vocalizing sounded more like a grunt than a groan.

Both he and Juliet looked from each other to Shelby and back again. "Was that a push?" Juliet asked with a wide smile.

Shelby looked frightened. "I don't know. Is that okay?"

"That's perfect. Are you still good standing, or do you want to try another position?"

"My legs are tired," Shelby said like she wasn't sure what to do about it.

Juliet helped Shelby recline against the back of the sofa, and positioned Ethan down at her feet, gloved and masked, so that Shelby could use him for counterbalance when she pushed and still keep her legs apart. Juliet prepared a few things from her kit, coaching Shelby the whole time to breathe down into the contraction, then push into her bottom. Whatever Shelby took Juliet's instructions to mean, it was working. He could see the baby descend just a little bit with each push.

"You're doing great," he said. His worry was ebbing as his natural need to nurture took over, even as his arms were starting to shake from the exertion. "Just a few more pushes and we'll have the head."

Juliet shot him a tight smile, but said to Shelby, "Did you hear that? Your baby's head is almost born. You're doing it, Shelby."

Ethan heard the difference in how she spoke to patients then, how it differed from the way he concentrated on outcomes and she centered all her words around the woman she was helping. He felt that pull in his gut again as he watched her hold Shelby's hand and reminding her to breathe again in a gentle voice, like she was her friend.

Juliet was built for this.

A bang sounded from somewhere deep within the house. A voice called "Shelby!" three times and footsteps sounded on the stairs.

"We're in the living room!" Ethan called, and a tall blonde man with a red nose sprinted into the room.

Shelby smiled and reached toward him with the hand that had been holding Juliet's. "Is everything okay?" he asked, eyeing Ethan.

Juliet gave up her spot next to Shelby. "Everything's great, Dad. You're just in time." She motioned toward Ethan. "This is Doctor Harvey, a colleague of mine."

The father-to-be only nodded and squeezed his wife's hand as another contraction started. Juliet nudged Ethan out of the way and took one leg. Pressing not just against Shelby's foot, but also her thigh, opening the woman's hips more, and Ethan followed her example.

In two more pushes, the baby's head was out, and Ethan took over holding Shelby's legs so Juliet could make sure the cord wasn't around the baby's neck and check it's shoulders. She gave Ethan a look, and he nodded. Of all the things he had thought could go wrong, shoulder dystocia was one of the milder, but no less serious. When Shelby failed to budge the shoulders, Juliet told her to stop pushing if she could.

Ethan itched to jump in but had worked with young doctors often enough to know to give them a chance. He checked his watch, deciding he'd give her two minutes, and then he was taking over. The fact that his Colorado medical license was still in the mail be damned. There were a couple of maneuvers that had never failed him. He expected Juliet to instruct him and the father to hold Shelby's legs back further, but instead, Juliet told them to help Shelby up on her hands and knees, while calmly explaining that they needed just a little bit more room to get the baby out.

They maneuvered her up between contractions, while Juliet supported the baby's head. As the next contraction started, Juliet applied pressure to the back of the pelvis, and the baby slipped into Juliet's arms. She took half a second to beam at him, then told them to help Shelby get comfortable.

When Shelby was reclined on the couch cushions, Juliet laid the baby on Shelby's chest and covered them both with a towel, then a light blanket, talking the whole time about what an amazing job the woman did and how great the baby was doing. Ethan watched the baby's breathing and color, which wasn't bad, but wasn't great either, but after a few minutes of rubbing and talking and being warmed by the towel, the baby looked pink and healthy. Ethan finally allowed his muscles to relax.

After another few minutes of watching the new family, Juliet asked, "What kind of baby do you have?"

Shelby and her husband laughed before peeking under the blanket, having forgotten all about the sex, and came up beaming. "It's a girl!" And they laughed some more because they didn't have a girl's name picked out yet. They hadn't been able to agree on one.

After Shelby delivered the placenta, Ethan examined the organ while Juliet took care of the stitching from a small tear, not nearly as large as the episiotomy he might have given her for the shoulder dystocia. And when the bleeding was a little heavier than he would have liked to see, Juliet gave Shelby a shot of Pitocin without any prompting from him.

The family's regular doctor arrived after they'd moved Shelby and the baby up to the bedroom, and Ethan helped Juliet clean up the towels, dousing everything with peroxide and throwing it in the washing machine. After Juliet filled out a small mountain of paperwork, they wished the new family well, collected Camille, who was asleep under the end table, and were on their way.

It was all Ethan could do to keep the grin off his face. It was his typical post-birth high, but this time heightened by Juliet's presence and poise. The way she handled herself, she might have been at this profession longer than he had. It was all he could do as the pulled away from the cabin to keep his eyes on the road and not sit back and be dazzled by her.

Chapter Twenty-Four

Juliet dragged herself up into Ethan's giant car and had never been more exhausted. The adrenaline rush had worn off, and while Juliet was proud of how well she'd handled her first home birth and her first case of shoulder dystocia, she hoped not every birth would be so dramatic.

Ethan had yet to say anything but was grinning like an idiot. Juliet had seen this before though. It's how he always acted after a good shift. She half expected him to suggest lunch at Dino's. Juliet so didn't have the energy for that. Her limbs had started to quake, she was so tired.

"Do you remember the way back?" she asked as she slumped against the window.

Camille curled into Juliet's lap, and Juliet buried her hand in the familiar bouncy white curls. She'd missed this dog so much.

"I think so. We're not far from where a friend of mine has a cabin."

"Is that where you're staying?"

He shifted his eyes to meet hers for a moment, and the reverie from the birth was gone. All that was left was a sad resignation.

"The cabin is available to me should I need it."

All day, Juliet had been hoping that perhaps him driving down her street was some cosmic coincidence. But she knew him better than that.

"Why didn't you tell me you were coming?"

"You would have told me not to."

"It would have saved you some time and money if I had." When he didn't say anything in answer, Juliet couldn't help but ask, "Is the hospital okay with you taking time off again so soon?"

"I'm not at the hospital anymore."

The words fell casually from Ethan's mouth, like he had said the sun was warm or the breeze was pleasant, but Juliet's neck popped she swiveled around so fast. "You're what?"

"I quit. My last day was Wednesday."

"Have you lost your mind?"

"It was a sound, well thought-out decision"

"You don't quit a job you love if you're sound of mind."

Ethan shook his head minutely. "I can do my job any-where. And the only place I want to be is where you are."

Juliet didn't let that comment sink in. He'd been saying the same thing for six months. "What makes you think I want you around?"

"I'm not giving up on us."

Juliet had nothing to say to that and turned her head to look out the window again. Ethan was silent until he turned onto her street when he said, "You were brilliant today. I'm grateful for the chance to see you in action."

"Flattery and grand gestures won't work on me."

"I've always admired how you work with patients," he said as he pulled into her driveway and parked behind her stuck car. "I want to be with you. Work with you."

That was when Juliet lost her hold on trying to be nice. She calmly placed a quick peck on the top of Camille's head before handing her back to Ethan. Then she allowed the cold void of the last few months to overcome her. "I don't want to be your nurse, Dr. Harvey. I am not the fulfillment of some boyhood fantasy of your perfect assistant. I am my own person with my own goals and my own needs. I deserve to be treated as more than a trophy for you or anyone else." Juliet got out of the car. "And if I have to move another ten hours away from you to find some peace, then I will."

She slammed the door, trudged through the snow with all the outrage she could muster, and locked her cabin door behind her. It was only as she slid to the floor, sitting in a puddle of melted snow from her new snow boots did she realize that she'd left her birth kit in Ethan's car—right as she heard him pull away.

Two hours and a good cry later, Juliet heard the scrape of a snow shovel in her driveway as she exited her bathroom where she'd hoped a long, hot shower would help wash away the evidence of the tears spilt over Ethan. When she peeked through the window, expecting to see her flirtatious snowboarding neighbor, she almost choked on her coffee when she saw Ethan had already shoveled out half her drive.

SHOVELING SNOW WHILE angry was almost better than rowing. Ethan made good time on Juliet's driveway, and he was able to stew in his fury over Juliet's dismissal. When he heard the door open and footsteps on her old wooden porch, he didn't look up. He'd started at the garage she apparently didn't use and was backing his way to where her little Toyota was stuck in drift.

He'd gone to Will's cabin, showered, and returned. His stomach was growling after skipping lunch, and he was stiff from spending most of the last two days in the car. He wasn't supposed to be spending his time here in exile. He was supposed to at least be able to grovel, but instead of saying, "I love you, please give us a chance. Let me take you out to dinner and convince you," when Juliet appeared on her porch to wordlessly watch him work, he looked up at her and half-shouted. "You need a snowblower, and something with four-wheel drive if you're going to live on a damn mountain."

"I won't use gasoline on something I can do just as easily by hand."

"But you're not shoveling the snow. I am."

"Nobody asked you to do it."

Ethan lowered the shovel to see Juliet standing on her porch with a mug of coffee in her hands. She wore the same purple snow boots she'd had on earlier and a big, boxy, gray sweater that fell off one shoulder to reveal a pink bra strap. He knew that bra. He knew how well the hot pink color contrasted against her creamy skin and red hair. The ache of missing her hit him in the gut again. The realization that she was right there, not twenty feet away, and he still wasn't allowed to hold her gnawed at his empty stomach worse than the hunger pains.

He sighed. "I couldn't leave and just let you be trapped."

"I would have gotten to it already, but it was supposed to be my day off," she said.

"Right," Ethan said, and didn't miss Juliet flipping him off as she sipped her coffee. He lowered the shovel again, chuckling. Just like that, his anger was replaced with amusement and longing.

"I made some coffee," she said. "Come in and warm up when you're done with that." Then she disappeared into the house.

While Ethan thought that maybe, she could have offered to help him with the shovel she'd thrown inside earlier, he also knew she was trying to make peace.

When he'd finished her driveway, Ethan cleaned off her car, then let Camille out of the Cruiser to do her business. He carried the dog and her food into the house for fear of the tiny white dog getting lost in the snow.

The inside of Juliet's little cottage was starker than he expected, as though she hadn't finished moving in. There was the furniture he'd seen on Instagram, all in tones of gray and blue, but the white walls were mostly bare, and the wood floor lacked the cozy rugs and tropical plants from the apartment she'd shared with Alex. There was a basket of yarn in the corner, a bowl of oranges and grapefruit on the counter in the kitchen. The smell of the strong coffee Juliet favored wafted throughout.

Juliet stood in the kitchen, washing dishes to music she played in her headphones, hooked up to the phone in her pocket. Her hips swayed in time to the beat only she could hear, but she didn't sing, and he wished she would, if only so he knew what she was listening to. He remembered her making fun of his Foo Fighters and Nirvana, but he didn't remember anything that she liked, and had the sudden desire to remedy that.

Juliet had set a clean mug out by the coffee pot, and he watched her hips twist, and remembered the night she'd lead him on the dance floor at Tokyo Nights. He wanted to wrap his arms around her waist and match his hips to her rhythm, letting her lead him into music he couldn't even hear, but instead he leaned back against her stove to watch her dance while he sipped at his coffee.

It was Camille that eventually gained Juliet's attention by jumping up on her hind legs and pawing at Juliet's knees. Juliet dried her hands and scooped the little dog into her arms, and almost walked right into Ethan. She tore the earbuds out of her ears, revealing what he thought was Beyoncé.

"Sorry," she said, and tried to dart around him, but his hands wrapped around her waist and she didn't fight as he drew her near, sandwiching Camille between them.

Juliet froze in his embrace, stiffening with obvious discomfort, and Ethan loosened his hold, but couldn't make himself stop touching her. The sweater was soft, and his fingers could feel the warmth of it as they traced her waist from back to front, then smoothed his fingertips over the curve of her slender hips.

"Did you knit your sweater?" he asked, even though he knew from her pictures that she did.

Ethan used his question as an excuse to keep touching her, and wasn't surprised when she nodded, and said, "I just finished it."

"It looks great," he said.

Juliet raised her bare shoulder, and Ethan actively fought the urge to kiss his way along her collarbone as she said, "I don't have anything else to do after work."

Camille squirmed between them, and Ethan finally stepped back so Juliet could put the dog down. Looking for something to do with her hands, Juliet refilled his coffee and was holding it out to him before he'd even taken his eyes off the dog.

"You look cold," was all Juliet said.

Ethan was anything but cold. Between the exertion of shoveling snow and the exhilaration of being in her presence, Ethan was pretty sure he could fry an egg on his skin. He took a sip of the hot beverage anyway.

"I've missed your coffee," he said.

"I taught you how to make it." Her words were dry, but a small smile played at the corner of her mouth as she looked at him over the fresh cup of coffee she'd just poured for herself.

"Yes, but I miss drinking it with you."

For the first time that day, Juliet really looked at him, parka hanging open, old jeans, old boots, and the new North Face he'd gotten for Christmas. Her gaze lingered on his chest, as she said, "Do you want some pie?"

Ethan's eyebrows rose and something that had been frozen at the core of him started to melt. "You have pie?"

Juliet nodded and pulled a pie plate from her refrigerator. She pulled the foil back to reveal a homemade, half-eaten peach pie.

That frozen core turned molten in the space of a heartbeat and Ethan laughed. "Where did you find peaches in February?"

"There's an orchard about an hour away. I went there for honey, but they had canned pie filling from last summer and . . ." Juliet shrugged her bare shoulder again as she trailed off.

Ethan tried, and failed, to school his grin. "But you don't like peach pie."

Juliet didn't say anything as she dished out a large piece of pie and handed it to him. He waited for her to meet his eyes before he accepted the plate. And Juliet made a scoffing noise in her throat at his wide smile. "Okay, so I missed you. Sue me."

"How about you let me take you out to dinner." Ethan set his mug aside to dig into Juliet's pie, then said around the sweet mouthful, "We can talk."

Juliet shifted her weight from one foot to the other. "I haven't had a lot of luck finding any good vegetarian options around here yet."

Ethan's grin returned the second he swallowed. "I know a bar. On the other side of the mountain. They make one hell of a black bean burger."

Juliet perked up, her shoulders straightening, her eyes brightening.

"The sweet potato fries are good too."

Juliet set her mug by the sink, then in a move he hadn't expected of her, she stood toe-to-toe with him. She set his plate aside with one hand, the other cupped his jaw, her fingernails lightly scraping through his beard, as she lanced him with searching green eyes. He wasn't certain what she was looking for, but he held her gaze, even as her touch bolt-ed through him like lightning. The desire he'd been staving off all day surged, but as he reached for her, Juliet slipped through his arms, and said, "What are we waiting for? I'm starving."

ETHAN DROVE HER TO a bar she hadn't found yet, though it was in the same town as the main hospital she was based out of. This town was bigger than the little village where her cabin was, and she hadn't spent much time explor-ing it because everything on the main streets looked tailored to tourists. She hadn't made it to the side streets yet, where this bar was hidden behind a bike rental place. It shared a parking lot with a rundown bowling alley.

Ethan helped her out of the car like he'd always done, then led her inside by the hand and up to the only two empty stools at the bar like he'd had them reserved. The bartender appeared immediately. She was a pretty woman in red buf-falo plaid that matched the rustic decor. She wore her long, wavy black hair pulled back in a ponytail and smiled all the way up to her olive-green eyes when she spotted Ethan. A pang of jealousy coursed through Juliet's veins. How well did these two know each other, exactly?

"Didn't take you long to make it back, Harvey," the pret-ty woman said as they both shrugged off their coats.

"Be back for a while, I hope," he said, then, wrapping his arm around Juliet's shoulders. "Marney, this is Juliet. Juliet, Marney."

If Juliet hadn't been paying quite so close attention, she might have missed the slight bulging in the bartender's eyes. The pretty woman held out a hand and said, "It's nice to meet you." She gave Juliet's hand one brisk shake and turned to Ethan and said, "I've got a local Saison on that I think you'll like."

"Perfect. Juliet?"

She had expected Ethan to order for her but appreciated that he didn't. "Gimlet, please. Double. And a menu."

When Juliet had her drink and her menu, she leaned into Ethan, not so much that she was touching him, but close enough to feel the warmth of his body through her sweater. The heat made her want to touch him. She wanted to snake her arms around his neck and crawl up into his lap, twining her legs around him like she might climb a tree. "Should I be worried about how well you know this bartender?"

"Are you jealous?"

Juliet sat back, purposefully turning her attention back to her menu as she took the first sip of her drink. "Mostly wondering if you've turned into a drunk while we've been apart."

Ethan chuckled, and told her more about his friend Will and his divorce, and how Ethan babysat him while he picked up women that were too young for him.

"You mean women who are my age?" Juliet asked, because she was never going to let him off that easy, even if she'd decided to be nice for today. He had driven all the way out here to see her. That he'd quit his job and had essentially offered to move here for her was something she wasn't ready to deal with yet.

Ethan was saved from answering when Marney returned to take their dinner orders. Juliet got her veggie burger and was relieved when Ethan ordered a regular burger. Him going vegetarian would have been a step too far, though she liked the idea of him ordering the black bean burger and sweet potato fries while thinking of her. She didn't mind a man who was a little sappy.

While they ate, they chatted about what Juliet's work had been like so far, what the hospitals were like, how much driving she did, and how she was making enough money to squeak by but hoped to prove her worth over the next year.

Ethan frowned at that and dipped four fries at once into his ketchup. "You should be making more money than that."

Juliet only shrugged as she downed the last of her drink, and asked Marney, who was nearby, but not hovering, for another. "I'm not bothered by it," Juliet said to Ethan. "I don't have much experience, and part of the reason there aren't enough people out here is that they can't afford to pay anyone."

Unable to talk with his mouth full, Ethan made a disgusted noise in the back of his throat and shook his head. After swallowing his food and a large gulp of beer, Ethan said, "Did you check the job listings for the hospital you work at before you moved?"

Juliet shook her head.

"Well, I did. They're offering about a hundred thou less a year than I was making for the same job in KC."

Juliet knew she looked confused. One hundred thousand dollars was a lot of money. More than she'd ever seen, or probably ever would see. "That's a huge pay cut," she said.

Ethan shrugged. "And still far more than I need, even after insurance."

"Did you take a job here already?" Juliet asked.

"I have an interview." Ethan shrugged. "So, I know the money's there. And yeah, maybe other assholes have been deterred by it being less than in the bigger cities, but that's no reason for them to give you such a bum deal."

"I like what I'm doing."

"I know, and you're good at it. Too good at it to be barely getting by, especially when they need someone like you around here."

Juliet's heart skipped a beat. Was he complimenting her work? Trying to play cool, she sipped at her new drink and asked, "Oh?"

Ethan wiped his hands and propped an arm on the back of her stool. "Of course, they do. What would have happened to that woman if you hadn't been here to drive to her. Her doctor wasn't going to do it. They would have sent an ambulance who may or may not have gotten there in time, and I can guarantee EMTs are not equipped to handle shoulder dystocia."

"I prefer not thinking in what-ifs," Juliet said, shuddering against the idea of Shelby having lost her baby.

"And I prefer handling births in a hospital, but that doesn't mean I don't recognize that you are worth your weight in gold out here."

Juliet cracked a small smile, and with it, she felt a little bit of the shell she'd closed around herself when it came to Ethan start to crack a little too. "So, you're saying I should ask for more money."

"And a mountain appropriate vehicle."

"I am not asking for a car."

"Why not? You just said you drive for work all the time, and you need something that's not going to get stuck in the snow."

"Any car can get stuck in the snow."

Ethan's answer was a set jaw to match his dubious expression. It was spoiled when a lock of too long hair spilled into his eyes, making him look young and petulant.

Juliet laughed, and pushed the hair off his forehead. "Don't worry, Colleen is taking me car shopping next weekend."

Ethan caught Juliet's hand by her wrist, holding her palm to his cheek, and she had to stop herself again from crawling up into his lap and digging both hands into his dark hair.

His eyes were alight as he said, "Good, I've always wanted to meet your sister." Then he kissed her palm, released her hand, and went back to his meal.

A few minutes later, when Ethan had excused himself to the restroom, Marney leaned forward over the bar, her head only inches from Juliet's, and asked. "You're that Juliet, right?"

"I'm sorry?" Juliet asked, not sure what the bartender meant.

"You're his midwife. The one he's in love with, but he can't be with because you thought he knocked up her best friend."

"He told you about me?"

Marney didn't look sorry as she said, "Well, you weren't talking to him."

"I guess I wasn't."

"But it looks like you guys got that worked out. You two here on vacation? A Valentine's getaway?"

Valentine's Day had been the week before, but Juliet ignored that and shook her head. "I live here now—well, close by at least. And Ethan just sort of..." Juliet trailed off, not sure how to explain it.

"Showed up to sweep you off your feet?"

A blush crept up Juliet's neck. "That was probably his intention."

Marney looked confused. "It didn't work? You guys looked pretty cozy."

"I—We—He—"

Marney flapped a bar towel at Juliet. "Don't worry about it. I'm not trying to grill ya. It's just that I've been a bartender for fifteen years and heard a lot of sob stories. Most of them were pretty self-indulgent, but he only worried about you."

"Oh," Juliet said.

"And was completely oblivious to all the ski bunnies trying to pick him up."

That got Juliet to laugh. "Really?"

"It was a little pathetic actually."

Ethan joined them then, and Juliet and Marney shared a smile.

"Uh oh. You guys were talking about me, weren't you?"

"Just how you spent your vacation oblivious to flirting ski bunnies," Juliet said.

"Not oblivious," Ethan said, sitting down next to Juliet, reaching for her hand. "Just not interested."

A thrill tripped up Juliet's spine as his fingers closed around hers, and when their eyes met, Juliet felt her heart softening. She wanted to let herself love this man, not just physically, though the temptation there was still strong. Juliet wanted to hold him, to laugh with him, to ignore him while he gutted fish, because the rest of it made him so happy, and the hush puppies later would be worth it.

Dimly, Juliet was aware of Marney asking if Ethan wanted another beer, and him asking for the bill, but his eyes never left hers.

The drive home was quiet, with only the low background of the fuzzy classic rock station to break the silence. Juliet traced the lines of lights leading to other towns and resorts around the mountain. When she passed the place where, during the day, you could watch the ski lift from the road, she asked, "When you were here a few weeks ago, did you ski, or did you hang out in that bar all day?"

"Will and I skied during the day. Not so much after he left. He's the one with the membership at the resort."

"So, it's pretty expensive then."

Juliet had looked up the cost of lift passes and ski rental, decided that she was better off not turning herself into a sled, and moved on.

She could hear the smile in Ethan's voice when he asked, "Do you want to go skiing?"

Juliet shrugged, "You get curious what all the fuss is about, living around here."

Ethan chuckled, picking up on what she wasn't saying, that she wouldn't let him pay for it. But she could tell that he was already plotting a way to take her, and when he did, Juliet wouldn't fight him on it—too much.

They were pulling into her driveway before the significance of that thought caught her attention. She hadn't consciously made the decision, but she was already planning what they would do next weekend and how she would introduce him to her sister.

Ethan parked behind her car, engine idling and unmoving, even as Juliet shifted out of her seat belt and gathered her purse. She opened her door and still he didn't move.

"You waiting for an invitation?"

He shook his head and shut off the engine, before following her onto the porch. She felt his hand at the small of her back through her bulky coat, and barely heard him whisper, "This doesn't feel real."

But then Juliet opened the door and Camille was yapping at their feet. Juliet picked her up and after a good scratch around her ears, handed her to Ethan.

"Maybe taking the dog out in the cold will help ground you."

Ethan scoffed, but took the dog. Then as Juliet turned away, he looped an arm around her waist and twisted her back into him, giving her a soft, too short kiss, then disappeared through the front door without another word.

Juliet was still turning on the various lamps in the small cabin when Ethan and Camille returned.

"That was fast."

"She doesn't like the cold."

Ethan plopped the dog down by the door and set about shedding his coat and boots.

"Do you feel like a fire?" Juliet asked, rubbing her still cold hands together.

Ethan grunted, but Juliet couldn't tell if that was from the effort it took to stand, or an assent, and she found herself staring at him as he stretched his arms up overhead. She watched the flex of his shoulders under his black fleece, and she remembered the feel of the muscles there under her fingers.

"Do you have a fireplace in your room?" He asked, finally turning around with a sexy half-grin on his face.

"Only in the living room," Juliet said, as Ethan stalked toward her. Her desire overruled her hesitation as Juliet tugged the zipper on his fleece down, then ran her hands over the soft fabric of his faded t-shirt and under the collar of his jacket, getting to know the cut of his beautiful shoulders again.

It took a minute before she realized he was staring at her, watching her admire his body with her hands. He looked undone, his lips were parted, his eyes focused intently on her face, his brow slack in awe. She traced one hand up to his hairline, touching the dark hair that had grown long enough to tuck behind his ear. There was a little patch of gray starting at his temple. That was new.

"So, fire?" she asked.

"Two things," Ethan said as he wrapped his arms around her waist, splaying a possessive hand over the small of her back. "I owe you a very long, very comfortable experience to make up for the last time." Juliet made to protest, but he silenced her with a kiss so soft and sensual that her socked toes curled into the rug under her feet. "Second, I don't want to stop touching you long enough to build a fire."

Juliet's response was to pull him into her room and down onto her bed with her.

They wasted little time divesting one another of their clothes, but neither seemed in much of a hurry to rush the experience. Each stroke of hand over flesh, each kiss, each nip, each flick of tongue was languid, luxurious, and almost tortuously slow. Ethan covered every inch of Juliet's body, while she did her best to return the favor pinned beneath him as she was.

He built her up with his mouth before bringing her to an agonizingly slow climax. And when he settled between her legs, finally sheathing himself in her with painful slowness, Juliet had to fight not to push him to hurry her to her next release. This slowness, this tenderness was so at odds with their last coupling, and she wanted it to be that way too, but now that they were here together, she was having trouble not eating him alive.

Not that she had any complaints about the pace Ethan set. The thrill in the suspense was exhilarating as each slow thrust touched every part of her. Finally, when she thought she might break from the intensity of it, Ethan gathered her in his arms and pulled her up onto his lap as he knelt on the bed. They fit each other like lock and key as her knees clenched his hips for balance and Juliet arched her back.

Gentle teeth tugged at her nipple. His arms encircled her, his hands spread wide against her back as he rocked into her. Despite the cold, sweat slipped down his chest, and across her belly. She never wanted to stop, but when Ethan whispered her name as he switched from on nipple to the other, the combination of longing in his voice and the tender nip of his teeth pushed her over the edge.

With a cry, Juliet fell backward, bringing Ethan with her as she pulsed around him. At last, Ethan lost his rhythm, and Juliet rode the frenzy that somehow kept pace with her pleasure. When he came, Juliet clung to him with her arms and legs, afraid to let go now that it was over.

Chapter Twenty-Five

Ethan wasn't sure what was better, making love to Juliet, or still being curled up with her just afterward. She smelled amazing, like the vanilla scent that must have come from her soap and the lime from her drink, and even a little bit like fresh snow, if that was possible. He rolled onto his side with Juliet pressed against his chest, their legs still tangled.

Juliet's fingers trembled as they skittered over his shoulder, down his arm, and back up again. Ethan pulled a blanket around her shoulders and squeezed her tight, hoping she was just cold. It would be easier to believe if her lips weren't set in a grim line. He kissed the corner of her mouth, but Juliet flinched away.

"What is it?" he asked, dread and fear gathering behind his heart and thumping through his veins.

"Why are you here?" she asked.

"This is where you are."

"Because you want to work with me? Are you working for Ski Valley?"

So far, Ethan had refrained from showering her with pretty words, and somehow, he knew that telling her he loved her wouldn't be met with any more welcome than it had been in the past. "Like I said, I have an interview on Monday."

Juliet sighed and tried to shimmy some distance between the two of them, but Ethan held tight.

"I can't be your nurse," she said, struggling against his hold. "I can't be your assistant. My job here is too important."

"What about my partner?" Ethan asked.

Juliet stilled. "What?"

Ethan stroked his fingers in her hair with one hand and raised the arm that had been wrapped around her waist to cup her cheek. "You were right last fall when you said I didn't respect you. I was being selfish because it hurt that you chose finishing your degree over our relationship. I thought we had something real. I still do, but I was clinging to a four-year-old fantasy that you didn't even know about, while also being pissed you wouldn't fulfill it."

"The nurse fantasy?" Juliet asked. Her limbs were relaxing again, but her eyes in the dim lamplight were sharp and icy.

"Yeah. I'm not sure when exactly it started. It couldn't have been long after we met, because I was smitten with you from the start."

Juliet huffed a dry laugh, and Ethan couldn't help but grin at his own understatement.

"Sometime during that spring, I got the idea that if I were to ever open my own practice, I would want you to do it with me. I could head the doctors, you would oversee the nurses, and we'd go into surgery together, deliver babies together. When we were done working for the day, we'd go home together and work on making some babies of our own."

Juliet snorted.

"I think I abandoned the idea of a private practice the second Rich found us in bed together. I felt like I'd never trust anyone again and going into private practice was always the first step toward starting a family."

Soft fingers feathered over his chest, past his ear and into his hair. "I'm sorry," Juliet said. "I shouldn't have used you like that."

Ethan ran the tip of his nose down the bridge of hers. "I don't regret it," he said, then stroked his lips against her mouth. Juliet didn't pull away this time but tightened her grip on his hair and opened her mouth so his tongue could delve inside. She still tasted like sweet limes. Juliet parried with her own tongue, the sucked his lower lip between her teeth before disengaging.

"What was that about being partners?"

"I knew that would get your attention."

"What kind of partners?" Her fingernails lightly scraped his scalp as she toyed with the strands of his hair, and he could feel himself starting to stir again.

"Every kind," he said. When Juliet gave him a shifty glance, even as her fingers still frolicked through his locks, he enumerated. "Business partners for one. I fantasize about a clinic that specializes in maternal/fetal medicine, but also functions as a birth center and well-woman clinic."

Juliet only hummed and waited for Ethan to continue. "You would head the birthing center of course, and I'd specialize in high risk cases, and sometimes we could meet in the middle."

"So, we'd share the practice?"

"Of course."

"And what else?"

"We would share a house, be lovers, husband and wife, maybe someday mother and father."

Ethan wasn't sure either of them were breathing. He held his breath waiting for her response. Juliet was either frozen in terror or shock or at best fervent contemplation.

Just as Ethan thought he might die of suffocation, Juliet said, "That's one thorough fantasy."

Ethan tilted Juliet's chin so that she was looking directly at him when he said. "I want the privilege of being near you."

Her lips were on his, her breasts pressed against his chest. He wanted her again as her legs slid against his, even though it had only been a few minutes.

When Juliet kissed her way over his jaw to his ear, he had expected something naughty or teasing to come out of her mouth. Instead she asked, "How tied are you to the idea of starting your own practice in order to have a family?"

Ethan had been leaving his own trail of kisses over her shoulder. It wasn't something he'd given much thought to. In his family, that was just the way things were done, but right now, with Juliet warm and responsive in his arms, Ethan didn't even need to consider his answer. "Not at all, unless that's what you want."

"I'm not sure what I want. Your clinic sounds amazing, but I like what I'm doing now. I'm not sure I'll ever want to run my own birth center."

"That's fine too," he said too quickly.

Juliet smiled and wiggled against him. "I may be willing to try some of the other things though."

"Yeah?"

"If you get that job, we could see where things might go."

"The job is mine if I want it," Ethan said. The recruiter sounded as if he'd nearly wet himself when he called after receiving Ethan's resume.

Juliet nuzzled Ethan's neck, and turned her wiggle into a slow grind. "Then stay." She licked up the column of his throat and Ethan rolled her onto her back while she giggled.

"You can't stay here though," she said. "Not yet."

"I want a bigger place anyway," he said. "A giant cabin higher up in the mountains, just like the one earlier."

Juliet nodded. Or at least he thought she nodded, Ethan was too busy kissing down her torso to know for sure. He made a note to ask again later,

"You should leave Camille here," Juliet's voice was a gasp as he dipped his tongue into her belly button.

He raised his eyebrows.

"So, you have an excuse to visit," she said.

Ethan laughed. "Deal."

Epilogue

Two Years Later
December Twenty-First

Juliet had left work two hours later than she'd told Ethan she would. The fresh dusting of snow had made the roads slick, even with the new winter tires on her hybrid SUV, so the drive home had taken twice as long. She sighed in relief as she pulled into the garage of the monstrosity of a house Ethan had bought a few months ago. Juliet still had a hard time believing that this was where she lived.

The house was a mix of rustic and modern that Juliet had come to associate with Colorado, with its soaring ceilings and exposed beams. It had more room than Juliet knew what to do with. The master bedroom alone was bigger than the little cottage she'd just moved out of. She was getting used to the open airiness and the walls of windows that overlooked the trees. Moving her plants in had helped make the giant rooms homier, but the small greenhouse that her cottage had become barely populated Ethan's living room—their living room now, Juliet reminded herself.

Camille greeted Juliet at the door from the garage, dancing and on her hind legs around Juliet's shins until Juliet crouched to scratch behind her ears. It was only as she stood that Juliet realized the whole house was dark. The only illumination came from the Christmas tree in the living room and a few candles spread throughout the kitchen and living room.

It wasn't unusual for Juliet to come home from work and find Ethan on his rowing machine in the bedroom, but she didn't hear the familiar clink and hum. She didn't hear anything. Juliet was still getting used to the quiet. Remote as her old cottage was, there had still been the sounds of regular neighborhood traffic, but out here, the only other people lived closer to the base of the mountain.

Juliet hung her bag on the hook by the door and did the same with her coat. Then she wandered through the dim kitchen. She opened the refrigerator to check if it was still working. The light came on, so the power wasn't out. Which was silly, if the Christmas tree was lit, they obviously had power.

There was a new pie box from Ethan's favorite bakery. Of course. She was going to have to talk to him about his sugar consumption. Juliet's stomach growled as she closed the refrigerator and made toward the pantry for a box of pasta and a jar of sauce since it didn't look like Ethan had made anything.

It was then that she heard the toilet flush, and a moment later Ethan emerged from the bedroom. He was dressed in a pair of black sweatpants and wore a t-shirt with the hospital logo on it. A smile lit across his face when he saw her. A gleam shone in his eyes as he crossed the giant room.

"You're home." With a quick peck on the lips he pulled her into a hug.

"Finally," she said. "Sorry I'm late." It was something they said to each other too often, but it was the nature of their jobs. Birth was unpredictable, and Juliet was thankful to have found someone who understood that.

"Are you hungry? I grabbed some food from Settler's on my way home."

Settler's Tavern was the bar Ethan had taken her to for her veggie burger that first night he'd been in Colorado. It had become one of their go-to places to eat in the last couple of years. Just the thought of sweet potato fries made Juliet's mouth water.

"That sounds amazing but let me change first."

Ethan looked down at her pink scrubs. There was a dark smear on her scrub top, likely blood. Juliet had been at work almost sixteen hours, she doubted she smelled pleasant. He squeezed her waist and placed a quick kiss to her forehead.

"You go get cleaned up, and I'll warm up the food."

When Juliet emerged from the bedroom fifteen minutes later in a pair of yoga pants and one of Ethan's old college shirts. She shivered and pulled a fleece jacket off a coat rack by the front door. Ethan was impervious to the cold, walking around on the hardwood floors in bare feet despite the chill, while Juliet contemplated whether she needed a hat too, but decided to wait until her hair dried more.

The smell of food pulled her into the kitchen where Ethan had set up their meal on the island. He'd grouped three of the candles in the middle and set out two glasses along with her favorite wine. A plate with her black bean burger sat next to his bacon burger.

"What's the deal with the candles?" Juliet asked as she seated herself and snagged a fry from her plate. "And the wine?"

Ethan tipped the baking sheet in his hand into the sink a brushed a hand over her shoulders as he passed to his stool. "You've lived here a whole three weeks. I think that's something to celebrate."

As if to punctuate his point, Ethan poured each of them a glass of wine and held his glass aloft.

Juliet raised hers. "To cohabitation," she said.

Ethan grinned. "To us."

Juliet's heart melted a little at the twinkle in his eye. "To us," she said, and they drank.

They shared about their days while they ate, and Juliet pretended not to notice when Ethan slipped Camille a few chunks of his burger, even though the vet has specifically told them not to feed her from the table anymore. She was too content to complain about anything as her belly filled and the wine relaxed her.

When she'd pushed her plate away and drained her glass, Ethan pulled her from her stool and led her front to the gigantic Christmas tree. Candles flickered around the room, and Juliet wondered where they had all come from. She'd moved in exactly three candles from her place, and Ethan hadn't had any as far as she remembered.

Ethan switched on the stereo and an older version of "Silver Bells" sounded from the speakers as Ethan pulled her into his arms and began to sway. He still wasn't a great dancer, but he'd made progress since that first time at Tokyo Nights.

"We're dancing now?" she asked.

"Is that a problem?" His voice was a seductive whisper in her ear.

Something strange was going on, but Juliet couldn't figure out what. She hoped Ethan wasn't buttering her up so when he broke the news that his mother was coming for Christmas after all she wouldn't be so mad.

Helen had only changed her plans three times so far. They expected Henry and Paige and their kids in two days, and Helen had been waffling about whether to accompany them.

"You don't usually dance."

"I dance with you," he said, and held her closer.

Juliet went with it. The song changed, and Ethan adjusted to the beat without any coaxing from her, and Juliet allowed herself to sink into his embrace. He smelled like home, and Juliet nuzzled a kiss onto his neck as he combed his fingers through the damp strands of hair on her back.

"I have something I've been meaning to ask you," he said.

"What's that?"

Ethan's voice once again came in a near whisper next to ear, "Will you marry me?"

Juliet jerked her head back so she could look him in the eye. "What?"

Ethan's grin was wide and mischievous as he said again, "Will you marry me?"

They'd only talked about marriage in abstract terms since he'd moved to Colorado. Juliet had moved into this house under the agreement that this was their forever home. Since then, it had been difficult to get Ethan off the subject of filling the bedrooms with children, but neither one of them had brought up the "M" word.

Juliet had been telling herself that she didn't need to be married. That having Ethan love her and respect her was enough. But now that he'd asked?

"Yes," she said. The word couldn't leave her lips quickly enough.

"Yes?" Ethan let out a relieved laugh, and Juliet didn't know what to do with her giant grin.

"Of course, you moron." She smacked him playfully on the shoulder, but he fielded any further abuse by pressing his lips to hers. Juliet could hardly participate for the smile that wouldn't quit.

Ethan let out another giddy laugh as he stepped back and pulled something from his pocket. When he opened his fist, a ring sat in the middle of his palm.

Juliet offered him her left hand and he slid the ring home. She angled toward the Christmas tree to get a good look at it in the glow from the twinkle lights. Her breath caught in her throat. The ring wasn't large, but the round moonstone was set into a little sun, a tiny crescent moon nestled into its side.

"Where did you even find this?" she asked.

"So, you like it?"

Ethan pulled her back into his arms at the same moment when she felt tears pool in her eyes. "It's perfect," she said. "You're perfect."

Ethan cupped her cheek and placed a soft, chaste kiss on her lips. "You're perfect."

"I was afraid you were going to tell me you mom was coming for Christmas after all" Juliet said as Ethan's hands began to wander.

"Oh, she's coming."

Juliet cursed, and Ethan let out a bark of a laugh.

"Sorry, but Henry spilled the beans about the proposal, and I couldn't keep her away."

"Damn."

"Play nice. She's excited."

With a deep breath in through her nose and out through her mouth, Juliet said, "Fine, I'll try to be charitable, but if she insults my ring the gloves are so coming off."

Ethan only kissed her, and whispered, "I love you," against her lips.

Keep reading for a preview from book two in the Try Again Series,

Sparkle & Shine.

Alex holds a special place in my heart, I really hope you love her story.
Look for *Sparkle & Shine* in early 2019!

THANK YOU FOR READING!

I hope you enjoyed reading *Ethan & Juliet*. This story took shape in my mind as I bounced my thirty-five pound then two-year-old on an exercise ball while I was eight months pregnant with my youngest. I wanted to write an opposites-attract story, much like I had done with *The Other Lane*, but I wanted it to be a different story entirely. I wanted the couple to have something essential in common, but I needed that to be a source of conflict somehow. Since I had spent much of the past four years pregnant or nursing, and in the care of midwives, it only seemed natural to make my heroine a midwife. And since there's an inherent tension between the midwifery model of care and the traditional, I knew my hero needed to be a hotshot OB-GYN. Over the months of drafting and revising, *Ethan & Juliet* became so much more than that. It had birthed characters that I truly loved, and I hope you love them too.

There will be two more books in this series coming out in 2019, featuring Alex's and Colleen's stories. Sign up for my newsletter[1] to get sneak peeks and released information!

---

1.   http://BookHip.com/QFDZZK

Want to Connect with Me?

I am @marlaholtauthor[1] on Instagram. I'd love to see you bookstagram posts or just chat about the book. I can't wait to meet you!

Finally, leaving reviews is one of the best ways you can support the Indie Authors you love. I'd be forever in your debt.

As Juliet would say, namaste, friends.

Sparkle & Shine

It was a fucking gorgeous day. Finally. What had been a mild and rainy spring so far had finally blossomed into a warm and sunny May full of green trees and flowers blooming everywhere. Of course, Rich might have a skewed sample since he was walking across the University of Kansas campus and they had it all done up for graduation weekend.

It had been a mistake to walk through campus. It was too crowded, but Rich hadn't been thinking. He'd just wanted to escape Lynette's place for a while. Taking Bijou for a walk had been a terrific excuse. He'd taken their normal route, and normally on a Sunday afternoon, the campus would be empty.

Now Rich was attempting to navigate through crowds and around barricades while keeping Lynette's little Bichon Frise from snapping at anybody's ankles.

It didn't leave much time for contemplation, which was why he'd wanted to get away in the first place. It wasn't a good sign when you couldn't stand your girlfriend for an entire weekend.

He should have broken up with her months ago, but how often did he meet someone who also spoke French and Italian just as fluently as he did?

Aside from his sister, Gina, Rich had never met anyone until Lynnette. That and the fact that Lynette had curves for days, and a sassy mouth, had Rich inviting her to his bed the first day of the teaching conference last spring, and asking her to start something serious with him after they left. That had been just over a year ago, and Rich was man enough to admit to himself that he should have ended the relationship by now.

He was not proud of the reason he hadn't. He'd wanted to make it one year. One whole year without cheating, and he couldn't make it a year if he wasn't in a relationship for a year. And now that he'd made it that year? He wanted out.

He knew it was time to get out because other women were turning his head left and right. The brunette in the yellow heels who smiled at him from beneath her cap as he ambled past. The blonde standing off to the side up ahead with her long hair blowing out behind her in the breeze. The girl with curly red hair that he could pretend was Juliet.

He sighed and tried to push that damn wedding invitation out of his mind so he didn't have to deal with the pain the sight of it had brought him.

It was Rich's own fault Juliet wasn't marrying him. She would have once upon a time. Rich had wanted to marry her, but he'd only been twenty-six when she'd lost the baby, and he'd been scared out of his mind. He'd wanted that baby. After losing Juliet and the baby all in one day, Rich had thought he might die from the heartbreak and regret. If he hadn't been so afraid of becoming his father, he might not have done the things that he hated his father for. He wouldn't have cheated. He wouldn't have abandoned Juliet when she needed him the most.

Maybe, if Rich had been less afraid, he might have been able to hang onto Juliet even after they'd lost the baby.

Finding out that he could have been a father again after it was too late to convince Alex to make a go of it with him had driven home how much he wanted the wife and kids thing. It had been almost three years since his affair with Alex, and he'd been searching for someone to do that with him since. It had been part of the reason he'd stayed with Lynette so long, but when he was honest with himself, he saw no future there.

The blonde's hair was still blowing in the wind as Rich approached her. She was small and wore black pumps with her cap and gown that made the little bit of calf he could see beneath her robes look strong and sleek. The urge to run his tongue over her ankle and up her leg hit. He was shaking it off when Bijou decided to dash toward where the pretty blonde stood in the grass, staring at her phone.

"Goddamn mother fucking asshole," she said, sidestepping the yapping, panting dog as if it wasn't there. "You'd think being on time to your fucking girlfriend's fucking graduation would be important, but no, Asshole of the Year missed it, and now he can't find a motherfucking parking place."

She finished her tirade before she'd looked up to meet his face, but Rich had recognized her voice the second she'd started to speak. Alex might be small, but she had the low, sultry voice that could sound like 900-number operator, but what usually spouting expletives instead. He hadn't recognized her at first, because she wasn't wearing her glasses.

When he said, "Hey, Alex," she flinched.

Flinched.

Then she looked anywhere but at his face, choosing instead to focus on the fluffy white dog jumping around her ankles. "Nice dog," she said, before reaching down to pet her. "I never pictured you with a dog," she said as Bijou rolled on her back. Lynette would have a fit if he brought her home with grass clippings in her newly groomed coat.

Alex just rubbed the dog's belly and babbled, "I mean, if you were going to have a dog, I always pictured you with something big and sleek like a greyhound or something, but you're really more of a cat person. Definitely not the fluffy lapdog sort of guy."

"She's my girlfriend's," Rich said.

Alex tapped the bow in the middle of Bijou's forehead. "Oh, that is more than obvious."

Rich knelt beside Alex to pet Bijou as well, but his eyes were on the white tassel that hung from her mortarboard. "What's your degree in?"

She met his eyes before answering, looking at him like he was daft. "The only thing I'm good at."

Rich wanted to crack a joke about how he didn't know they offered degrees in fellatio, because damn, the woman gave a hell of a blow job, but knowing Alex, she'd knee him in the balls for saying so.

When he only raised his eyebrows in question, she rolled her eyes. "Metalsmithing. You know, for jewelry making."

She stood brushing her palms over her gown. "And a minor in business."

"You're still doing the jewelry thing then?"

She nodded, regarding him the way a cat might when it's noticed a strange person in the room, cautious, but still a little curious. "Full time and ever expanding. I'm throwing a swanky party next month when I launch my new line."

Rich smiled. "That's great news," he said, and he meant it. He was glad Alex was doing well, even with everything between them that he suddenly grew aware of. The disappointment from when she'd broken things off, the anger and betrayal of learning she'd terminated her pregnancy and never planned to tell him about it, and the sadness of the knowledge she'd gone through all that alone. Not knowing what else to say, Rich said, "Sounds like you chose the right degree."

Alex snorted and looked up to the hill crowds of people, mostly dressed in black robes still swelled one second, then contracted the next like a flock of starlings. "Not that anyone was here to see me walk, apparently."

"Nobody?" he asked, furrowing his brow.

But Alex's phone buzzed and she was cursing again. "I swear to God he better have something really fucking good planned for tonight or I am going to kick his ass. The one thing I wanted out of today—the only goddamned thing was to have a nice picture of me all decked out," she motioned to her cap and gown, "to send to Gran, and he wants me to pick me up at the fucking Kwik Shop. I can't send my Gran a photo of me with an advertisement for dollar off Red Bull in the background."

She meant for the words to sound frustrated and annoyed he knew, but all Rich heard was the distress in her voice that bordered on panic.

"I can take your picture, *Piccolina*," he said.

Alex's eyes widened, and she took a step away from him. "I don't want to trouble you," she said. Meaning she didn't want to ask him for anything, not even a simple photograph. Not that he blamed her. Not really.

"It's no trouble," he said, holding out his hand for her phone. "You deserve better than a Kwik Shop parking lot."

Alex hesitated, then placed her phone in his hand. The case was black and sparkly, and it made him chuckle. The only time he'd seen her in something that wasn't black was the one time she'd worn a matching red lace bra and panty set beneath her little black dress. It had been the hottest thing he'd ever seen.

Rich almost fumbled the phone in shock, and he couldn't even pretend it was Bijou pulling on the leash, because the dog was lounging in the grass, panting. He just looked like the stunned clutz he was.

Was Alex in red lace the hottest thing he'd ever seen? If anyone had asked him five minutes ago he would have said that time that Julie had—but Alex was talking to him and he hadn't heard what she was saying.

"I'm sorry?" he said.

"Can you get the Campanile in the background or are there too many people?" she asked, enunciating the words like he was an idiot.

"Of course. Smile." Rich framed the shot so the bell tower reached into the blue sky in the background and Alex stood, smiling, in the foreground. He took a few, then focused close on her for a few shots, the hill and the path to Potter's Lake in the background. There were also a few people's butts, but that couldn't be helped with the lawns as crowded as they were.

Alex flipped back through the pictures. "Thanks. Gran might not like what my degree is in, but she'll be glad for the pictures all the same."

"She couldn't come?" Rich asked, remembering that her grandmother was the only family Alex had left.

Alex scrunched her nose. "No. She was sick all winter, first with the flu, then with pneumonia. She's been going back and forth to the doctor . . ." Alex trailed off.

"I hope she feels better," Rich said, feeling more shy and awkward than he had since he was a teenager. Teasing, flirting, testy Alex he could handle, but today Alex seemed fragile, like one more ounce of pressure might break her.

Alex slid her phone back in the neckline of robe. Was she stashing it in her bra? He remembered the way that red lace had wrapped around her breasts, exposing just enough skin to make him want to peel it off to expose the pale peaked nipples he knew he'd find below.

No. He could not be thinking about Alex's nipples right now.

"I better get moving, Ben's probably waiting."

"Can I walk you?"

She shook her head. "It's only a block away." Kneeling again, she patted Bijou on her ridiculously puffy head. "Nice to meet you pup." Then she stood, her fingertips grazing the exposed skin on his forearm as she passed. "See you around, Rich."

"Congratulations!" Rich called after her and watched her walk away until she blended in to the sea of other black robes headed off campus. He knew that Alex only meant that she'd see him again when they ran into each other in another three years, but Rich didn't want to wait that long. Yes, seeing her again had stirred up a ton of bad memories and mixed emotions about their past, but there was something else there too. Not just that he couldn't get the picture of Alex in red lace out of his mind, though he'd likely spend more time contemplating that than he should.

What he really wanted to know was why Alex looked like she was about to shatter.

"Come on, Bijou." Rich tugged on the leash. "We better head back."

About the Author

Marla Holt grew up wishing the heroines in the fairy tales she loved had more to choose from than marrying the prince or utter devastation, so now she writes modern day fairy tales with a feminist flare. She's living her own dream come true, writing and knitting in Topeka, Kansas with her husband and three boys.

Read more at tinydinostudios.com.

Made in United States
North Haven, CT
18 April 2022

18373428R00209